About the Author

I've really enjoyed the feedback from my first book. There are a lot of naughty people out there, including me.

There have been a lot of questions about my life. I'm a regular everyday housewife who has had three children, a reasonably amicable divorce, and been tested by the normal trials and tribulations of life.

I have always been very good at enjoying myself and appreciating the wonders of this brilliant world. I love reading, watching films and going to the theatre, and having exciting adventures. Love Sheila.

Sheila's Little Black Book
Vol 2

Sheila Allen

Sheila's Little Black Book
Vol 2

Olympia Publishers
London

www.olympiapublishers.com
OLYMPIA PAPERBACK EDITION

A CIP catalogue record for this title is
available from the British Library.

ISBN: 978-1-80074-151-5

This is a work of fiction.
Names, characters, places and incidents originate from the writer's
imagination. Any resemblance to actual persons, living or dead, is
purely coincidental.

First Published in 2021

Olympia Publishers
Tallis House
2 Tallis Street
London
EC4Y 0AB

Printed in Great Britain

Dedication

To my three sons: Michael, Adrian and Christopher

Introduction

I, like most people, was surprised just how successful my first book was. So, firstly, I would like to thank everyone who purchased the book and for all of the kind comments. It's always great to get some positive feedback.

For those who thought that the book was a collection of 'vile, disgusting, sordid tales for the depraved and sick of mind', thank you for buying the book and thankfully this book continues in exactly the same vein.

The stories continue with many of the characters that were introduced in the first book. I need to stress that the characters are fictitious and any resemblance to people in real life is purely coincidental. I mention this because some of my fans have been trying to track down both the people and locations in the book. Mostly they don't exist.

Anyway, back to this book. I believe that it is sexier and funnier than the first book. I enjoyed writing it. I enjoyed thinking of sexy situations for our heroine — Sheila. She has a sexy old time but is placed in predicaments that also offer a revealing reflection on life. So, please continue to enjoy her ongoing adventures.

Look after yourself, but have some fun.

Love Sheila

New Business: Part 1

Ken, Sheila's agent, asked if she could meet with him regarding a new opportunity. Sheila was quite excited as business had been a bit sparse recently. She put on her prettiest underwear, as Ken took every chance to take advantage of her. He was a great lover, and she was looking forward to a good seeing to. It would set her up for the week.

Sheila arrived on time and shook Ken's hand. She was a bit surprised that he did not attempt to grab her arse or fondle her tits. She thought that he might be having a bad day. Ken asked if he could be excused for a few minutes, as he had to meet some potential customers in reception. He said that his secretary might even bring them up to the office later.

In the meantime, Sheila thought that she would lay on a little treat to cheer Ken up. She stripped off completely and laid on his desk. She decided to arrange herself so that her fanny would be immediately visible when he entered the room. She grabbed each leg with her hands, and pulled her legs apart, exposing her fanny to the best effect. If this didn't get Ken going, nothing would.

She realised that she looked a bit like a Christmas turkey ready to be stuffed, and that was precisely what she was hoping for — a good stuffing. She could hear footsteps and prepared herself for the big surprise.

The door opened and in walked Charlotte, Ken's

secretary, and two men. Sheila just froze. Charlotte said, 'Let me introduce you to Sheila, she is one of our best entertainers, very flexible as you can see, and almost game for anything.' The two men moved close to Sheila and just stared. It is not every day you see a gorgeous naked woman exposing herself on an office table.

Charlotte saw this as an opportunity to get the job done. She said to the men, 'Feel free to fondle her.' Darren, the older of the two men, looked at Charlotte, and she nodded her permission. Darren stroked Sheila's thighs and gradually moved his hands upwards towards her vagina. He carefully stroked the hood of her clit and gently slid his fingers down each side of her fanny. Charlotte walked over with some massage oil and poured it onto Sheila's cunt.

Darren saw this as permission to go for it. He steadily fondled each labia, gently pulling them apart so that he could finger Sheila's vagina. Two fingers entered her love hole while two fingers on the other hand teased her clit. Sheila's arse was finding it hard to stay still, and her bum was wriggling all over the place, putting pressure on her arms, which were trying to keep things in place.

Charlotte calmly walked up to Darren, unzipped his trousers and pulled out his stiffening penis. Without saying a word, she positioned it directly in front of Sheila's fanny but held it in place. She then said to Sheila, 'Is it all right if Darren enters you?' Sheila nodded. Charlotte then said to Sheila, 'Is it all right if Darren fucks you?' Sheila nodded again. Darren was now really keen to enter Sheila's fanny.

Charlotte could feel that Darren's cock was really firm. She could feel that the steady pressure she was maintaining on his glans was also having its effect. Charlotte said to Sheila,

12

'Is it all right if Darren fills you up with his hot white spunk?'

Sheila nodded and said, 'Yes, please.' Charlotte rubbed Darren's cock against Sheila's clit. Both of their bodies responded. Charlotte continued the cock to clit rubbing. Both bodies were finding it hard to maintain control.

Charlotte could see Darren's pre-cum. Charlotte could sense the lust in the room. Charlotte could feel the control she had over two adults. She held Darren's cock even tighter, twisted it slightly and plunged it into Sheila's fanny, pinching her clit on the way. Darren came with an audible roar, firing his seed deep into Sheila's fanny. Charlotte pulled him out as she wanted to see the effect of her machinations.

Spunk was still erupting and shooting everywhere. A pool rested on top of Sheila's fanny. Her belly-button was steadily being filled up. Darren couldn't believe the sheer volume he produced. Sheila had only experienced a small orgasm but was now totally engrossed in the spunk experience. It was beyond anything she had seen before.

Charlotte turned to the other man and said, 'Do you fancy some sloppy seconds?'

Sheila thought to herself, '*Well, there is sloppy, and there is sloppy.*' Brian wasn't sure what to say. He had never seen such a performance, and he wasn't sure that he wanted to, although he really did fancy Sheila.

He thought to himself, '*You don't get many opportunities to fuck a stunning woman.*'

Charlotte said, 'Can I tempt you?' She walked over and rubbed his already erect penis through his trousers.

Brian said, 'I really shouldn't, I've only been married a year, and I have a little girl.' But he did nothing to stop Charlotte freeing his cock. Charlotte led him by the cock towards Sheila, gently pushing Darren out of the way, who was still leaking.

Charlotte said, 'You have the choice of Sheila's mouth, arse or fanny?'

Sheila thought, '*What a cheek*, but was hoping that he would choose her fanny.'

'Fanny,' 'he mumbled.

Charlotte said, 'Sorry, I didn't get that.'

'Fanny,' he said, a bit louder.

Charlotte told Sheila to get off the table and bend over the armchair. Sheila did as she was told. Charlotte told Sheila to spread her legs further apart. Sheila did as she was told. Charlotte told Brian to remove his trousers and pants. Brian did as he was told. Sheila thought to herself, '*Charlotte is a real bully.*'

Charlotte grabbed Brian's cock and sucked it so that it was absolutely rigid. Charlotte could feel the veins on his cock pulsating. Charlotte said to Brian, 'Do you want me to put your cock in Sheila's fanny?' Brian nodded. Charlotte said, 'Did you say "Yes"?'

Brian shouted, 'Yes.'

Charlotte said to Sheila, 'Do you want Brian's cock in your fanny?' Sheila nodded.

Charlotte said, 'Do you want Brian to fuck you?'

Sheila said, 'Yes.'

Charlotte rubbed Brian's cock against the crack of Sheila's arse. She rubbed it up and down relentlessly. It almost entered the fanny on several occasions, but just missed and moved on. It rubbed the clit a dozen times. Charlotte asked them both, 'Shall I put the cock in the fanny?'

Both replied, 'Yes.'

Charlotte said, 'Shall I do it now?'

Both said, 'Yes,' loudly and aggressively.

Charlotte said, 'Did you say please?'

Both shouted, 'Please.'

In it went. Brian's large, stiff, engorged cock entered Sheila's tight little fanny. Just at that moment, Darren took some photos capturing both the point of entry and the full thrust. Brian partially withdrew, and Darren took another picture. Sheila came hard, holding Darren's cock tightly in place. As he finally withdrew, Sheila received a second shower of cum all over her bum.

Brian just shouted, 'Fuck all three of you.' He pulled his trousers up and left.

Darren said, 'Thank you, ladies, that was masterful. It served that blackmailer right. He had been ripping me off for years. Your money will be in the account this afternoon.' He turned to Sheila and said, 'Thank you for a delightful experience. I will never forget you.' Charlotte showed Brian out of the door.

When Charlotte returned, she said to Sheila, 'It was a good job that Ken briefed you. Do you want a cheque for one thousand pounds now, or shall we do an electronic transfer this afternoon?' Sheila took the cheque.

Charlotte then said to Sheila, 'Ken is now my husband, and you will keep your hands off him. I know that in the past you have taken advantage of his good nature, but things have changed.'

Sheila said, 'Thank you for updating me. I'm sure that you will both be very happy together.'

Sheila thought to herself, '*A charlotte is a pudding made of stewed fruit with a casing or covering of bread, sponge cake, biscuits, or breadcrumbs. Ken can't have his cake, and eat it.*'

New Business: Part 2

Sheila congratulated Ken on his marriage to Charlotte.

Ken said that he had no choice, 'Bun in the oven, and she is a right bully.'

Sheila said, 'She does seem quite strong-willed. I've been warned off already.'

Ken said, 'I have agreed to behave myself, but she is not as pure as the driven snow; it's going to be interesting to see who breaks the rules first.'

Ken asked how she got involved with the blackmailing case. Sheila explained that she planned to give him a surprise and had stripped off and was waiting for him to return. 'I thought that you needed cheering up.' Ken asked Sheila if she was totally naked. Sheila said, 'Yes, totally nude, on my back, with my legs apart, waiting for a good shafting. Everything was hot, just waiting for your todger.'

Ken simply said, 'Bugger.'

Ken then said, 'I suppose Charlotte turned up with Darren and Brian?'

Sheila said, 'That's right, and Charlotte effectively invited them to fuck me. During the process, Darren took photos of Brian, which meant that he had lost his ability to blackmail.'

Ken said, 'Bit naughty of Charlotte, but at least you made some money.'

Sheila said, 'Yes, that was good. Anyway, you mentioned

on the phone that you might have another job for me.'

Ken said, 'I do, but I don't think you will like it much. None of the nice girls stay. I just thought you might need the cash.'

Sheila asked, 'What info do you have on the job?'

Ken said, 'Very little, but you get fifty percent of your earnings.' He gave Sheila the details and said that it was up to her to contact them if she wanted to.

Sheila decided not to pursue the opportunity based on Ken's comments, but then she had to find a way of paying the gas bill. The other unexpected money would be enough to pay for her car repairs. *'Life is not easy,* 'she thought to herself.

After a quick call, and the texting of a few saucy pictures of herself, she got the job. There wasn't even an interview. They asked her to start immediately, and told her to ask for Millie when she got to "The Sunrise Men's Club". Sheila arrived at seven p.m. as requested, and asked for Millie.

Millie met Sheila in reception in a giant, pink, fluffy dressing gown. Sheila suspected that she was naked underneath. Millie asked Sheila if she knew what the job was all about. Sheila said 'she had no idea, but knew that she would almost certainly be naked.'

Millie said, 'Well, that's a good start; at least you are not a prude. There is also every chance that men will take advantage of you.'

Sheila said, 'Nothing new there then.' Millie didn't want to say too much, as it put the girls off.

Millie said, 'Can you strip and follow me?'

Sheila said, 'Everything?' Millie nodded.

Sheila thought to herself, *'Here we go again.'* Sheila quickly stripped, piled her clothes up neatly and followed

Millie, who was also naked now. They were soon joined by three other naked girls. Apart from Millie, she thought that the other three were a bit plump; one, in particular, had obese legs. Another one was very spotty. She was worried about getting too close to her. She guessed that she was probably the oldest, but apart from Millie, easily the prettiest.

In front of them was a rack of tubes on wheels. It had five tubes for five girls. The girls laid in the tubes face down, with their bottom and legs exposed. The pipes could rotate so that the legs could also be in the air. This arrangement gave anyone full access to a girl's private parts. Sheila was immediately reluctant to enter, but the others encouraged her, and she didn't want to seem wimpy.

When all five girls were in the "rack", a shutter came down so that nothing above the waist could be seen. A young man then wheeled them around. The first stop was outside the men's toilets. While the movement was going on, Sheila asked Millie for more details. Millie explained that each section on the rack had a credit card reader. A person could pay one hundred pounds for ten minutes.

Sheila asked, 'What are they allowed to do?'

Millie replied, 'Whatever they want.'

Sheila said, 'So we are going to be fucked, aren't we?'

Millie said, 'More or less, but we get half the takings. On a good night, I get five hundred pounds.'

Sheila said, 'But that means that you get fucked ten times.' Millie just smiled and nodded.

Sheila said, 'I'm not doing that; how do you get out?'

Millie said, 'We are effectively prisoners until the club shuts down for the night.'

Sheila said, 'When is that?'

Millie replied, 'Three in the morning.' While they were chatting, Sheila heard a clang, and someone was pressed against her bottom. She could tell that he was removing his trousers, and in no time at all, she had a prick in her fanny.

Sheila said to Millie, 'I've got a prick in my fanny.'

Millie said, 'Well done. You have made fifty pounds.'

Sheila said, 'He is certainly fucking quite quickly.'

Millie said, 'They have no choice, they only get ten minutes.' Millie then said, 'I've got a punter now. The funny thing is you have no idea who they are. They could be a young lad or a dirty old man. I try to imagine a face, but it's very difficult.'

Sheila said, 'What's happening now?'

Millie said, 'Louise will wipe you down and spray you with some disinfectant.' Sheila felt the cloth wiping her private parts, and then the coldness of a spray, and then she felt another cock pushing its way into her fanny.

Sheila said to Millie, 'I've now got another cock in my fanny; it feels a bit bigger than the last one.'

Millie grunted a few times, and said, 'I've got quite a large one in me too; I prefer the smaller ones, you can relax more. They are in and out in no time. The big ones move your whole body around.'

Sheila said, 'I think he is gone; I didn't feel him come.'

Millie said, 'That happens a lot; ten minutes is not enough time to get their rocks off. A lot of them just like the feel of a fanny. Some seem to enjoy the entering process.' Louise did her wiping and disinfecting.

Sheila was just going to say to Millie that it's not as bad as she thought it was going to be, when suddenly her fanny was bitten. Sheila said, 'Millie, I've just been bitten.'

Millie said, 'That is probably Dracula.'

Sheila said, 'Are you serious — Dracula?'

Millie replied, 'Yes, he is an old bloke who bites the fannies of all the new girls.'

Sheila said, 'What else does he do?'

Millie replied, 'Nothing, he bites once and leaves.'

Millie said, 'Just got my second of the day. Have you got any children?'

Sheila replied, 'Three boys, what about you?'

Millie answered, 'Two boys and a girl, all under the age of five.'

Sheila said, 'I bet that's a handful; just got another one.'

Millie, 'A boy?'

Sheila, 'No, a punter, he seems to be playing with my labia, no he is looking for my bum. Are they allowed to fuck your bum?'

Millie, 'Oh yes, they can fuck anything they can get their hands on, or rather their cocks into.'

Sheila said, 'I don't think he will get any joy there, it will be far too tight. No, I'm wrong, he is in.'

Millie said, 'They can be determined buggers; I'm not so keen on it up the old arse hole.'

Sheila said, 'Nor me, I've just felt him come.'

Millie said, 'I must admit this whole thing is a bit degrading, we are really just cum receptacles, but the money is good; so far you have earnt four hundred and fifty pounds, and the night is young.'

Sheila said, 'Does your husband mind you doing this?'

Millie replied, 'No, he got me the job; I keep him in fags and booze, and he looks after the kids. What about you?'

Sheila said, 'I'm divorced now; just finding work to pay

the gas bill. Just got another one.'

Millie said, 'Gas bill?'

Sheila said, 'No, a punter.'

Millie said, 'You are doing well; sometimes there are no punters and you can wait around all evening. I don't think the other girls are doing too well. When they get a pretty one like you, it takes the trade away from the other girls.' Sheila started to feel guilty.

Sheila said, 'I think he has gone.'

Millie said, 'I don't think so, I think he is a torcher.'

Sheila said, 'What do you mean?'

Millie said, 'I think I can see the light of a torch. He is just having a good look at your fanny. Anyway, we will be on our travels soon. We go to the main bar area next to where the striptease dancers are. The dancing tends to make the punters randy, and we get more business.'

Millie was right, and off they went. As soon as they got to the bar, a queue formed. It got around that there was a new girl with a fine arse. Sheila was in peak demand, being shagged every fifteen minutes. Sheila asked Millie how long they had to go.

Millie said, 'Two hours; it will soon go quickly.'

Sheila said, 'I'm not sure if the punters are enjoying it or not as my fanny is so wet. Can they feel anything?'

Millie said, 'Surely you aren't worried about them, are you?'

Sheila replied,' 'Well, they are paying good money, they should get a reasonable service. What's all that noise?'

There was lots of shouting and banging. The noise was getting deafening. The rack was being aggressively shaken backwards and forwards until it tipped over. Sheila was confronted with over fifty men all waiting to take advantage of her. She tried running, but they grabbed her. They grabbed her everywhere; no part of her body was safe.

Luckily, the bouncers arrived, and she was rescued. One of the bouncers picked her up, took her to a back room, put fifty pounds in her hand, turned her over and fucked her. It was the last thing Sheila needed after a night of continuous fucking. He took his time. Sheila didn't dare to say that there was a ten-minute limit. He came, he thanked her, he took her to the cashier to get her pay, and then took her to where her clothes were. When she bent down to pick her shoes up, he entered her again and came for a second time. He pushed another fifty pounds into her hand and kissed her on the cheek. Sheila grabbed her clothes; she didn't dare bend down again and rushed out of the door.

Sheila counted up her money — nine hundred pounds, better than a car boot. However, she worked it out that she had been shagged eighteen times. She felt ashamed of herself. On the other hand, she didn't come once. Somehow, she was disconnected from the entire process. She thought that she had probably done some good. Regardless, it was just another adventure, but she was not going back again.

The moral of this story is, "Check out the job specification before you are put on the rack".

Love Actually: Part 1

Jack had noticed Sheila a few weeks ago. Apart from being gorgeous, she was alive. She had a genuine love of life. She laughed, she cared, she loved Maltesers. He loved the way she walked. He loved the happiness in her eyes. He loved the way she said, "Morning, Jack" as she walked by.

Clearly, she was totally out of his league. It occurred to Jack that he wasn't even in a league. Why would she be interested in someone who was leagueless? But she always seemed to be alone. Did she have a Mr. Right hidden away? Was she someone's bit on the side? Someone must be paying for that distinctive look she had. No normal person could colour co-ordinate her clothes the way she does.

What right did he have, a common restaurateur, to even talk to her, but he was allowed to dream? Most of his dreams ended up with him taking Sheila's clothes off. They were pleasant dreams — no, they were great dreams! Dreams of lust, dreams of love, dreams of hope. Hope of a future where loneliness deserted him. Sometimes, he could feel her in his arms. Sometimes, he could smell her breath. Sometimes, they even argued about how much they loved each other. He even had a dream where he wanted to die before she did, as he didn't want to live in a world without her.

Then the day came when she popped into his café. She wanted a cappuccino in a china cup. With a twinkle in her eye, she said, 'Can you make the coffee a bit stronger than normal.' He could hardly talk. His occasional stutter became his only means of communication. His hand acquired a shake that had never been there before. Close up, she was even more beautiful. The way she held a cup was almost a piece of art. He then realised that he was smitten. He was in love.

Sheila thanked him and left a small tip. He put the coin in his pocket. It was precious. She had touched it. He started having "Carpenter" moments — the grass was greener, the birds sang sweeter, and every love song on the radio was about him, and for him. No, it was for us. He spent hours looking out for her; a day without seeing her was a day lost. Sheila was obviously oblivious to all this.

Ken, her agent, had got her another job where she would appear naked, and would probably have to fuck someone. There was always someone. Sometimes she just wanted an ordinary life. A life where she cooked a meal for her husband, a life where he cut the lawn, a life where they went for a walk on a Sunday afternoon, or perhaps a drive. Mostly, she wanted someone to love her for herself. She wanted sex, but love was the aim. Then she remembered Wormy, her first and only husband. It was not a pleasant experience.

Perhaps there is a force in the galaxy that brings people together. On a wet Saturday evening, Sheila appeared in Jack's café. She had just done an afternoon stag party, where she had jumped naked out of a cake, and was eaten by the future bridegroom, and the best man. It's not every day that two men chew your fanny. They had no right to push cake into her most private part and then lick it out. She had spent an hour de-caking herself, but then that's business.

While she was sitting there sipping a cappuccino from a

china cup, she noticed the waiter walking up to her with a red rose. He said, 'Pretty lady, I have a rose for you.' Sheila was quite touched by this simple act of kindness. She noticed that he was not that good looking, his nose was too big, his eyes were too close to each other, he was slightly overweight, but there was something about him. Was it a sense of fun? Was it humility? Was he the one to cut her lawn?

Jack summoned as much courage as he could. In fact, he managed to summon every single bit he had and went for a blurt. He may have said, 'Do you fancy dinner sometime?' Or he might have said, 'Dinnery fancybum,' 'or even, 'Someertime dinner fan.' No one could have made sense of his utterance.

Sheila said, 'Could I have the bill please,' and thought to herself, *'he didn't seem foreign at first.'*

Jack did more courage summoning and managed a second blurt, which did sound a bit more like an invitation to dinner.

Sheila said, 'Are you inviting me out to dinner?' Jack nodded, and Sheila said that she would be delighted to accept. Jack was more than stunned, more than speechless, more than hope personified.

He said, 'Thank you so much, pretty lady. What is your name?'

Sheila said, 'Sheila,' although she had wondered about calling herself Alice, Alice from Wonderland.' Jack lifted Sheila's hand and kissed it, and she left after giving him her mobile number.

There were now two delighted people — a delirious cafe owner and Sheila. Sheila wondered if she should buy a new lawnmower. Then she wondered how she could tell him about her career, but she decided that it was a bridge that could be crossed at a later date.

Sheila prepared for her first date in years. Although she regarded herself as a "Woman of the World", or rather society regarded her that way, she was rather naïve in the ways of romance. She washed and polished herself, selected her prettiest underwear, knowing that things would never get that far, and then spent ages choosing her favourite Desigual dress. With a final spray of Armani, she was ready.

Jack was dead on time. In fact, he had been outside for nearly an hour, making sure that he would not be late. Off they went to see La Bohème, followed by a fish and chip supper. Sheila saw Jack in a new light. He was starting to look more attractive. Jack couldn't believe that he had just taken a stunning woman to the opera. They had chatted like old friends. She was so easy to talk to. Jack gave up stuttering. Sheila was dropped off with a quick kiss on the cheek, and another date was fixed.

The next day Jack was in Heaven. He had kissed his dream girl. Sheila had thoroughly enjoyed the girlfriend experience, but now she had to jump out of another large cake. Ken had managed to get another five or six cake bookings, as the first one had been so successful. It appeared that each one included some sexual activity. Sheila tried to get an exact requirement, but Ken just said, 'You will just have to judge it for yourself. *So in other words*, 'she thought, '*I could get humped a dozen times if I don't put my foot down.*'

Sheila waited in the cake for the clock to hit the designated exit time. This time, she was determined not to get cake in her fanny. At precisely seven p.m. she jumped out of the cake, into the weedy arms of a lad who had just turned eighteen. And he was really weedy, skinny, spotty, bespectacled and already going bald. His pot-bellied dad was there shouting, 'Now it's your chance to become a man.' He pulled his son's trousers and pants down to some applause. Sheila decided that she wasn't going to enjoy this, as his cock was also pretty pathetic. Within minutes, Sheila was bent over and "Spotty", as they called him, was in her fanny. Seconds later, the job was done, and he was out.

The father escorted her over to the dressing room which to most people was a nice thing to do, but Sheila knew the ways of men. Immediately inside the dressing room, he pushed her over, and quickly entered her. He was no better than his son. He came, withdrew and slapped her bum, calling her a "slut". She called him a pig, and they went their separate ways.

The second date was at the pictures. It was a re-run of *Gone with the Wind*. Jack was a gentleman. He held Sheila's hand, and at one stage even touched her knee. It was just a touch; not a fondle at this stage. After a very successful evening, Jack dropped Sheila off. He opened the car door for her and gently grabbed her face and kissed her on the lips. It wasn't that Jack was slow, he just didn't want to screw things up. Sheila was looking forward to getting more intimate, but she was also enjoying the growing tension between them.

It was time for yet another cake job; what was she in for this time? She knew that it was an LGBT affair. At seven p.m., she did her regular leap to find a room full of glamorously dressed women. There were shouts and screams, and lots of applause. It appeared that two women had just got married, and they were going to have her. The song being played was, *Isn't she lovely?* Everyone had to agree that Sheila did look lovely.

The two brides lifted their wedding dresses to display two

massive black strap-ons. Sheila was carefully laid on a table, and after some breast massage and general fingering, the brides entered her one at a time. Sheila thought it was not the same as a cock. The dildos were too hard, too inflexible, too cold.' She tried to imagine what Jack's cock would feel like, but struggled. When the second bride finished, she was surprised to find that the shared best man entered her.

Now here was a real cock — firm, warm flesh. He knew what he was doing. The girls counted each stroke amongst much laughter and gigglement. The best man pulled Sheila towards him so that his penis could enter her as far as possible. He was keen to put on a bit of a show, but his resolve was weakening, as he responded to the deliciousness of Sheila's cunt. He was still resisting when he came. He pulled out to display a spray of spunk. Love was in the air. The crowd laughed and whooped. Fun was had by all. Even Sheila enjoyed herself.

The third date was a steak dinner, followed by *Les Miserables*, one of Sheila's favourites. Alfie Boe was performing. It was a fabulous night, and they started holding hands. They had suddenly gone from being two individuals to being a couple, but they were not yet lovers. Sheila wondered when he would make his move. As he dropped her off, they French kissed, and Jack held her bum.

Jack still couldn't believe his luck. He enjoyed other men looking at Sheila, as it made him realise that he had a real beauty on his hands. Sheila just enjoyed the normality of the situation. She wondered if she needed to encourage him more, as he was obviously a bit hesitant. Sheila was ready for more. However, she was getting more worried about him discovering what she did for a living. He had asked her once or twice, and she had murmured marketing.

Sheila couldn't believe how many cake events there were. The next one was a conference for a publishing house that specialised in kinky books. At midday, she jumped out of a cake which was in the shape of a vagina. Thousands of camera lights shone on Sheila. After much cheering, she was walked down to a stage. Sheila's body was put on public display with her legs spread apart. Her fanny was open for all to see.

A queue quickly formed. The conference attendees were invited to throw sponge darts, which were in the shape of a penis at Sheila. It didn't take much imagination to guess what the target was. One of the stand organisers had to remove piles of penises from Sheila's vaginal area regularly. He always managed to fondle Sheila's private bits in the process. Sheila didn't mind, as being on public display was getting her hot.

Then someone shouted, 'We have a winner.' A pillow was placed under Sheila's bottom, and a video camera was set up. A nice-looking young man, who lacked both trousers and underwear, was presented to Sheila.

The organiser said, 'Joss has won the right to fuck you.' There was a considerable amount of cheering, and Joss bent down to suck Sheila's fanny. Sheila was quite impressed by his technique. With the use of his tongue, he brought Sheila to a climax — it was the first time that oral sex alone had achieved that.

Joss then parted her labia and pushed first one and then two fingers into her now very juicy fanny. Most of the crowd watched the activities on the giant TV screen. Sheila's fanny was at least a foot across. You could see every curve, every facet of her cunt, even the juice. You could see Joss' two fingers diligently ploughing in and out. You could see the pinkness of her fanny walls. You could see her little soldier standing to attention. You could see Joss' cock approaching the entrance to the fanny.

On the screen, his cock looked like a monster. A giant snake head with a slit at the end. It was shiny and leaking pre-cum. In the distance, you could see two large hairy balls. Joss' fingers pulled the labia apart to let the cock in. It rested on the entrance. It didn't seem possible that his cock could enter. It looked far too big. Joss pulled Sheila's labia further apart and stroked her clit. Sheila immediately juiced up. Her cunt was glistening and eager. Her cunt had a life of its own. It was trying to suck Joss' cock in.

Joss resisted and continued to stroke Sheila's clit. Little strokes around the edge, a quick flick of the hood, then a few strokes down each side of her fanny. He played with the inside and outside of her labia. Sheila was now very juicy indeed. Joss used some of the juice to play with her anus. A finger was inserted and left there. Joss was now ready to enter. Sheila had been ready for a while. Her body was aching to be fucked. She wondered if he would be gentle or rough.

She didn't have to wait long. Joss simply thrust into her with no finesse whatsoever. She hadn't really expected that and came immediately. Her fanny simply contorted and flooded the pillow with vaginal juices. Musk was in the air. If he stood up, his erect cock would probably lift her. He was so entrenched in her.

Joss tickled her, which immediately relaxed her, and he started the fucking process. Someone put on the song *Sledgehammer* by Peter Gabriel, and that was what Joss was. Sheila began to suspect that he was a gigolo; he was far too good at this fucking business.

On the giant TV, you could see the "Sledgehammer" in action. He made most men seem inadequate. With the thrust of his mighty dick, Sheila's whole body quivered. Her boobs were dancing around in a rhythmic manner. They seemed to move in one direction and then another; they couldn't make their mind up, but they knew that Joss was the boss. Sheila came a few times, but she knew that a mighty orgasm was building up. There was nothing she could do about it.

Joss just ploughed away, increasing both speed and levels of penetration. There was no rest, just continuous fucking. Joss was sweating, Sheila was sweating, and most of the crowd were sweating. When would it end? Sheila could tell that the end was coming, as his thrusts slowed down, but were becoming more potent. She knew that he would let go in a few seconds, and she was ready.

He came with a roar, and so did Sheila. Her whole body bent and stretched; it may have been agony, but it was delicious. That was the best fuck of her life. There was shouting and clapping from the audience as they saw Sheila's orgasm on the big screen. They saw Joss' cock depart from Sheila's cunt, spraying semen everywhere. They saw Sheila's fanny make a series of contractions as she relaxed. They saw the spunk dribble out of Sheila's fanny. The organisers congratulated Sheila and then she made her way home.

She had another date with Jack that night. They were off to see Star Wars at the pictures. It wasn't easy for Jack to get away, as he had a restaurant to run. He hadn't invited her to a meal at his restaurant as he didn't want the staff to know about his amorous intentions, although they suspected that something was up, as he suddenly seemed so happy.

During Star Wars, Jack made his first serious move. It

may have been the power of the music, or perhaps it was the Luke Skywalker effect, but he put his hand on Sheila's knee. As time went on, Jack gradually edged his hand under her skirt. As there were no objections, he slowly moved further upwards. He was undoubtedly enjoying the feel of her naked thighs. As he approached the knicker line, the scorpion struck. Sheila grabbed his hand and put it back on her knee. Sheila then decided to buy the new lawnmower next week.

Jack was quite pleased with the progress he had made. He now knew the acceptable boundaries. He also knew that Sheila wasn't an easy catch, which pleased him. Sheila felt a bit sorry for him. Earlier today, she had been put on public display and had her brains fucked out in front of two hundred men. Here she was stopping one nice guy touching her panties. Isn't life strange?

Sheila's next cake assignment was a masked charity ball for men only, where she was the first, second and third raffle prize. Tickets had been sold well in advance. Once again, she jumped out of the cake at precisely seven p.m. Like the rest, she was masked, but unlike the rest, she was totally naked. Sheila was walked around the tables in a final attempt to sell more tickets. Once they saw her body, it led to a rush of ticket sales. The sales office was then closed, and the mayor was asked to pull the three winning tickets out of the hat.

The first-place winner was selected, and Sheila did her duty. She was fucked on stage by a very portly gentleman, who thanked her for her services to charity. The second-place winner was younger and much more eager. In fact, he was far too eager and came before he entered her. She thought, *'Serves him right for coming second.'*

Then the third-place winner had his turn. He turned Sheila

around so that the audience could see him entering her. He fucked her hard in an unpleasantly aggressive way. He wasn't making love. He was punishing her. She thought she could hear him sobbing. He continued to fuck her, but it wasn't a pleasant experience. At the point of coming, he pushed her over and threw his mask at her. It was Jack! He just stormed off.

Sheila stood up, bowed, and left the stage. Tears started welling up. She wondered why life played these sorts of tricks. She felt sorrier for Jack than herself, but she knew that this day was inevitable. Should she run after him, or just move on? It would take time for her to decide, but then it would probably be too late. Not many men could cope with the skeletons in her cupboard.

Then she thought, *'What was he doing at an event like this?'* Later, she discovered that he had supplied the catering, and had just purchased a ticket as a charitable act. Would he have fucked an alternative girl? She would never know.

The moral of the story is to "choose the right moment when to buy a lawnmower".

Love Actually: Part 2

Sheila was walking to the shops when she heard steps behind her. She turned to find Jack with a white rose. Jack said, 'A rose for a pretty lady.' Sheila wasn't sure what he wanted. A white rose represents innocence. He knew that Sheila wasn't innocent, but then, in some ways, she was. She stopped, and Jack said, 'I have a business proposition for you.'

Jack said, 'I have been looking for ways of generating additional business for my restaurant. I wondered if you would consider a striptease night.'

Sheila said, 'Why now?'

Jack replied, 'Business has been OK, but I need to discover ways of finding new clients. A gentleman's night could open up an entirely new type of clientele for me. I would pay you two hundred pounds. If it worked out, it could be a regular session.'

In some ways, Sheila was disappointed. Here was a man who was treating her as a girlfriend. Now he was just another man who wanted to use her body for personal gain. But then his money was as good as anyone else's. Sheila accepted, and they agreed on a time and date.

Sheila wasn't really a stripper. She wasn't sure what she was, but somehow, she always ended up naked on stage, and quite often found herself having sex with strangers. She was not a hooker. She had never been paid for sex, although sex was often part of the job. Perhaps, she was a totally new category, but then what was the point of compartmentalising? *That was a good word,* 'she thought. As far as she was concerned, she had no discriminating tendencies, and that was the case with her work.

She turned up on Friday night as agreed with Jack. She just looked fabulous. She had gone out of her way to look the best she possibly could. No expense had been spared. She kept telling herself that this was not a date with Jack, but somehow her mind kept telling her it was.

She noticed that a small stage had been prepared in the corner of the restaurant. A DJ had his rig set up, and even a seventies-style disco ball had been installed in the ceiling, that was already throwing out patterns of light. The tables had been arranged so that everyone had a good view.

Jack was getting quite excited. Perhaps, Sheila was not good girlfriend material, but he fancied her rotten. Jack couldn't wait to see her naked again. He even considered the possibility of fucking her again. It's incredible what a rose can do. When Sheila arrived, he was stunned. She was a seriously beautiful woman. It crossed his mind that he had no right even to consider fucking her. She was way outside of his league.

They kissed, and Jack showed Sheila to a small area that she could use as a dressing room. It was hardly private, as the kitchen staff had access to it, but it would have to do. The restaurant was filling up. The idea of a men's night seemed to be succeeding, or was it the attraction of having Sheila there? She was becoming quite infamous.

The time had come for Sheila to display her charms. She arrived on stage to the song *She's a lady*, and she was. Sheila was not an experienced stripper, and she tended to remove her

35

clothes far too quickly. Sheila had agreed to do four songs, but found herself removing her panties at the end of the first song.

During the second song, she grabbed a red napkin, and displayed herself in several positions, to the song *Lady in Red*. She was on her back with her legs wide open. She bent over with her legs wide open. She tried to do a handstand, but by then she couldn't get her legs wide open. The audience seemed to appreciate the wide-openness. This seemed to be the case, as so many photos were being taken. She managed to complete most of the second song, but what was she going to do for the third song?

Sheila decided that the only option was audience participation. She went up to a bald man in a tracksuit and rubbed her breasts in his face to the song *The Lady is a Tramp*. The poor man almost suffocated. Well, he was asthmatic and was totally unprepared for a full-on mammary experience. He managed to recover his decorum and was soon sucking away like a trooper. Gradually, his hands started caressing Sheila's arse, and as he got fruitier, she decided to move on.

Sheila extracted herself and ran to the next table with her breasts swinging all over the place. She sat on a young man's lap, with her bottom on his knees, and her breasts in his face. Effectively, their faces were touching. She started kissing his face while he played with her tits. She moved forward so that she could feel his erect penis beneath her fanny. They had sex through at least two layers of clothing. The crowd was cheering, but what was she going to do during the fourth song?

The fourth song started, and she moved on to find a good-looking man in a business suit. It turned out that he was the local bank manager. Sheila had little time for bankers and immediately carried on from the previous position. She rubbed her fanny up and down his lap while licking his ear. The bank manager was checking out her assets, firstly those upstairs, and then downstairs. He had his finger in her pussy.

Sheila saw that Jack was close by taking in everything. He was also taking photos. She thought, 'I will show that bastard,' and lifted herself, opened the banker's flies and pulled out his penis. In no time, the banker was up her fanny and fucking her to the tune of *Lay Lady Lay*. *'I will give Jack some photos,'* she thought. She lifted herself up again so that the tip of his penis was just touching her fanny. Lots of photos were taken. She plunged down hard; the bank manager's eyes almost popped out. She repeated this a few times so that every aspect of her fanny was fully on show. The poor bank manager was almost suffering from cardiac arrest.

She could tell that he was about to come. She made one last heave and then jumped off him. The photos of his ejaculation were magnificent. No one had caught that moment so well. It was unlikely that the bank manager would keep his job. She left the stage to the song *Three Times a Lady*.

When she got to the changing room, she found Jack waiting for her. He didn't say a word and just watched her. She took a flannel and cleaned her fanny, making sure that Jack saw everything. She took her time delicately washing her labia, clit, and vagina. Sheila then moisturised the entire area, making sure that he could see her finger entering her fanny. She deliberately had a nonchalant expression. She was enjoying this.

She rubbed moisturiser onto her breasts. Two big dollops that she proceeded to massage in slowly and sensuously. Her nipples were unbelievably erect. Sheila put her black lacy bra on, which caused problems as her nipples ached for attention.

Her cardigan followed. Each button took an age to do up. During this process, neither of them said a word.

Then Sheila bent over, exposing her naked rear to Jack. She took her time undoing the laces on one of her shoes. Her bottom wiggled occasionally. She bent over further, which fully exposed her recently moisturised fanny. It was almost iridescent. Jack just stared. He could not take any more, took his cock out of his trousers and fucked her.

This was the second punishment fuck. Jack totally ignored her needs and just fucked her hard and mercilessly. It was brutal. Sheila was just pushed back and forward as his large todger relentlessly ploughed in and out. He came like before, with a mighty roar. He wondered, *'What power does this woman have over me?'* Sheila really enjoyed it; there was a pleasure in making a man come. It was definitely a type of power.

Jack left the room without saying a word. Sheila got dressed and went back into the restaurant. Jack was waiting with some money in his hands. He said, 'Here is two hundred pounds for the strip, and one hundred pounds for the fuck.'

Sheila threw the one hundred pounds back, and said, 'I'm not a whore, but you, sir, are a rapist.' As she left, she shouted out again, 'Rapist.' Both of them knew that it wasn't true, but both of them wondered if their adventure would continue.

The moral of the story is "Sometimes a banker is a wanker, especially when the Lady Sings the Blues".

The Supermarket Job

Sheila wasn't sure if she could walk down the road without being presented with a rose. Jack was at it again, but this time he had a yellow rose, which represents friendship. Sheila said, 'Jack, what do you want?' He replied that he wanted to both apologise, and to offer her another business opportunity.

Sheila said, 'Well, go on?' Jack wasn't sure what she meant. Sheila said, 'Let's hear your apology.'

Jack said, 'I should not have taken you like that; I apologise.'

Sheila said, 'That's hardly an apology for raping me.'

Jack said, 'You provoked me. You deliberately made me rape you.'

Sheila said, 'So I grabbed your cock and forced it into me!'

Jack said, 'Well, not exactly, but you did entice me.'

Sheila grinned, and said, 'What's this business opportunity?'

Jack explained that three men saw her striptease. They would like to meet with her. Sheila said, 'You mean that there are three blokes who want to fuck me.'

Jack said, 'You are right, but they will pay one thousand pounds each.'

Sheila said, 'Jack, I've told you before, I'm not a whore; I don't fuck for money. Anyway, I'm off now for an interview.'

Sheila had been contemplating her life and decided that she needed some normality in it. She was on her way for an interview at the local supermarket. They always had vacancies. They never seemed to keep their staff.

Sheila arrived on time. She went to the manager's office to meet the manager and receive a large mug of tea. That didn't go down too well, as Sheila was a coffee drinker and only drank from a china cup and saucer. The manager simply asked when she could start. She replied almost immediately.

He said, 'Fair enough, go downstairs, and Toots will show you the ropes.'

Sheila said, 'Do you mean start right now?'

He replied, 'Is that a problem?'

Sheila said, 'No,' but wondered why he hadn't asked for references.

She went downstairs and asked for Toots, who was a pretty girl with short blonde hair and a perky bust. Her overall was a bit too short. Her knickers were on show when she bent over. Toots took Sheila to the canteen, where she asked why she wanted to work here.

Sheila said, 'I need a job, and this is very local.'

Toots said that they only pay minimum wage and that the conditions are poor, very poor indeed. Few people stay.

Sheila said, 'Give me the dirt, I need to know more.'

Toots said, 'I'm not trying to put you off — you are a particularly pretty girl, and consequently you will attract problems.'

'Problems?' Sheila said, in a questioning way.

Toots was very hesitant as they desperately needed more staff, but she wanted to be fair to her sex. 'Sheila,' she said, 'You may have noticed that my overall is too short. When I bend down, my underwear is displayed. That is one of the rules here. Pretty girls wear short overalls.'

Sheila said, 'That is totally unacceptable.'

Toots said, 'Try telling that to the management, you will be straight out of the door. I might as well be honest — you will get groped, and you will suffer sexual abuse.'

Sheila said, 'Why has no one complained?'

Toots stated that there had been hundreds of complaints. There is no legal aid any more, so the staff just leave. Sheila asked if Toots had been abused. She nodded and said, 'I have two young boys, I need the job; I treat the abuse as an occupational hazard.'

Sheila said, 'Well, I'm not putting up with that.'

Toots said, 'You will if you want to keep your job.' Sheila wanted to ask what was the worst abuse she had received, but it was obvious that Toots didn't want to talk about it.

Toots issued Sheila with a uniform. It was probably shorter than the one Toots was wearing. Sheila told her that it was far too short. Toots said that she was just following instructions. Sheila stripped off her skirt and top and put the uniform on. There was no way she could bend down, or reach up, without exposing herself. Sheila had effectively accepted the first level of abuse.

Toots took Sheila to the warehouse, which was directly above the store. She said, 'I need to warn you about the debagging ceremony.'

Sheila said, 'Debagging?' Toots explained that new girls, well the pretty ones, are formally debagged on the first day. It can be done voluntarily or by the warehouse staff.

'Sheila said, 'What is meant by debagging?'

Toots said, 'I guess that you have never worked on a shop

41

floor. In a factory full of women, they remove the trousers and pants of new male starters. It happens in lots of factories. Here the knickers are removed. On the second day, the girls can put them back on again.'

Sheila was horrified, but as she stood there, the manager and a large group of warehouse workers started gathering. The manager introduced Sheila as a new starter. They weren't particularly interested, but they wanted to see her debagged. Sheila was probably the most attractive starter they had ever seen. The manager turned to Sheila and said, 'I believe that Toots has explained the debagging procedure. Are you going to volunteer, or do you need assistance?'

Sheila looked around at the motley crew. It didn't look like she was going to get out of the warehouse with her panties on her. Sheila slowly lifted her uniform and pulled her knickers down. She displayed her charms in a confident and dignified manner. The manager was shocked as it usually was a rapid display, and then a rapid cover-up. What made it even more impressive was the sheer beauty of Sheila's body. The crew stared and then clapped.

Sheila then handed her still warm knickers to the manager. She said, 'I think you normally keep these.' Toots then took Sheila down to the shop and showed her the ropes — well, how shelves are filled. Most shop staff who had a short uniform with no knickers on would be somewhat discreet. Sheila did the opposite. She went out of her way to show her fanny to the shoppers.

After a few hours, the manager asked to see her. At this stage, he had no idea that she hadn't been that discreet in the shop. The manager invited her into his room and asked how she was doing. She said that she was enjoying it so far, but that the uniform was a bit too hot. He suggested that she tried on the new lightweight outfit.

Sheila agreed and took off her uniform, standing there in just her bra. Sheila said, 'I guess that it can get rather hot with a bra on.' So she took it off. The manager was gob-smacked. He had spent most of his adult life abusing young female shop staff, and here was one of the most beautiful women he had ever seen, naked in his office.

The manager pointed to the box of lightweight uniforms. Sheila bent over to check them, making sure that the manager could get a good look at her vagina. She wiggled her arse in a very tempting way. In minutes he entered her, and being the bastard he was, came almost immediately. Coming quickly suited Sheila perfectly.

Sheila said to him, 'I will go and get some tissues.' She deliberately walked into the warehouse stark naked, and asked one of the lads for some tissues, as the manager had just raped her. She went back to the manager's office, wiped her fanny in his presence, and grabbed one of the lightweight uniforms.

The new uniform was even more revealing. Even the bust was not adequately covered. Sheila continued displaying herself in the shop. The complaints soon started coming in. At the same time, a crowd began to form. Young lads were following Sheila around hoping to get a glimpse of her private parts. She didn't disappoint. A reporter from the local paper turned up and started photographing her. Her poses were not discreet.

The police eventually arrived and warned Sheila that she was going to be arrested for indecent exposure. The manager was called. The police asked the manager if this uniform was the official company issue. He could hardly deny it.

The police asked why Sheila wasn't wearing any knickers. There were too many witnesses for him to deny the debagging ceremony. While the manager was protesting his innocence, Sheila admitted that he had raped her in his office. She handed over the tissue containing his semen. The police said that it was his word against hers. Sheila said, 'Firstly there was the short uniform, then the debagging, then the new uniform. It was all leading towards the rape.' Then she mentioned all of the staff that had left due to sexual harassment.

Sheila left, the manager was sacked, but not jailed, and Toots took over. On reflection, Sheila decided that her entertainment career wasn't that bad after all, but at least she had done some good. What was more distressing, was that she owed the supermarket some money. Her wage had two uniforms charged against it. Hard to believe.

The moral of the story is "the debagger rarely bags it all unless it is Harry Potter".

Anyway, Sheila decided to push her entertainment career forward. The only rule that she would stick to was that she would not sell her body for sex, but everything else was up for grabs. Literally everything else. She would be like a premiership footballer. She would make money while her body was in a good state.

The Photographic Exhibition

Sheila was actually a bit disappointed. There was no sign of any roses today. Anyway, she had decided to pop in and see Jack. She arrived at the restaurant and entered via the side entrance. She knew that his flat was above the restaurant, but she had never been in it.

In she walked to find Jack lying flat on the bed, with a young girl on top of him. Her fanny was grinding away at his cock. Sheila sat down on the bed next to him. Jack looked stunned. He really hadn't expected to see Sheila again.

Sheila asked if this was a staff relations exercise, or was he in the process of creating a new relationship? Sheila recognised the girl as Anna, one of the waitresses. Anna seemed more or less oblivious to Sheila's presence and just carried on grinding away. You could tell that Jack was approaching his climax from his facial expressions.

Sheila could tell that the girl was young, as her nipples were still pink and soft. Her breasts were perky, but probably still not fully formed. They still managed to put on an excellent gesticulating display. Sheila desperately wanted to hold them down, but you would have to catch them first.

Sheila said, 'Regarding the three businessmen, she was interested after all, but he would have to think of a way of her providing a service of some sort. It couldn't be just money for sex.' She asked if he understood. Jack nodded, but she thought for some reason unbeknown to her, he seemed distracted. On the way out she gave his protruding testicle a firm tug. This pushed him over the edge, and he shot his load into the waitress' willing vagina. Her job was done.

Sheila continued her walk into town. After some window shopping, she noticed that there was an X-rated photographic exhibition in the Town Hall. The Council had always been very forward thinking. She paid the entrance fee of five pounds, to see naked photos of herself.

Inside there were pictures of her being fucked on stage at the Theatre. There was no filter at all. You could see a large cock entering her fanny. There were, in fact, ten photos showing the process in great detail. To say that it was embarrassing was a colossal understatement.

In the next section, things got worse. There were nude photos of Sheila as Lady Godiva in Pershore High Street. There was one clearly showing the horse rider entering her from behind. There were pictures of her being taunted on the rack, with her boobs covered in rotten tomatoes.

She wasn't sure if she dared to move on. The next section was the *Snow White* experience. There were numerous photos of her being raped by the huntsman, but worse was to come. There were a series of over three hundred photos of her being fucked by the dwarves. Lots and lots of them, although the Grumpy images were a bit sparse. These photos clearly showed Sheila's fanny close-up, being fucked by all seven dwarves. She wondered what her mother would think.

There were other photos from the club at Thornton Heath, and from the Rugby Club. There were even photos of her being left naked on the M1. There were also explicit photos of her from the calendar shoot. Someone had done an excellent job of collating all of these photos.

Suddenly, there was a tap on her shoulder. A middle-aged man said, 'We thought that you would eventually turn up. My name is Roger. I either took these photos or purchased them from other collectors.' He offered Sheila his hand. Sheila shook it but was still dumbfounded by the whole experience.

'Why me?' she managed to stutter.

Roger said, 'You are a remarkable woman. Not only gorgeous but gregarious and fun-loving. Wherever you go, you spread happiness and joy. I've not heard a single bad word about you. It's really my pleasure, and indeed, a great honour to meet you.'

Sheila said, 'Could I have the five pounds entrance fee back?'

Roger laughed and said, 'Of course, but I owe you far more than that. So far, I've calculated that I owe you twenty-two thousand nine hundred and forty-five pounds in royalty fees. I will do an electronic transfer when you give me your bank details.' Sheila thought that this man was starting to look very attractive.

Roger then said, 'What's more, I had a model booked for tomorrow. If you want, I could cancel and you could take her place.'

Sheila said, 'I wouldn't want to deprive another model of her work.'

Roger said, 'I will pay her a cancellation fee. It's also worth pointing out that we could sell a portfolio of photos. A complete set of pornographic photos on Sheila.'

Sheila asked, 'How rude would they be?'

Roger said, 'Very rude indeed, but no worse than the collection on display.'

Sheila wasn't too sure, but the photographic fee was two thousand pounds and she would get thirty percent of any sales, plus he would pay her the twenty-three thousand pounds. Things were looking up.

Sheila arrived back at the Town Hall at the designated time. There were already two or three hundred people, mostly men, queuing up to see a photographic master at work. Or did they just want to see Sheila naked in compromising positions? Either way, it was going to be a sell-out.

Next to the gallery, there was an auditorium with tiered seats. It could only hold one hundred and fifty attendees, so there was not enough room for all of the people queuing. In the centre of the stage, there were several props, including a bed and some racking.

Roger welcomed Sheila and introduced her to Peter, Michael, and Ben. He asked if they could all strip off next door, and wait for his call. Sheila was amazed how only a few years ago this would have horrified her, but now it was second nature. She was, in fact, the first to get her kit off. The others followed. Peter was embarrassed that he already had a massive erection. It was in anticipation of entering Sheila's cunt. He had quite a few of her photos in his collection, but they were nothing compared to the real thing. He just couldn't believe that he was getting this opportunity.

Michael and Ben were also reasonably eager to get the action underway, but they had more control. There was a call for Sheila. She fluffed up her hair and checked her face in the mirror. The lipstick was OK, her nose was powdered, and she walked out to great applause. The crowd stood up and clapped. She didn't know that she had a fan base, let alone such an enthusiastic one.

Roger took Sheila through an extensive range of poses, with the photos being displayed on the largest screen Sheila had ever seen. Roger showed how the use of light could change the entire mood of the photo. He then focused on close-ups displaying Sheila's fanny to great effect.

Tools were introduced, and Sheila had a dildo up every orifice available, sometimes two at a time. She wasn't sure if this was entirely necessary, but then it was Roger's show. She just supplied the body. The crowd was probably on Roger's side and seemed to enjoy an enormous black dildo being pushed into her tight little cunt.

Roger shouted for Peter, and he was introduced to the crowd. His job was simply to fuck Sheila's fanny. He was soon on the job. His engorged cock slipped in and out, as requested by Roger. Usually, Peter had a lot of control, but Roger could see that he was losing it. From Peter's perspective, this was a dream job, fucking a goddess, and despite his efforts to resist, he came. He roared, the crowd roared, and Roger shouted his annoyance. That was totally unprofessional. What were they going to do for the final act, with one down?

Sheila tried to clean herself up, but it was not easy with one hundred and fifty people watching. Anyway, what did a little bit of spunk matter? Roger carried on taking photos. A beautiful woman covered in spunk was definitely erotic, and photos of her cleaning herself would go down well.

Roger called for Michael. His job was to fuck her in the arse. Sheila had never been keen on this, but perhaps it was an acquired taste. It wasn't, but the job was done. Roger had numerous photos of her bum being violated.

While Michael was in her arse, he asked Ben to take advantage of her mouth. Again, this wasn't Sheila's favourite, but the job had to be done. Perhaps it was an acquired taste. It wasn't, but the audience enjoyed her breasts swinging in tandem to the fucking.

Roger then asked for a volunteer to fuck her fanny. Loads of hands went up, and Roger chose a large lad called Les, from the front row. He was stripping his clothes off as he walked towards Sheila. He had absolutely no problem getting a hard-on.

Roger then organised all three. Sheila sat on top of Les and put his cock in her fanny, and then managed to lean forwards but stick her bottom outwards. Michael entered her anus, and Ben put his cock in Sheila's mouth. It ended up being a confusing picture, but it seemed to work. The close-ups on the large screen were particularly impressive.

Sheila found the two cocks in her neither region rather interesting. They were only separated by a thin piece of skin: the perineum. She could feel the two cocks rubbing against each other. She wondered how the men felt about it.

Roger then put some music on and asked them to fuck in unison to the tempo. It was not easy keeping all of the cocks in Sheila's body. Occasionally one would pop out, and Roger would have to return it. There was no way that any of them were going to come. He asked Sheila to stay where she was and asked the other three to disengage.

Roger pulled his cock out of his trousers and entered Sheila's fanny. Sheila said, 'What are you doing?'

Roger said, 'I was not going to miss a chance of fucking you.'

Sheila said, 'I don't think that is very professional, you are the photographer.' While Sheila was discussing it, Roger came. He was a very happy man. Sheila had never seen such a big smile before.

Roger declared that the photographic session was over and had the whole team bowing in front of the audience. Sheila was the star and received one standing ovation after another. She didn't feel like a star, as warm spunk was running down her legs.

Roger thanked Sheila and apologised for his final action. Sheila said, 'That was very naughty.' She forgave him, as he was only a man.

The moral of the story is "Two cocks in the bush, beats one in the hand any day".

The Wheelchair

Jack had arranged for Sheila to meet one of the businessmen in Purley. She had made it clear to Jack that it couldn't be just "Sex for Money". Both Jack and the man she was going to see had agreed to this. As a result, the customer asked if she could arrive in a skimpy waitress outfit, and make his day by carrying out some domestic duties.

Sheila hired the waitress outfit from the local shop. Sheila tried it on in the shop, and she had to agree that she looked great in it. The knickers only just covered her arse. Her boobs were only just held in place. The stockings were held up by a very fragile suspender belt. Obviously, it wasn't a proper waitress outfit, but it would do the job. The shop owner obviously agreed as he took some photos for marketing purposes.

She caught a taxi to an imposing house on the Purley Way. It reminded her of the time she saw Queen perform at the Purley Ball Rooms. What a night, Freddie Mercury was just amazing. He dominated the stage. The audience was his to command.

As Sheila lent forward to pay the taxi driver, her boobs popped out. He simply said, 'Nice pair.' Sheila wasn't sure what he meant at first and then saw her dilemma, as she handed him the money. She quickly returned them to their proper home and pressed the doorbell by the gate, which slowly opened.

The taxi driver watched Sheila walk up the long and winding drive to the house. He was mesmerised by the way her buttocks moved. *'What a delightful sight,'* he thought to himself, *'What a lucky man.'* Sheila pressed the electronic doorbell, and a man's voice asked who was there.

Sheila said, 'Sheila, your waitress.' The front door swung open.

Inside, Sheila found a very good-looking man in a wheelchair. He introduced himself as Derek. He said that he had organised a coffee for her in the kitchen. Sheila was delighted to find a bone china cup and saucer. They both enjoyed a coffee and some chit-chat. It appeared that he lost the use of his legs in a car accident. Sheila wanted to ask if he could still use his todger, but was too embarrassed to ask.

Sheila asked what tasks he wanted her to do. He said some light dusting, and perhaps preparing some lunch. He asked if she minded him watching her, as he didn't get much female company. In response, Sheila stood up and asked if the outfit was OK. She did a twirl so that he could see the full effect. She asked if there was any garment that he wanted removing. Before he could answer, there was a tremendous crash, and two men wearing balaclavas entered the room. Both were brandishing knives.

Before a word was said, one of the knives was at Derek's throat. Sheila just stood there, stunned. The other masked man started ransacking Derek's home. Sheila didn't think he was very professional at his job, but kept silent. The man holding Derek in place started shouting, 'Where are your valuables?' Before Derek could answer, the burglar hit him, and then hit him again.

The other burglar returned from his pillaging duties, and said, 'No sign of any money or valuables.' Derek was hit again. Sheila thought that things were starting to look a bit dark; it was getting serious. The ransacker took his balaclava off. Sheila started to worry, as that meant that they could recognise him. She had seen on television that this meant that they were doomed. They were going to be killed.

The burglar grabbed Derek by the throat and said 'it was his last chance.'

Sheila then blurted out that they should not attack a man with disabilities, and that they would have to get past her first. She followed up with, 'You are just cowardly bastards.' She was trying to work out who said that and was then shocked to hear that it came from her mouth.

All three stared at her. The nearest burglar said, 'Perhaps we can retrieve something from this after all.' He told Derek to pull Sheila's knickers down. Derek looked into Sheila's eyes, and she nodded. Derek then lent forward and slowly grabbed the waist of her knickers, and then slowly pulled them down. All three men were entranced with what they saw—a beautiful pussy surrounded by a suspender belt. There were immediately three erections.

Sheila noticed the bulge in Derek's trousers. *'Well that answers one question,'* she thought. The burglar then told Sheila to take Derek's cock out of his trousers. She unzipped him and removed a fine specimen of manhood. The burglar then pushed Sheila's head down and told her to suck Derek's prick. Sheila obeyed and started sucking as instructed.

Sheila was effectively bent over with a cock in her mouth. Her fanny was exposed to the world. Well, it was actually exposed to two burglars who were admiring her arse, and more specifically her fanny. Both were rubbing their cocks. One said to the other, 'Who is going first?' They tossed a coin, and the first burglar entered Sheila's tight little cunt.

Sheila thought, *'At least I'm going out with a bang.'* He was quite well-endowed and took his duties quite seriously. He soon had a good rhythm going, with Sheila being rocked backwards and forwards. Both cocks were being pushed in as far as they would go. Sheila thought that one was banging against her cervix. The other burglar then decided that it was his turn and literally pulled the first burglar out.

Sheila soon had the second burglar in her fanny. She wasn't as keen on this one, as he was much rougher. Then she thought to herself, *'I'm not keen on any of them.'* He asked the other burglar for a knife. Sheila started to panic. He took the knife and literally sliced the waitress outfit off. He said, 'I want to see those tits swinging free.' He got his wish as two magnificent dangling breasts swung in partnership to his thrusts.

The cock in Sheila's mouth was making her cough. The coughing caused her vaginal muscles to contract more than usual, which made him thrust harder, which caused her to cough more. Sheila was too frightened to come, although she had an intense tingling sensation; the other two had reached the end of the line. Both erupted at the same time. Sheila wasn't sure which way to turn.

Should she swallow or spit? In the circumstances, she decided that it was safer to swallow. Both withdrew, and Sheila fell to the ground, exhausted. The unsatisfied burglar demanded Derek's car keys. He took the keys and frog-marched Sheila to the car. She thought her time had come.

In was the first time that she had experienced the joys of

being in the boot. She wondered if she was breaking the law not wearing a safety belt. She tried to work out the route he was taking, but it was too difficult. She knew that he was driving up a hill, as her ears were popping. She was ready to scream, kick him in the balls when they stopped, and then make a run for it.

When they stopped, she just silently laid there. The burglar undid the boot and pointed for her to walk between two bramble bushes. On the floor was a thick blanket. He pointed at her to lie down. She was ready to scream and kick, but decided to lie down. She was wondering how come the blanket was there when he parted her legs and finished the job.

Without saying a word, he picked up the blanket, forcing her to roll over, and gave her an envelope. He simply walked off, leaving her lying there stark naked.

She undid the envelope to find three thousand and fifty pounds. The fifty pounds was for the outfit. Inside there was a telephone number for a taxi that been paid to rescue her. Sheila thought, *'They are all bastards, how could they do that to me?'* She rang the number, and the taxi was there in ten minutes. It was the same guy as before. He refused to give her any covering or his jacket.

He could have dropped her outside of her house, but he refused. He was enjoying her humiliation, watching her walk nude up the road to her home. We all get our kicks in different ways.

Sheila got dressed and headed for Jack's restaurant. She knew that someone was going to suffer. Sheila stormed in and said, 'You knew, didn't you?' He smiled, and she kicked him hard in the balls.

The moral of the story is "You need balls to be a Sheila".

A Chat about Sex

Fortunately, Jack didn't need medical attention for the attack on his groin. He still wasn't sure why Sheila attacked him. She asked him to organise "an event" where it wasn't "Sex for Money", although everyone knew it was. He probably should have told her that it was going to be simulated rape, but if he had told her, would it be "Sex for Money"?

He found Sheila very confusing. He never saw it, but apparently her waitress outfit was so skimpy that it hardly held anything in place. He tried to imagine her delightful, voluptuous boobs bursting free. He tried to imagine those black stockings. He could feel his somewhat aching balls responding to his mental images. She was expecting to have sex with Derek, so why all the fuss?

Anyway, he had sent her some yellow roses which represent an apology. He wondered why he was doing this. He wondered if he was still in love with her. He wondered what he was apologising for, but then it is easy to say "sorry". Sheila was coming to the restaurant at mid-day. He had organised fish and chips for lunch, which was one of her favourites.

Sheila's first reaction on receiving the roses was "to stuff them up his arse". Hopefully, half a rose bush up his rectum would be as painful as the kick she gave him. She was starting to regret the kick. He was so pleased to see her, but not so pleased when the "boot hit the nuts". She had never seen so much pain in one man. He just collapsed on the floor in complete agony.

It was rather amusing seeing Pedro, his head waiter, rubbing ice cubes all over his naked testicles. She wondered what the clients thought, seeing this half-naked man sprawling on the restaurant floor shouting, 'Oh Shit, Oh Shit, I've never felt anything like it.' It definitely put one woman off eating her cheese soufflé.

Sheila had agreed to meet him for lunch at mid-day, but she was a bit worried about what sort of reaction she was going to get. He did set her up. She genuinely thought she was being raped. Surely a simulated rape is the same as a normal rape if the person involved didn't know that it was simulated? If she had got the police involved, they would question her about her dress, or rather the lack of it.

On the other hand, a lack of clothes doesn't mean that rape is acceptable. Far from it, there is no excuse whatsoever. But Sheila was going there to have sex, or was she? She tried to convince herself that she was just going there to entertain, but was she only deceiving herself? She even asked Derek if he wanted her to remove any of her clothes, and she wasn't wearing much anyway.

When it came down to it, the real issue was not the violation of her body, but fear. No man or woman should be put into a position where there was fear involved. No man or woman should be forced into any form of sexual activity under the threat of violence. She had been frightened. It was wrong.

Sheila waited outside the restaurant, trying to build up some courage to enter. Jack saw her, rushed out to meet her, and kissed her on both cheeks. Sheila felt immediate relief. There was no apparent anger. He did rush out, but he hobbled back. Sheila was hoping that the hobbling wasn't down to any injury that she had inflicted. Jack sat her down at the table and lit a candle.

Sheila asked how Anna was. Jack replied that she was working this evening. Sheila asked if she was working at the restaurant or working on him. Jack wondered why the questions about Anna. Sheila thought the same — why did she bring that up, it was nothing to do with her? They both concluded that jealousy was involved in some way.

The fish and chips arrived, and Sheila had to agree that it was probably the best she had ever eaten. The coffee came in a bone china cup and saucer. This was followed by an Eton Mess. Sheila had to admit that it was a cracking meal. She had been treated like a lady. Sheila wondered when they would discuss the recent events.

Jack was the first to crack. He simply said, 'My behaviour was unacceptable. I apologise with no reservations.'

Sheila said, 'I accept your apology.' Jack was hoping for an apology regarding the testicular damage he had received. Then Anna turned up for work.

She stopped at their table, and said, 'Are you still OK for tonight?' Jack just nodded.

Sheila looked at Jack and said, 'So she is going to do some overtime tonight?'

Jack said, 'I need to explain the situation. Anna is working her way through university. She is in her second year, where she has to find her own private accommodation. She works in the restaurant at times that suit her, but she simply doesn't make enough money to live.

'Some of the younger restaurant staff agreed to pay her for sex. I know that it is shocking, but there was a schedule on the kitchen noticeboard. The boys pay her fifty pounds for a couple of hours after work. I simply make use of the facilities on an occasional basis.'

Sheila said, 'So, Anna is really a part-time prostitute.'

Jack said, 'Technically, I guess that you are right, but that word has lots of connotations. She is a really nice girl. There is no way that I see her as a whore.'

Sheila said, 'But you are taking advantage of her.'

Jack said, 'Am I? She is offering a service, and I am simply a client.'

Sheila said, 'But she is being forced into it by economic circumstances.'

Jack said, 'She doesn't want to take out a loan like most other students. You seem very interested in her, why don't you have a chat with her about it?'

Sheila said, 'I would like to talk to her; I will be back tonight.' Before Jack could argue, Sheila said, 'Thank you for a great lunch. See you later.'

Sheila walked back home, thinking about the conversation. Is Anna just being more honest than me? Am I really the whore? That was not the way Sheila saw herself, but then she was criticising Anna's behaviour. Was it because she was so young? Sheila thought that a chat with Anna might help clarify her own thoughts. Perhaps it was just the way society was. The Church had spent decades trying to control what women did with their bodies; that didn't seem right.

Sheila had a relaxing soak with a lavender bath bomb, listening to Mozart's *Cosi Fan Tutte*. She sampled the delights of a fabulous box of Belgian chocolates, helped down with the odd sip of Baileys. Sheila knew how to have a great bath. She realised that you couldn't afford this on the wages of a supermarket till operator. Sheila, without realising it, slowly entered the land of nod.

When she woke up shivering in a cold bath of water, she realised that she was late for her meeting with Jack. She quickly dressed, putting on warm clothes to try and get some heat back into her body. By the time she got to the restaurant, she was forty minutes late. She popped into Jack's flat to find that the action had already started.

As before, Jack was lying on the bed with Anna sitting on his assets, screwing him for all he was worth, well fifty pounds actually. Sheila could see that Anna was a pretty girl, with a good figure, a fine set of immature tits, and long blond hair. Sheila simply said, 'Hi guys, how are you doing?'

Jack said, 'I didn't think you were coming and Anna has to get home, so we thought we would start.'

Anna said, 'Hi, Sheila, I like the red streaks in your hair.'

Sheila said, 'Do you mind me asking you some questions?'

Anna said, 'Not at all, fire away.'

Sheila said, 'How did you get into this?'

Anna said, 'Some of the girls have joined a modelling agency where they meet strangers as requested. I thought about it, but it seemed a bit dangerous to me. You have no idea who you are going to meet. You are travelling late at night. I just didn't fancy it, but the girls can make a lot of money. It certainly solves the problem of paying student fees and accommodation.'

Sheila said, 'Why didn't you take out a loan?'

Anna said, 'I'm studying to be a lawyer. I would end up with costs of over seventy thousand pounds. I'm not prepared to get into that sort of debt.'

Sheila said, 'But you pay it back when you get a job.'

Anna said, 'What if I don't finish the course?'

Sheila asked how she got into it without going through an agency.

Anna replied, 'Well, it happened by accident. I was working here in the kitchens on a hot summer's day. I was wearing shorts and a very skimpy top. We had a few drinks, and the boys dared me to take my top off. After much bantering, I obliged. The boys were delighted, and I found myself really enjoying the attention. My shorts soon followed, and two hours later, I had lost my virginity.

'In bed that night, I wondered what sex was all about. It seemed OK, but it wasn't the mind-blowing experience that I had expected. Back in the kitchens, the boys wanted a repeat of the previous night. I told them that it was going to cost them, without really thinking about it. They asked how much, and I said fifty pounds. I just blurted it out. The next day there was a schedule on the noticeboard, and that is why I'm here now.'

While the conversation was going on, Anna was still screwing Jack. Sheila asked Jack how he felt about it.

Jack said, 'I'm enjoying the feel of my prick rubbing against the walls of Anna's fanny. I would accept that it is taking advantage of Anna, but I do have a normal man's needs. I don't feel guilty as it is doing some good.'

Sheila asked Anna, 'How do you feel about having Jack's cock in your fanny?'

Anna said, 'If you asked me a few years ago, I would have said that it is disgusting, immoral and reprehensible. My secret place was mine, and would only be shared with my husband. Then both my parents had affairs and got divorced. My grandmother has been having an affair with a younger man for the last ten years. What does it all mean? Here I'm letting Jack rub his skin against my skin. Hopefully, he will ejaculate soon, and I can go home.'

Sheila realised that Anna wasn't that keen on sex. Sheila asked Anna, 'Have you ever had an orgasm?'

Anna said, 'No, but I can tell that Jack is not far away from his.'

Sheila said, 'How can you tell?'

Anna said, 'His cock is getting harder, much harder, his cock has grown a bit, his temperature has gone up, his breathing pattern has changed.'

Sheila said, 'That is quite perceptive.'

Anna said, 'That is my legal training.'

Jack had been listening, but he knew that he was about to come. He quite enjoyed having sex with Anna, as there were no obligations. He didn't have to worry about giving her a good time. He could just focus on his orgasm. It was very liberating. He was only using her as a source of relief, but she did know his ways.

She knew that he liked to feel his ejaculation, so before he came, she pushed hard and withdrew slightly so that he could feel his load being discharged. At the same time she contracted her vagina; Anna enjoyed men enjoying her. It was fulfilling in its own way. The time had come, Jack screamed. It quite surprised Sheila.

Sheila sat there thinking, *'Am I living a normal life? I've just watched a "friend" being fucked by a waitress, and I quite enjoyed it.'*

Anna means graceful, beautiful and popular. It seemed to describe the situation quite well, and the moral of the story is that everyone needs some love. If you can't find it, then perhaps buying it is OK.

Crocodiles

Sheila lay in bed that night, thinking about her conversation with Anna. It was odd in some ways that Jack was just incidental. He was just a minor player in a much larger game. It was a bit sad that Anna had such fixed views about sex, at such a young age. She has probably missed the joy of first love. The joy of a first valentine. The joy of a furtive and hurried kiss. The joy of a quick one behind the cycle shed. Or was this just Sheila being sentimental, she asked herself?

Then Sheila thought about her own life, and what she was missing. Sheila had little time for Wormy but missed the simple things of life. Like having someone making you the occasional cup of coffee. The joy of cuddling up on a cold winter's day. The pleasure of watching an annoying video on the box and arguing about it. The holding of hands, the intertwining of fingers. Now, it was the quiet horror of going home to an empty house, the lonely silence of an unshared home, the nagging unhappiness of loneliness.

Sheila shook her head and wondered where these thoughts came from. Was she wrong to think of Jack as a potential soul mate? She didn't feel jealous about Anna shagging him, which surprised her. Jack had his own life. He had his own needs. He needed a mechanical release, and Anna performed that function. Sheila understood that the desires that men had needed to be satisfied. Marriage wasn't really a natural institution, but then what was? Perhaps, the only thing that mattered was happiness? She wondered if she would be happier as half of a couple, but the price was freedom. The price was a loss of independence.

She never used to give any thought to the philosophy of life. But now she could ponder these mysteries, as she had more time on her hands. Her children were grown up and doing their own thing. She had pushed her boundaries beyond what she thought was possible. She was her own woman. She had money in the bank for the first time in her life. She could turn work down if she wanted to. She was alive.

The phone went, and she was grateful that this period of reflection had come to an abrupt end. It was Ken, her manager. He asked how she was, and several pleasantries were exchanged. Sheila asked how married life was going. Ken said, 'Fine,' which Sheila interpreted as "It is facing major problems".

Ken said that there was a new men's club in Aldershot that had specifically asked for her. They were staging a jungle game where Jane would be fed to the crocodiles. Sheila intimated that she didn't really fancy being eaten by aggressive reptiles. Ken said, 'I doubt if it will be the edible threat that you should be worried about.'

Sheila said, 'What could be worse than that?'

Ken said, 'Knowing Thomas, the owner, he has a more intimate threat in mind.'

Sheila said, 'How many crocodiles are we talking about?'

Ken said, 'I've no idea, but the fee is very handsome. You are going to be saved by Marzipan.'

Sheila said, 'Marzipan?'

Ken responded, 'They couldn't use the name "Tarzan" for

copyright reasons.'

It appeared that the event was a one-off. No rehearsals were needed. Sheila just needed to turn up, do her stuff, and that was that. It was "doing her stuff" that concerned her. Clearly, she was going to be the focus of attention at a stag do. Clearly, she was going to be naked. Clearly, she was going to get shagged. The plot had already been agreed. It was now time for the drama.'

Sheila arrived on time. She was always on time. She was taken to a very nice dressing room where Dingo, the Performance Director, met her. Sheila had to ask him about his name. Apparently, as a child in Australia, he was rescued from a fire by a dingo. No one knew why he was called Dingo from then onwards, but then life plays these little tricks.

Dingo said to Sheila, 'Can you slip your clothes off please.' Sheila did as requested, and stood there totally naked. Dingo said, 'You are a gorgeous woman.' Dingo thought that Ken had delivered what he promised: a beauty without inhibitions. Dingo asked Sheila if Ken had explained the rules of the game.

Sheila said, with some honesty, 'All I know is that some crocodiles are involved.'

Dingo explained the game. 'You will go down a slide into a pool of warm water. Waiting for you will be five crocodiles. Their task is to score points by taking advantage of you. You will be covered in grease to make you slippery and, consequently, make it more difficult for the crocs. Tarzan, sorry Marzipan, has the job of rescuing you, and eventually claiming his reward.'

Sheila asked, 'Exactly how will the crocodiles take advantage of me?'

Dingo said, 'The crocs will be wearing suits that cover most of their body except for one part.'

Sheila said, 'So what you are saying is that their cocks will be sticking out.'

Dingo said, 'That is the plan, but the boys have found it difficult to keep their erections going. The suits are a bit constraining, but I think things will change when they see that naked butt of yours. It would be hard for any man to keep control,' and he pointed at the erection in his pants.'

Sheila said, 'And Marzipan's reward is?'

Dingo said, 'I suspect that you have already guessed.'

Sheila thought, *'It looks like there is going to be a fair amount of willy action. My fanny is going to go through it.* Anyway, she wanted some action after seeing Jack and Anna at it.'

Dingo introduced his son, "Little Dingo", who had volunteered to grease her up. After seeing Sheila, Dingo also decided to assist. They both grabbed large dollops of grease and started rubbing it all over Sheila's body. It wasn't an easy job, as Sheila was quite sensitive, especially around the fanny and the boobs, which seemed to be the areas that most of the grease was applied. Sheila was very slippery. It was going to be difficult for the crocodiles to succeed in achieving sexual intercourse. Penetration was not going to be easy.

Sheila stood at the top of a long slide. In the distance, she could see a small pool, a few plastic palm trees and five, somewhat suspect looking, crocodiles. There were a few hundred spectators with cameras surrounding the pool. Some even had tripods, obviously hoping to catch the moment when the crocodile captured its prey. The crocodiles looked rather pathetic, with flappy jaws, deformed feet and very stiff, immobile tails. At this height, their penises didn't look very threatening.

Down she went, much faster than she expected, and much quicker than the crocodiles expected. Two of them were at the end of the shoot with their arms ready to catch her. She was so slippery that she shot through their arms and landed on top of another crocodile. Sheila wasn't that heavy, but the speed of descent caught the victim unprepared, and one of Sheila's legs knocked him out. The unconscious reptilian was hastily removed, and despatched to hospital. Sheila wondered what they would make of it — a comatose alligator with a dangling prick.

The game was restarted, and Sheila was put down the shoot for a second time. She tried to slow herself down, but the grease eliminated most of the friction. She shot down like a bullet, crossed the entire pool, over the protective fence and into the arms of a security guard. The poor man was knocked head over heels into a giant cactus. To say that he was pricked all over would be an understatement. Fortunately, he saved Sheila from a similar fate. Another ambulance was called, and the second casualty was despatched to the hospital.

Two members of the audience attempted to pick Sheila up. This was a mistake as Sheila was pushed upwards, as they gave her a bear hug. It was a bit like grabbing a creased balloon. Sheila eventually returned to Earth with each of her legs landing on the rescuer's' feet. There was the sound of crushed bones, and another ambulance was called.

Sheila managed to walk back to the pool, somewhat disheartened by the number of medical mishaps. She got back into the pool to face four randy crocodiles. Two leapt for her and smashed their heads together in mid-air. One of them was bleeding profusely. Sheila tried to comfort him, but he wasn't having any of it, calling her a jinx. She thought that was a bit unfair, as the fourth ambulance carted off two further victims.

Then there were two. Sheila was getting concerned, as the number of accidents was getting quite silly. The NHS would not be able to cope with this onslaught. There was a danger that they would call this a disaster zone. Consequently, she decided to help the crocodiles and used a palm tree to hold herself in position. She was still in the pool but holding on. She stuck her bottom out so that penetration could be more easily achieved. One of the crocodiles managed to get an erection, but it was too challenging to get the angle right for coitus. Every time he put his hands on Sheila's hips to steady himself, he slid down. He tried entering Sheila's vagina without the use of his hands, but this was a rash and dangerous action. Down he went, pulling Sheila on top of him.

Crocodiles drag their victims down under the water. In this case, Sheila was sitting on top of a drowning croc. Every time she tried to get up, she fell on top of him again. Luckily, he was resuscitated, but it was a close thing. He wasn't so lucky regarding his other injuries: dislocated shoulder, two broken ribs, water on the lungs and a torn penis. It appeared that the zip on the crocodile suit molested his cock and one of his testicles. The hospital thought that he still had a good chance of having children, but there were no guarantees.

The last crocodile did a runner. Well, you couldn't call it running, it was more of a totter. In his eagerness to flee, and the fact that he was taking off the costume as he ran, he fell down a flight of steps. The injuries he received looked worse than they actually were. Modern plastic surgery can achieve wonders, and he was expected to return to work within a year.

Sheila felt a bit disappointed. Five "good men and true" had failed to satisfy the needs of this damsel. The audience had expected a sex-fest but instead had encountered a great theatrical experience. They had probably laughed more than they had ever laughed before.

Sheila was still hoping that Marzipan would save the day. It turned out that he had been injured in a car crash. An ambulance leaving the club had hit his car headlong. He was taken to the nearest A&E in just a loin cloth.

It wasn't easy getting the grease off. At one stage, Sheila thought that she might have to go to the hospital.

Ken phoned the next day. Apparently, they were going to pay her the agreed fee, but they were not happy. Five crocodiles, Marzipan, a security guard, and two members of the general public were suing the club for damages. The club did not believe that it would survive a health and safety inspection, and may have to close.

Sheila protested her innocence. She asked Ken, 'Why did the crocodile cross the road? To eat the chicken. Remember, in this world we are all chickens.'

The Chef Hits One Thousand

After talking to Ken, she felt a bit guilty about the whole crocodile affair. She decided that she was totally innocent and she had carried out her duties as instructed, but the customer defined success. In this case, the customer was not a happy bunny. Ken told her that the crocodiles had paid a lot of money to fuck her. Instead, they were all hospital cases. What was worse, the press had found out, and there was likely to be at least two divorces.

Anyway, she had decided not to be a chicken. She was going to visit Jack and give him the todgering of his life. She wasn't being altruistic. She needed a good seeing to. Sheila discovered that her body needed it when it had been promised. The crocodile incident had not delivered. Jack was a lucky man.

Sheila arrived at the restaurant and entered the back stairs to Jack's flat. She wondered why the door was never locked. It appeared that Jack had been caught a few times with the "wrong" lady and had to make a rapid escape. On other occasions, it was the lady who needed a fast exit route. Nevertheless, it suited her.

Sheila stripped off. She would confront Jack in her birthday suit. That would guarantee to get his juices flowing. She approached the bedroom door, which was ajar. She thought to herself, *'It doesn't look a bit like a jar.'* It was funny how the jokes of childhood reappeared at the strangest moments. She stopped at the entrance as she could hear voices. Sheila thought, *'That's strange, as Anna usually works nights. Jack must have another guest.'*

Sheila hesitantly looked around the door to see Jack in his usual position, on his back being ridden. His cock was deeply entrenched in a young lady's pussy. Sheila thought to herself, *'That appears to be Jack's favourite position.'* Sheila didn't mind it, as it gave the woman a lot of control, but she liked to be taken by the man. She probably preferred a more passive position. Was this a reflection of Jack's character?

Sheila actually enjoyed a bit of voyeurism. It was interesting seeing how other people fuck. She was starting to feel a bit sorry for Jack. At first, he was being ridden. Now he was being abused. His passenger was using his tool like a gardening implement. Jack was being abused. You could tell by the look of agony on his face. She wondered if she should rescue him.

The woman's thighs were simply eating Jack. She had nearly consumed most of his lower body. Jack was twisting and turning, clearly trying to avoid contact with her. Then there were two piercing screams. Sheila wasn't convinced that they would both survive. The woman literally leapt into the air, shouting, 'Serves you right; I've got to get back to my husband now.'

Jack looked shagged, really shagged. His cock was beyond being limp. It had reverted to being the cock of a little boy. There was a smile on his face, but he had lost the ability to talk. In fact, he had lost control of most of his bodily functions.

The woman had a cracking body, with long legs and a fine

set of lungs. Sheila could see that she was a natural blonde. Then it dawned on Sheila that she knew this woman. It was Ken's wife. As she was getting dressed, Sheila decided to hide. Sheila had been watching *The Walking Dead*. She knew how important it was to hide from the zombies.

Sheila dashed downstairs into the kitchen. She managed to crawl head first into a gap by the sink. Her bottom was somewhat exposed, but Sheila would only be there for a few minutes. Then she would go home, as Jack wasn't going to be of any use to her. Fancy Ken's wife getting her oats here. She thought it odd, as Ken was such a good lover.

Jerry, the head chef, had just caught the flash of a naked girl entering his kitchen. He was feeling a bit randy, as Anna was on holiday. Jerry thought it strange how his Monday evening session with Anna had become such an essential aspect of his life. In some ways, he lived for Mondays. He suspected that this girl was one of Jack's protégées. Jerry thought to himself, *'That Jack is a real man, but I'm sure he won't mind me having some of his cast-offs.'*

Jerry quietly tracked Sheila down. He was delighted to see a beautiful arse protruding from the gap by the sink. He thought, *'That will do very nicely.'* He slowly rubbed his finger up and down the crack of Sheila's arse.

Sheila said, 'Nothing.'

Jerry said, 'Nothing.' Jerry entered his finger into Sheila's tight little cunt.

Sheila said, 'Nothing.'

Jerry said, 'Nothing.'

Jerry unzipped his flies and freed his steadily hardening cock. He slowly rubbed his cock up and down the crack of Sheila's arse.

Sheila said, 'Nothing.'

Jerry said, 'Nothing.' Jerry entered his cock into Sheila's tight little cunt.

Sheila said, 'Nothing.'

Jerry said, 'Nothing.' Jerry started to fuck Sheila slowly.

Sheila said, 'Nothing.'

Jerry said, 'Nothing.' Jerry had the habit of counting the strokes. It wasn't particularly romantic, but then Jerry wasn't particularly romantic.

Twenty-six, Jerry was enjoying the softness of her fanny. Seventy-three, Jerry liked the way her cunt grabbed him. One hundred and thirty-six, Sheila liked the brutal stiffness of his cock — it was hard, really hard. Two hundred and eighty-five, Jerry started quickening the strokes. This was a bad sign. Jerry had spent most of his adult life trying to get to one thousand strokes. He usually got to about three hundred and he would come. Jerry decided that there was not a lot he could do; it was such a beautiful fanny — tight, moist and eager. Three hundred and twenty-three, he wasn't going to be able to hold on much longer, then Jack entered the room.

Jack couldn't see what was going on, as the sink was in the middle of the room. All Jack could see was the top half of Jerry chopping up some onions. 'Three hundred and ninety-six,' he mumbled.

Jack said, 'Pardon?' Jerry explained that he was counting the number of chops he was making. Four hundred and ten.

Jack said, 'You are really putting your heart into the chopping, and that is some chopper you are using.'

Jerry explained that he was trying to combine exercise with cooking, and he upped his rate. He didn't think that he would come with Jack in the room. Five hundred and thirty-

74

six. He had passed the halfway mark.

Jack said, 'What is that smell? It reminds me of a knocking shop.'

Jerry said, 'The smell of onions can be quite deceiving,' six hundred and fifty-eight.'

Jack said, 'I know what you mean, but surely you have enough onions now?'

Jerry had to slow down a bit, as it was getting quite exhausting. Sheila was quite grateful as the piston in her fanny was pushing her towards a massive orgasm. She wouldn't be able to scream. If she came now, how could she explain the situation to Jack? Six hundred and eighty-nine.

Jack said, 'I think I will go back to bed for a couple of hours. I feel quite exhausted.' Sheila knew precisely how he felt. Seven hundred and twenty-two.

Jack then said, 'Before I go, can you organise a really nice cake for a good friend of mine? It needs to be a really big cake.'

Jerry said, 'What's her name?'

Jack said, 'Sheila; I think I may be falling in love with her.'

Sheila thought two things, *'That's really nice, and what a bloody cheek. He has just been fucking another man's wife.'* Seven hundred and ninety-one. Jerry asked what he wanted on the cake.

Jack said, 'Red roses, she is going to be the only woman that I give roses to.' Thinking about Jack, Sheila's fanny contracted a few times, causing Jerry to stutter. He was struggling to maintain the fucking process, but he was getting so near to his target. Eight hundred and twenty-three.

Jerry said, 'Jack, are you serious about Sheila?'

Jack said, 'Yes, she is just so beautiful. Her smile would

out-perform that of Helen of Troy. Her personality is just so sweet, honest, caring, loving, exciting, funny, engaging.'

Before he could carry on, Jerry said, 'Stop, you have got it bad.'

Jack said, 'I know, I just can't help thinking about her. When I fuck another woman, all I think about is fucking her.'

Eight hundred and eighty-six. Jerry said, 'Have you fucked her yet?'

Jack said, 'Yes and no; I've fucked her twice, but we haven't really made love yet. I want to suck her toes. I want to chew her breasts. I want to caress every part of her. I want my cock to investigate every crook and cranny.'

Sheila thought, *'Dirty bugger'*, but she had no idea that he felt this way. Nine hundred and twenty-seven.

Jerry was still enjoying the todgering, but his cock was starting to ache. Sheila started to feel guilty; Jack was proposing his undying love, and his chef was porking her. She needed to keep quiet and hope that Jack would go back to bed. Jerry said, 'Do you want any text on the cake?' Nine hundred and eighty-four.

Jack said, 'Yes please.' Nine hundred and ninety-one.

Jerry said, 'What exactly?' Nine hundred and ninety-six.

Jack said, 'Sheila, I love you.' One thousand. Jerry came; it had just been too much for him. Sheila was swimming in vaginal fluids and Jerry's come. Jack noticed that something was wrong. He asked Jerry if he was OK.

Jerry said, 'I'm OK; just give me a few moments.' He had achieved the one thousand mark. He started to wonder who the girl was, but then Jack wanted to show him the card he had purchased for Sheila.

Jerry quickly zipped up and followed Jack out of the

kitchen. Sheila managed to reverse out. She also managed to fight off cramp, and clean herself up. After one thousand strokes, Sheila still didn't feel satisfied. She still needed an orgasm.

She grabbed a tablecloth to cover herself up and hurried home. What a day — she had caught Ken's wife in the act, and learnt how Jack felt about her. But how could she trust a man like that? It was shocking — doesn't the man have any morals?

Talking about morals, the point of this story is that it is not all about numbers.

The Great Cake Story: Part 1

Sheila had a restless night. Should she tell Ken about his wife's affair? How should she react to Jack's proposal, if it was a proposal? Was he the sort of man she wanted, could she ever trust him? Would Ken shoot the messenger? How would Anna regard the situation? Sheila's head swam. There was no clarity, just a drunken emotional hotchpotch.

Jack wasn't sure how Sheila would react to the cake. Was it effectively a proposal? What was he proposing? He thought he loved her, no he knew that he loved her, but he hardly knew her. What was he trying to achieve? Would she move in with him? He knew that he would have to change his ways, but would she? Did she already have a boyfriend? He had never experienced such emotional turmoil before.

Ken was trying to decide if he ever really loved his wife. Did she love him? He thought it unlikely. The marriage was only six months old, and she had already mentioned the word "mistake". When he fantasised about a woman, the image was always Sheila. Did he love her? He thought he probably did. She had a remarkable effect on him. He always got the impression that she loved him. She seemed to give herself wholeheartedly to all of his projects. Or was this just another fantasy? Ken considered himself to be a reasonable man, but he had a strong jealous streak. He might not love his wife, but he could not tolerate another man fucking her. Ken would kill that man. What should he do? The indecision was affecting his work and stressing him out.

Anna had gone home to see her parents. There she was confronted by a furious mother and father. They had discovered that she had been selling her body to pay for the university fees. How could she bring such shame to the family? How could they ever look her in the eyes again?

Anna raised the issue of her father molesting her on many occasions. He had never raped her, but it had been very close. That was one of the reasons she went to university to avoid his unwelcome attentions. That was one of the reasons she was training to be a lawyer, to help protect the innocent against fathers like hers. Her mother was as bad. She knew what had been going on. She used Anna to stop her husband from abusing her. Anna cried; Anna's mother cried. Anna's father had no answers. No answers at all, but they all had questions.

Ken's wife had enjoyed her night of passion with Jack. He was a real man. Ken was a great lover, but he was far too nice. She realised that she was attracted to bastards. She wanted to be treated badly. She wanted to be used and discarded. She would always crave more of that. She wondered what was wrong with her. She couldn't think of anything or anybody to blame. She was just a bad penny. She knew that Ken would be history in the next few days. She would be gone, gone from his life forever.

Jerry couldn't stop thinking about the woman he had just fucked. She took one thousand thrusts without saying a word. That was a woman in a million. At that moment in time, he loved her, but who was she? He had to track her down. He had to have her again.

Wormy, Sheila's ex-husband, wanted her back. He

realised that his life had no value without Sheila. It wasn't her housekeeping skills. It wasn't her culinary excellence. It wasn't her organisational abilities. It was her. Just Sheila. He just wanted Sheila. He just wanted her in his arms again. How could he get her back?

Jack phoned Sheila and invited her to dinner at his restaurant. Sheila accepted, but she still wasn't sure what the best way forward was. She experienced butterflies in her stomach for the first time in years. She tried to remember when she last had them. It was her prom. Was that significant? Sheila packed a skimpy nightie. She assumed that it might be needed.

Ken phoned Sheila for a chat. He didn't have any work for her, but he was hoping that she could help clarify things. Ken said, 'I think my wife is having an affair.'

Sheila said, 'What makes you think that?'

Ken said, 'The whispers, the lies, the hidden conversations, odd receipts, nights spent away from home. I'm not sure who the philanderer is, but I have a private eye on the case.'

Sheila wasn't sure what to say, but she said, 'I think you are right, the bitch doesn't deserve you.' Sheila was surprised how much venom there was in her voice. Ken took that as positive advice; he knew that he could count on her.

Anna had a new life with her friends at the restaurant. They were her family now. She wanted to be back in Jack's bed. She wanted to tell her parents to "fuck off", but she calmly told them that she would probably never see them again. She cried, her mum cried, her father had regrets. She caught the train home.

Ken's wife decided that the time had come. The time had come to move in with Jack. She decided that she would just turn up. Ideally, she would just sneak into his bed. Jack could do whatever he liked with her.

Jerry wondered how he could track his new woman down. Then he had a brainwave. There would be some security footage from the cameras in the restaurant. At least he would have a picture of her.

Wormy, for the first time in his life, was going to be spontaneous. He booked a restaurant for tonight near Sheila's house. His only problem was getting her to go there with him. She had to come, as he had paid a deposit.

Sheila arrived at Garibaldi's Italian Restaurant on time. She was always on time. Jack was waiting for her with a bunch of twelve red roses. He led her to the best table in the house. A small band was playing *When a Man Loves a Woman*. Sheila's butterflies were fluttering. Sheila ordered a medium steak. Jack ordered steak tartare and a jeroboam of champagne. Sheila thought, *'No expense has been spared.'* Jack complimented her on her silver threaded dress, and her matching shoes. She did look lovely. Little did Jack know that Sheila was only wearing the dress and shoes.

Ken's detective had tracked the bastard down. He was the owner of an Italian restaurant a few miles away. He grabbed two bouncers who were on his books and prepared to make his way there.

Anna was naked, waiting in Jack's bed for the restaurant to close. She hoped that he would be pleasantly surprised. She desperately needed comforting.

Ken's wife was in a taxi on the way to Jack's restaurant. She was wearing a fur coat, with nothing underneath.

Jerry had been through the security footage. He had a perfect photo of a goddess. She was one of the most beautiful women he had ever seen. He wanted her more than ever. He thought that there was a fair chance that Jack would recognise her. He asked one of the waiters to see if Jack could spare a few minutes in the kitchen. He said, 'Tell him that it is very urgent.'

Wormy couldn't make contact with Sheila. As he had paid a deposit, he decided to have dinner at the restaurant, although he wasn't dressed for the part.

As the band was playing *You Look Wonderful Tonight*, a very large cake was wheeled in. It contained the words, *Sheila, I love you*. Jack looked into her eyes and was about to speak when a waiter asked Jack to go to the kitchen. Jack said, 'Not now, I'm busy.'

The waiter said, 'Jerry said it was very urgent.' When the head chef says it's very urgent, then it's normally very urgent. Jerry had no choice but to go.

Sheila looked across the room and thought she saw Wormy sitting there on his own. He was busily tucking into a spaghetti Bolognese and making a fine mess of himself, the tablecloth and the floor.

Ken's wife crept up the stairs into Jack's room and assumed that the body under the quilt was Jack. She stripped off her fur coat, jumped on the bed and shouted, 'Take me, I'm yours.' Anna hadn't expected a naked woman landing on top of her, and thought it was some sort of attack. Her natural reaction was to defend herself, and she gave the woman a severe left jab.

Ken and his two bouncers arrived and demanded to see Jack. The head waiter wasn't sure where Jack had gone. Ken decided to create an incident to draw Jack out, and started emptying the client's' dinners on their heads. This didn't go down too well with the customers, and fisticuffs broke out. Ken was glad that he had the two bouncers with him.

Jack wanted to know what the crisis in the kitchen was all about. Jerry explained that previously in the week when they were discussing onions, he was secretly shagging this beautiful bird behind the sink. Jack said, 'I thought you were drunk because you were acting so strangely.'

Jerry said, 'No, I had achieved a life time ambition by giving this woman one thousand thrusts.'

Jack said, 'One thousand thrusts of what?'

Jerry responded, 'I gave her one thousand thrusts with my todger, and she didn't say a word. She took it like a trooper.'

Jack said, 'That is some sort of whore.'

Jerry said, 'I'm not having you call my woman a whore.'

Jack said, 'Sorry, I didn't mean to offend; where did you meet her?'

Jerry replied, 'Well here; I came into the kitchen, and there was this beautiful arse sticking out next to the sink. I just took advantage of her.'

Jack laughed, 'You took advantage of her one thousand times?' Jerry admitted that he had. Jack said, 'I don't see how you can call her your woman; the only part of her you would recognise is her arse.'

Ken's wife responded with a well-timed right hook. This knocked Anna off the bed onto the floor by the stairs. Anna wasn't sure who this woman was, but if she wanted a fight, she was going to get one. However, before she could respond, Ken's wife moved into kick-boxing mode, and Anna went sprawling down the stairs onto the restaurant floor. Ken's wife followed her down the stairs, preparing to deliver the killer blow.

Sheila thought she saw a naked Anna tumble down the stairs. She was planning to help, when Wormy's spaghetti Bolognese was deposited on his head. The sauce was running down his neck. It actually made her day. Wormy stood up, ready to retaliate, but seeing that the bouncer was twice his size, decided to resist and said, 'Thank you.'

The bouncer asked, 'Are you being funny?'

Wormy tried to say, 'No,' 'but it was too late, the remains of the spaghetti were poured down the back of his trousers. This was followed by a round of garlic bread, the salt and pepper pot, and a Fanta Orange with straw. The bouncer then told Wormy to sit down, and Wormy obliged. Sheila's day had already been made, but this topped it all.

Jerry said, 'I'm not even sure that I would recognise the woman's arse, but I have been through the security footage from the cameras. I'm pretty sure that this is the woman.' Jerry presented Jack with a photo of a gorgeous naked woman. Jack couldn't believe what he saw. It was Sheila. Jack grabbed the photo and stormed back into the restaurant.

For the second time that day, Jack couldn't believe what he saw. Two naked women were fighting by the stairs. Thirty-odd customers were brawling, mostly covered in a variety of Italian dishes. The man nearest to him had his trousers down and appeared to be extracting a salt pot from his rectum. Anyway, enough of this, his temper was in charge and he had to confront Sheila. He started shouting, 'You are a whore, a filthy whore.'

On the way to Sheila's table, Jack's leg was mistakenly grabbed by Anna, which sent him flying. His body smashed against Sheila's table, knocking the cake onto Sheila's lap. Anna's blood was boiling, and she gave Ken's wife a great uppercut, followed by a left hook and some pretty brutal hair pulling. Anna was making significant headway, and Ken's wife ended up head first in the cake. Sheila's chair collapsed under the combined weight of two people and the cake. Unfortunately, Sheila's dress was ripped off in the process.

Wormy, who was now trouserless, was trying to help Ken's wife escape. Ken then spotted his wife's naked bottom sticking out of a very large cake. He assumed that Wormy was Jack, and immediately attacked him with two breadsticks. They went straight up Wormy's nostrils. Ken couldn't believe his luck — what a brilliant move. Ken then spotted Sheila on the floor with her dress ripped off. A good-looking man was calling her a stinking whore.

Ken wasn't having anyone being rude to "his 'Sheila'" and leapt onto Jack's back. Ken's wife came to Jack's defence and smashed Ken with a model of Madonna. Anna still saw Ken's wife as the enemy and stuck a tiramisu straight up her arse. It wasn't the most effective of weapons, but it did surprise her adversary. She followed up with a raspberry panna cotta. Jerry came to the rescue of his boss, but then spotted Sheila, and declared his undying love.

The police had a field day. Thirty-four arrests, including three for indecent exposure. The press, as usual, got it wrong. In one paper it appeared that it was football hooliganism from supporters of Arsenal and Spurs. In another article, it was women carrying out a naked protest against the fur trade.

Well, how do we sum it all up? Jack never proposed and was unlikely to in the future. Ken and his wife split up. Jerry was still in love with his record-breaker, but Sheila was not interested. Ken's ex-wife and Anna were now living together. Wormy was still wondering what happened. He was still removing pieces of glass from his arse. Anyway, he decided to stick with the single life.

So what did our heroine do? She just carried on.

The moral of the story is 'that "too many cooks spoil the broth, but many hands make light work". And then Sheila thought, *'Who put the turd in Saturday?'*

The Great Cake Story: Part 2

'Well, well, well,' Sheila thought, *'What happened?' I was sitting there in my most elegant attire, waiting for a proposal of marriage. Three hours later, I was stark naked, facing indecency charges in Wellesley Road Police Station in Croydon. For the life of me, I'm not exactly sure what happened in between those events.*

I remember that Jack was being particularly romantic. I remember the red roses and the band playing You Look Wonderful Tonight *. I remember the steak and champagne. I remember that I was only wearing my silver dress and a pair of matching shoes. I remember this truly massive cake arriving with the words,* Sheila, I love You *on it. I remember being absolutely thrilled and somewhat light-headed from the champagne.*

I remember Jack preparing to kneel when he was interrupted by a waiter. I remember Jack rushing off to the kitchens.

I remember spotting Wormy having a meal and then minutes later seeing him removing spaghetti from his head. I was even more surprised to see that he had removed his trousers and pants. He has been known to do that before, but not in an upmarket Italian restaurant. I was even more surprised to see Anna put some kitchen tongs up his anus. It's not the sort of thing you expect to see in polite society.

It was clearly a night of surprises, as Anna managed to extract a pepper pot. If you had asked me what was most likely to come out of Wormy's arse, I would not have said a pepper pot. What made it worse was that Wormy was screaming, 'That really hurts, it really stings.' Sheila could almost feel the pain that fresh pepper would cause in a rectum. She had to laugh. At the same time, she thought it was a waste of valuable condiments.

Sheila didn't think she could cope with any other surprises when Anna forced the tongs back up Wormy's arse. She shouted, as there was a remarkable amount of din in the room, 'I think it has gone too far up. Our chances of getting it out are very slim. Nature will have to take its course.'

To be honest, I had lots of questions. Why was Wormy there? Why did he have spaghetti on his head, and of course I wanted to know why he had a pepper pot up his arse? Sheila wondered if she was just too curious. What else was up his bum? Why was Anna naked and covered in bruises, but then the evening progressed?

I also remember a rather large, well-endowed woman trying to remove a hot lasagne from her bra. Her husband, or should I say "life-partner" had his hands in there, assisting as much as he could, but his cigarette somehow managed to set her dress on fire. Another man was liberally spraying them from a soda syphon.

On the next table, three society ladies were trying to remove a variety of pastas from their heads. A linguine, a vermicelli, and a tagliatelle had already been deposited. A middle-aged woman with mauve hair, and a large pearl necklace, was using a wooden chair to hold back a bruiser of a man, who was trying to land a tasty looking, cannelloni on her. I won't forget her words, "Keep your distance young man, you are not gonna get pasta me". Sheila wasn't sure if she was joking or not, but the look in her eyes was quite terrifying.

Sheila said, 'Wherever I looked, food fights were in progress. I've absolutely no idea what caused this. I remember ducking to miss a giant, spinning Margherita. It was a war on a scale unknown to Croydon.'

Inspector Knight said, 'I understand that Wormy is your ex-husband?'

Sheila said, 'Yes, that is correct, we divorced a few years ago.'

Inspector Knight said, 'I find it hard to believe that it was just a coincidence that he was at the restaurant at the same time as you. Was he following you?'

Sheila said, 'I can understand where you are coming from, but I think it was just a coincidence.'

Inspector Knight said, 'In my experience, there is no such thing as a coincidence. If you are holding things back, we will find out, and you will be in trouble. Wormy is one of our chief suspects here! Please continue with your statement.'

Sheila said, 'Is there any chance of some clothes?'

Inspector Knight said, 'Not at the moment, please continue.'

Sheila said, 'As I've already pointed out, there was a lot of disruption in the restaurant. Suddenly, Jack, the restaurant owner, came running out of the kitchen shouting, 'You whore.' I'm not sure who he was directing his anger at, but it must have been something to do with the kitchens. I can't really explain what happened next, but Jack came flying through the air, and hit my table.'

Inspector Knight, 'What do you mean flying?'

89

Sheila said, 'That's what it looked like. He flew into my table.'

Inspector Knight, 'Did someone push him?'

Sheila said, 'I don't think so. He just arrived and slammed against my table, sending everything flying. Sadly, the fabulous cake that was made for me flew up in the air and landed on my lap. I was covered in chocolate icing and marzipan. I'm talking about a seriously large cake.'

Inspector Knight agreed that it was indeed a large cake, as he had seen the remains.

Sheila then said, 'Things got even more surreal, as the wife of my manager dived into the cake, which as you know was on my lap.'

Inspector Knight said, 'Can I stop you there; we had reports that two naked women were fighting, and one received a punch that knocked her into the cake.'

Sheila didn't want to get the girls into trouble, and said, 'I think you will find that it was a dive.' Inspector Knight looked quizzical.

Sheila said, 'Well, the force of Ken's wife landing on the cake caused my chair to collapse. I guess it was the combined weight of two women and the cake. Chairs aren't designed for that.'

Inspector Knight, 'I understand that you claim that this collapse ripped your dress off?'

Sheila said, 'Yes, that was the case.'

Inspector Knight, 'This is an important point, it has a direct bearing on the indecency charge against you.'

Sheila said, 'It was a skimpy dress, held in place by a couple of clips. It doesn't take much to dislodge them. Believe me, that collapse was enough to do it.'

Inspector Knight, 'I'm not sure if I believe you. Anyway, what happened to your underwear?'

Sheila went bright red and said, 'I wasn't wearing any. I was just wearing a dress and a pair of shoes.'

Inspector Knight, 'Is that why Jack was calling you a whore?'

Sheila said, 'I'm not sure if I want to carry on with this conversation. Regarding the underwear, I didn't want there to be a knicker line.'

Inspector Knight, 'I suggest that Jack was calling you a whore because you were not wearing any underwear.'

Sheila said, 'Fine, if that is what you want to believe.'

Inspector Knight, 'So, now you are naked, what happened next?'

Sheila said, 'Wormy, my ex-husband, was trying to help Ken's wife get out of the cake.'

Inspector Knight, 'So, you are saying that a naked man who had been covered in spaghetti, and who had just had a pepper pot removed from his arse, came to the rescue of a naked woman in your cake. What sort of sex party was this?'

Sheila said, 'Wormy was just trying to be helpful, that's the way he is. Then two breadsticks were stuck up his nostrils.'

Inspector Knight, 'Why, and who did it?' Sheila didn't want Ken to get into trouble and, to be honest, she had no idea why he did it.

Sheila said, 'I'm not sure. I just saw the results. Wormy was standing there naked from the waist down, with Ken's wife's bottom in his hands, with a one-foot-long breadstick up each nostril. He didn't look happy. I even thought I saw some tears in his eyes.'

Inspector Knight, 'For God's sake, woman, if I had two

hard Italian breadsticks up my nostrils, I would shed more than a few tears.'

Inspector Knight, 'I understand that things then got a bit violent?' Sheila nodded.

Inspector Knight, 'Tell me what happened.'

Sheila said, 'It was a bit of a blur.'

Inspector Knight, 'We find that these things normally are.'

Sheila said, 'There was some name-calling, and then my manager jumped on Jack's back. Ken's wife went to Jack's rescue.'

The Inspector said, 'Stop there. Are you telling me that Ken attacked Jack, but Ken's wife attacked Ken?'

Sheila said, 'I think so; it's all a bit confusing, isn't it?'

Inspector Knight said, 'Can you elaborate further?'

Sheila said, 'Not really, but Anna went for Ken's wife and stuck firstly a tiramisu, and then a raspberry panna cotta up her arse.'

Inspector Knight, 'Why would Anna attack Ken's wife? Why would Ken's wife attack Ken?'

Sheila said, 'It's all beyond me.'

Inspector Knight, 'What happened next?'

Sheila said, 'I caught Wormy removing the Italian delicacies from Ken's wife's arse.' He then asked what happened next. Sheila said, 'Wormy started eating it.'

Inspector Knight, 'He starting eating her out?'

Sheila said, 'No, the Italian desserts. He has always been a sucker for coffee flavoured puddings.'

'Then Jerry rushed towards me, shouting his undying love.'

Inspector Knight, 'Did you know him?'

Sheila wasn't sure what to say, but she said, 'Yes and no;

we were two ships that met in the night. In other words, I was a kitchen utensil.' The Inspector had no idea what she was talking about, but was now keen to finish the interview.

Inspector Knight, 'I need to point out that you have been arrested for indecent exposure before. It can't go on, but I can't see any point in pursuing this. We will not recommend that any further action be taken against you.

'However, we are concerned about this wormy character. Would you say he is dangerous?' Sheila shook her head. The Inspector asked if he was a drug taker or dealer. Sheila shook her head again.

The moral of the story is:
- A kiss without a beard is like an egg without salt.
- Trust no one till you have eaten a bushel of salt with him.
- I peddle salt, it rains; if I peddle flour, the wind blows.
- A dry finger cannot pick up the salt.
- As a daughter grows up, she is like smuggled salt.
- Too many cooks over-salt the porridge.
- Before you make a friend, eat a pack of salt with him.
- The cure for anything is salt water — sweat, tears, or the sea.
- Give neither counsel nor salt till you are asked for it.

Sheila didn't understand the moral either.

The Great Cake Story: Part 3

'I planned everything down to the last detail. I organised red roses, steak, and champagne, the best table in the house, and I even managed to get the band to play *When a Man Loves a Woman*. I even organised a massive cake. I was in love with her. I planned to propose that night.'

Inspector Knight asked him to confirm who his intended was. He replied, 'Sheila, of course,' wondering why he even asked the question.

Inspector Knight could see Jack's quizzical look and responded, 'I only asked because there appear to be several other women who have the hots for you.' Jack wasn't sure who he was on about.

Inspector Knight asked him to continue. Jack said, 'I was about to propose when one of my waiter's demanded my attention in the kitchen. I told him that I was busy; I was beginning the kneeling down process, so it was a critical moment. He was so insistent that I really had no choice but to go to the kitchen. I'm now so grateful that I did.

'When I got to the kitchen, Jerry, my head chef came clean.'

Inspector Knight couldn't resist saying, 'An admirable quality in a chef.'

Jack didn't even smile, and continued, 'It appears that Jerry gave this woman an education in thrusting techniques.'

Inspector Knight, 'Thrusting techniques?'

Jack said, 'Yes, he found this bit of crumpet by the sink in the kitchen, with her arse sticking out. It was on public view.'

Inspector Knight, 'That doesn't sound too hygienic.'

Jack said, 'I agree, so he went to investigate and was overcome with lust. Here was a, to put it mildly, juicy fanny ready for the plucking.'

Inspector Knight, 'So he plucked her?'

Jack said, 'Yes, to be exact. He entered her vagina one thousand times.'

Inspector Knight, 'So he gave her one thousand thrusts? What made him do that?'

Jack said, 'Apparently, he had always counted the number of thrusts during love making, and his life time ambition was to hit one thousand. On the final thrust, he came.'

Inspector Knight, 'You have to admire the man, he is clearly a romantic. Did the woman object?'

Jack, 'Apparently not; she took it like a trooper without saying a word.'

Inspector Knight, 'That is some tart.'

Jack, 'I'm glad that you see my position. That is why I was calling her a whore. That is what she is, a fucking whore.' Inspector Knight could see that Jack was getting angry, in fact, very angry.

Jack, 'She meant everything to me; I was going to marry the bitch.'

Inspector Knight, 'Who are we talking about?'

Jack, 'Sheila, of course.' 'For the second time, Jack wondered why the inspector was not keeping up.

Inspector Knight, 'You are saying that Sheila was the arse sticking out by the sink?'

95

Jack, 'Yes, my intended had just been fucked by a member of my staff; it was embarrassing, it was devastating, it's just so hard to believe.'

Inspector Knight, 'I also find it hard to believe that it was Sheila — she seems so refined, so demure, so much a lady.'

Jack, 'She might appear that way, but clearly, she is not. The odd shag I could probably accept, but to receive a thousand thrusts from my head chef, in my kitchen, is just too much.'

Inspector Knight, 'Can I ask what she was doing naked in the kitchen?'

Jack, 'Absolutely no idea.'

Inspector, 'What happened next?'

Jack, 'My blood was boiling; I had never felt so angry in my life. I decided to go and confront the harlot, so I rushed out of the kitchen. I had contemplated taking a chopper with me, but I'm not sure if she could cope with another big chopper, after what she had been through.

'Then, I was gobsmacked. What had happened to my restaurant?'

Inspector, 'What do you mean?'

Jack, 'Two naked women were fighting by the stairs, a half-naked man was walking around aimlessly, and at least a dozen food fights were going on.'

Inspector, 'I assume that this is not a typical Friday night?' Jack responded with an angry frown.

Inspector, 'Who were these girls?'

Jack, 'One was Anna, one of our waitresses, and the other was just a friend I know.'

Inspector, 'Why were they fighting?'

Jack, 'I've no idea, but they were really going for it. It was rather erotic — two beautiful, naked women slamming into each other. There was punching, kicking and a fair amount of hair pulling. They totally ignored the diners, who were watching attentively. They were just totally consumed with each other. It gradually turned naughtier, as fingers were entering very private places, and breast sucking broke out. Some of the diners were clapping. They seemed to think it was a show put on by the restaurant.'

Inspector, 'Do you know these girls?'

Jack, 'Yes.'

Inspector, 'Do you know these girls intimately?'

Jack wasn't sure how to respond, but he thought that he had better be honest. Jack, 'Yes, I know both of them intimately. I have sex with Anna every Tuesday and Sunday, and the other woman was just a friend, that I occasionally have sex with.'

Inspector, 'What days do you manage to fit Sheila in?'

Jack, 'It wasn't like that. Anna needed some additional funding for her university course, so the boy's set up a schedule of love-making.'

Inspector, 'And this was formalised?'

Jack, 'Well, yes.'

Inspector, 'This could be construed as maintaining a house of ill-repute, or even a brothel. At the very least, it is aiding and abetting prostitution.'

Jack, 'But Anna was quite happy with the situation.'

Inspector, 'That doesn't change the law.'

'It seems to me that you are criticising Sheila for the thrusting episode, but you are maintaining a brothel, and fucking one of the girls two days a week, and then also fucking this other woman occasionally.'

Jack, 'I can see where you are coming from, but Sheila knew about Anna.'

Inspector, 'And she didn't mind?'

Jack, 'I don't think so; she even watched Anna and me performing.'

Inspector, 'This whole debacle is just getting sicker and sicker; what sort of man are you?' Jack was starting to get the feeling that things were not going his way.

Inspector, 'After your voyeuristic viewing of the two naked wrestlers, what happened next?'

Jack,' 'I decided to confront Sheila, but then Anna grabbed my leg, which sent me flying. I smashed into Sheila's table and knocked the massive cake into her lap. She was absolutely smothered in cake debris, but she still managed to look absolutely beautiful. I'm not sure how she does it.'

Inspector, 'Please continue.'

Jack, 'I was in a slightly dazed state, but I saw several weird things going on. There was a woman whose dress was on fire. She looked like she was covered in layers of aubergines and minced meat. It might have just been my imagination, but there may have been a man playing with her tits. There may have been three other ladies covered in a variety of pasta dishes. I remembered thinking that the vermicelli didn't go well with her dress. I may have seen a Margherita flying by. It was very surreal.

'I doubted my sanity, when I saw Anna, who had just been in the fight, pushing a kitchen utensil up the arse of one of our customers. This is totally against our rules, fraternising with a customer. Anna had always been willing to try new things, but this sort of sexual deviation was totally unacceptable. I wouldn't normally mind, but this was taking place in the middle of the restaurant. What are our customers going to think regarding our hygiene standards? That is no way to treat a pair of tongs.

'I was also concerned that the customer was not enjoying the experience. My years in the trade have given me a genuine insight. I can typically spot when a customer is not happy. However, I was rather shocked to see that Anna had removed one of our standard pepper pots from his arse. They are not designed to be deposited there. They are meant to be tableware.

'I made a mental note to carry out a salt pot inventory. He made me wonder how many other diners were secreting our cruet sets up their arses. Whatever happens, I will get to the bottom of it. Anyway, it was good news that once the pepper pot was removed from the man's arse, he seemed a lot happier. At least the screaming stopped.'

Inspector, 'I've already got some statements regarding the pepper pot. What do you know about this man?'

Jack, 'Never seen him before. He is not typical of our clientele. Most of our customers do not come to the restaurant wearing tracksuit bottoms and a T-shirt with the logo, "My other woman is much prettier than this one". It took us quite some time to get him to remove his stained duffle coat. He found it very difficult to select something from the menu, and pointed at another table, and said I would have that one. The man on the table thought that he was referring to his wife, and we only just managed to stop a fight by offering them free drinks.'

Inspector, 'Is he a drug dealer?'

Jack, 'No idea, but he did smell funny.'

Inspector, 'In what way?'

Jack, 'I would say, 'a mixture of stale farts, cabbage, paint, motorcycle oil and beans, lots of beans.'

Inspector, 'You seem quite specific.'

Jack, 'It's part of the job to develop our sense of smell.'

Inspector, 'You know, of course, that he is Sheila's ex-husband.'

Jack, 'I can't believe that, Sheila is a lady; she is so sophisticated. What would she be doing with that bundle of rags? What was he doing here?'

Inspector, 'That is what we would like to know.'

'Do you have the pepper pot?'

Jack, 'I hope not. Well, after Anna extracted the pepper pot, I was surprised to see the tongs re-enter his rectum. It's the sort of thing that could lose me my licence.'

Inspector, 'What happened next?'

Jack, 'He seemed to wander off with the tongs dangling from his backside. I also thought that he needed to wash his hair; it looked like he had some spaghetti on his head.'

'I may have got the sequence slightly wrong, such a lot of stuff was happening, but the woman who was fighting Anna dived into the cake.'

Inspector, 'Was she pushed?'

Jack, 'I'm not entirely sure, but she appeared to dive in head first, leaving her naked arse for all to see. Her legs were dangling all over the place. You could clearly see her erect clitoris. A number of the men were using their phones to take photos.

'The arrival of this woman knocked Sheila's chair over and wedged the woman further into the cake. It's a big cake, you know.'

Inspector, 'I agree that it's a big cake. I've seen the

remains.'

Jack, 'Then Sheila stood up, completely nude. I don't know why she did it. Perhaps, she wanted to beat her recently acquired thrust record. She did look gorgeous. The cameras were then directed at her. I heard someone say, "It's a bit like that play called 'The Play that Goes Wrong". Some of them seemed to think that all of these events were planned.

'I didn't think that the situation could get any worse, but then the strange trouserless man attempted to rape the woman in the cake. I could understand where he was coming from. Here was a beautiful, naked woman covered in butter icing. His gander was up, probably from the rectal probing, and he decided to give her one. It crossed my mind that she was going to be disappointed, as his erect penis was rather challenged.'

Inspector, 'Challenged?'

Jack,' 'It was so tiny, a puny little rose bud. She might get more of a thrill from the kitchen utensil that was still protruding from his arse.'

'I thought I had seen everything when this man approached the rapist and stuck two breadsticks up his nostrils. He looked angry, and I assumed that he was going to punch the rapist. To be fair, I don't think it was a rape attempt after all, as he was pulling the woman out of the cake. It was entirely accidental that his wee little cock entered her cream filled fanny. Perhaps, he deserved the forced entry of a twelve-inch breadstick up each nostril. I don't know. What I do know is that it would be a very painful experience. One would hurt, two would be excruciating.'

Inspector, 'Is that the end of the affair?'

Jack, 'No, there was much more to come. I think I was shouting obscenities at Sheila. My emotions were in such a state. Sheila was cleaning herself up. A young man was wiping her naked body down with tissues that got me even angrier, especially as her breasts seemed to need a lot of attention. Another man was cleaning her bottom, possibly with his tongue. Sheila seemed to lap it up. Then the man who attacked the rapist jumped on my back. I've no idea why he did it. I, of course, immediately covered my nostrils for protection.'

'The woman in the cake hit the man on my back with my mother's figurine of Madonna. This figurine is a prized family heirloom brought all the way from Pisa. To be honest, it's head has been lost twice before, so it was no great surprise when it came off again. Then, Anna arrived and stuck a tiramisu up the woman's arse. I think a raspberry panna cotta was also despatched to the same area. To be honest, it didn't make much impact, as her arse still contained a fair amount of cake.

'Jerry then rushed in to assist me, spotted Sheila and fell on his knees, proclaiming his undying love for her. That got me annoyed, especially when he chased off the two guys who were cleaning Sheila. He was quite terrifying, running through the restaurant with a cleaver in his hand. It should have been me protecting my woman.'

Inspector, 'Do you have anything else to add to your statement?'

Jack, 'Have I committed a crime?'

Inspector, 'It's not for me to decide.'

The moral of the story is, "A cake on a plate, is better than two up your arse".

The Great Cake Story: Part 4

'I used a detective agency to track down the bastard who was having an affair with my wife. I have only been married to Charlotte for six months, and I suspected for a while, that things were not going well.'

Inspector Knight, 'Can you give some examples?'

Ken, 'Firstly, she kept trying to avoid sex. I'm a damn good lover. Most women want more. I've never had any complaints, well, perhaps a few, but then again too few to mention.' The Inspector could tell that he had a musical background.

Ken, 'I'm a very attentive lover; I'm not sure what is wrong with her. There have been too many lies to mention. There are some strange purchases on her credit card. Who was she buying Old Spice for? Why did she buy an Arsenal season ticket, when I'm a Spurs fan? Who is getting the nude photos of her? Lots of secret telephone calls. She disappears for the odd night, coming back looking thoroughly shagged.'

Inspector, 'I guess that's because she has been completely shagged.'

Ken, 'Manners, please.'

Inspector, 'Sorry. Which detective did you use?'

Ken, 'Bill Pants.'

Inspector, 'You mean old smarty pants; he is a great detective. I bet he hunted the man down?'

Ken, 'It wasn't that difficult — Jack phoned my home asking if Charlotte can come out to play.'

Inspector, 'Never.'

Ken, 'Charlotte had told him that I was her disabled uncle who had piles, gout and dementia. Is that how she sees me? Anyway, ignoring all of that, I wasn't having another man shagging my wife, well not without my permission.'

Inspector, 'So, what did you do?'

Ken, 'I rounded up two of my employees.'

Inspector, 'You mean the two bruisers you brought with you?'

Ken, 'Yes.'

Inspector, 'You know that both have been done for grievous bodily harm?'

Ken, 'Yes, but there were extraneous circumstances, mostly recreational fun.'

Inspector, 'One was done for using a Millwall supporter as a cricket bat, the other had the habit of scalping Pekinese dogs and their owners. This cannot be regarded as recreational fun in my book.'

Ken,' 'It was funny seeing Doug score a boundary with the football fan's head.'

Inspector, 'Why Pekinese dogs?'

Ken, 'His mother had been abused by a Chinese docker after an alcohol-induced riot. He mistook her for a gargoyle and attempted to amputate her horns.'

Inspector, 'What horns?'

Ken, 'I couldn't possibly say, but some of these East London lasses can appear fairly intimidating in the wrong sort of light.'

Inspector, 'What sort of light?'

Ken, 'Bright light.'

Inspector, 'So, you arrived at Garibaldi's Italian Restaurant, then what?'

Ken, 'I asked for the owner. I was told that he was indisposed. I suspected that he was giving Charlotte one.'

Inspector, 'Did you know that she was there?'

Ken, 'No, but I had my suspicions. I was in a bit of a quandary on what to do. I discussed with my two business colleagues, and they suggested that a mild distraction might flush him out.'

Inspector, 'Then what happened?'

Ken, 'Doug accidentally lifted a plate of linguine, and accidentally dropped it on this woman's head. I believe that it was a tuna linguine, with a fair amount of almond pesto. I think I also detected a touch of lemon. These sorts of accidents can happen in a restaurant. I was a bit surprised to find that the woman's reaction was catatonic. Doug tried to calm her down, but in doing so accidentally knocked another woman's pasta dish onto her head.'

Inspector, 'This doesn't sound plausible.'

Ken, 'I agree that it was a shame to waste the vermicelli, especially the dumplings. I had to laugh that it is sometimes called "angel hair". Well, it was certainly in her hair, down her face, dripping between her breasts and covering her Armani dress. To be fair to Doug, he was helping her clean her bust. I'm not too sure that she appreciated this, and she swung out at Doug, causing him to knock a bowl of tagliatelle onto the third woman. She kept screaming, "Not on my Stella McCartney". Those women were very violent. There was another purple-coloured woman who attacked Doug with a chair. It was disgraceful.'

'We then made an effort to avoid these delinquent women. In a rush to get by, my other colleague managed to knock a lasagne onto this woman's bust.'

Inspector, 'This was the second accidental bust-up.' The Inspector was enjoying his little jokes, but no one else was.

Ken, 'She was very well-endowed, and the lasagne was very hot. Quite a few people we're helping, but my colleague had no alternative but to de-bra her. It was for her own good, but unfortunately, it was not the way she saw it.'

'Her husband, or "life partner" as she wanted him called, attacked my colleague. His punch missed, and he mistakenly hit a nearby bystander, who had sneaked a crafty smoke while all the commotion was going on. As he fell, his cigarette set the de-braed woman on fire. It was not her day. Someone was spraying her from a soda syphon, but this seemed to get her even more annoyed. The dress continued to burn, and my colleague had no alternative but to de-dress her. Underneath she was wearing yellow, leather knickers with the words, "Take me, big boy". She ran off down the road, screaming. I also remember Doug trying to stop people from throwing pizzas around the room.'

'We think we identified one of the trouble makers. He was a shifty-looking guy wearing tracksuit bottoms and a duffle coat. He had painted his hair orange and may have had a ventriloquist's doll on his arm. Not the sort of thing you would expect to see in an upmarket restaurant. For no apparent reason, he started making fun of Doug.'

Inspector, 'What did he do?'

Ken, 'He looked at Doug in an arrogant and slightly enfeebled way, saying that the spaghetti needed more spice.' Doug thought that he was accusing him of being a drug dealer.

The guy kept smirking and making pathetic little laughs. He was clearly provoking Doug, a man known for his impatience.'

Inspector, 'What happened next?'

Ken, 'Well, Doug could take no more of this provocation and deposited the spaghetti on his head, and the rest of the table's contents down the back of his trousers. I mean, the little shit was asking for it.'

Inspector, 'I agree there comes a time when action is needed. Please go on.'

Ken, 'I glanced up, and there was Charlotte, my wife, running down the stairs of the restaurant, stark naked. She appeared to be dishevelled and bruised. What had that bastard done to her? I realised then that I had been too soft with her, but then I cannot stand to see any woman getting abused. Then I spotted another naked woman, and it became apparent that they had been fighting. What was going on?'

'To be honest, it was quite erotic seeing these two women fight. On the other hand, it was rather embarrassing that one of them was my wife. There was no sense of modesty. People were taking photos and cheering them on. I had thought about stopping it, but it was just too much fun. Then, I noticed that the dark-headed girl had her fingers in my wife's fanny, and then my wife started sucking the girl's breasts. As the crowd cheered, the girls got even more intimate.

'Then, a strange thing happened; a man who I hadn't seen before flew across the room and crashed into the table holding this huge cake. It was a large cake.'

Inspector, 'I know, I've seen the remains of it.'

Ken, 'Then, I spotted Sheila — she looked lovely before the cake hit her, and just as lovely afterwards.'

Inspector, 'Do you know Sheila?'

Ken, 'Of course, I'm her manager.'

Inspector, 'She seems to have a lot of admirers.'

Ken, 'You can add me to that list, I would love to marry her.'

Inspector, 'But you are here defending your wife's honour.'

Ken, 'No, I'm not, I just want justice. Charlotte is history as far as I'm concerned.'

Inspector, 'I'm trying to untangle the emotional ties here; have you slept with Sheila?'

Ken, 'Yes, on many occasions, and hopefully that will continue.'

Inspector, 'I've never seen so much social interaction, or do I mean sexual interaction. Please continue.'

Ken, 'I'm not exactly sure how, but my wife seemed to dive into the cake.'

Inspector, 'I had a report that the other girl punched her.'

Ken, 'Do you mean the one that had her fingers up my wife's fanny? It doesn't seem likely, does it? Anyway, there she was, her rear end sticking out of the cake for all to see. It was embarrassing before, but this was a lot worse. My colleagues were killing themselves laughing. Then, the weirdo in the duffle coat raped her.'

Inspector, 'Before we investigate that, did you see any other suspicious activity regarding him?'

Ken, 'I certainly did; I'm not sure if I've got my head entirely around it yet. Firstly, he was just sitting at the table with spaghetti on his head, and the table contents down his trousers. He was not a happy bunny. He kept asking why him? Apparently, he wanted a simple life. He just wanted his woman back, but mostly he wanted his bum put back to normal. We just left him to his own devices. It seemed the best thing to do.'

'Later, I spotted him again without any trousers or pants on. I just caught it out of the back of my eyes. Initially, I thought the dark-haired girl had her fingers up his arse, but that clearly wasn't the case, as we know that she was a lesbian. Then, I realised that her fingers were up there. Clearly, her sexuality was confused. I then saw her run off to the kitchen.'

Inspector, 'We have our suspicions that he might be a mule and that Anna, the dark-haired girl, was one of his accomplices.'

Ken, 'Do you think the restaurant is just a cover for a world-wide drug operation?'

Inspector, 'It wouldn't be the first time. Is that it?'

Ken, 'No, there's lots more. The dark-haired girl returned from the kitchen with a large spatula, shook her head and ran back. She then returned with what looked like a robot arm, shook her head and went back to the kitchen. After a few minutes, she came back with a pair of nutcrackers. I had no idea what she was going to do with them. She spat on the end and stuck them up his arse. I've got to be honest, I never expected that. Who would?'

'When I looked more carefully, they weren't nutcrackers, they were kitchen tongs. Not that it surprised me any less. I heard the girl say, "It's coming". That caught my attention. Now, this is the funny bit. You won't guess what came out of his arse.'

Inspector, 'A pepper pot!'

Ken, 'You've already heard this story. I found it funny, but Doug was on the floor in actual pain. I've never seen a man laugh so much. The girl said that she couldn't go any further. As far as I was concerned, I thought she had already gone far enough. I thought I was fairly liberal-minded, but I had never seen anything like it. Totally perverted. Then, it got worse.'

Inspector, 'In what way?'

Ken, 'Well, he rushed towards my wife in only a T-shirt, and a pair of tongs dangling from his arse, and proceeded to rape her.'

Inspector, 'There is a view that it was an accidental rape, and that he was trying to help her.'

Ken, 'Most men on a mercy mission are not trouserless with a full erection.'

Inspector, 'Apparently it was not a large specimen.'

Ken, 'That might be the case, but an erection is an erection, and a rape is a rape. I'm not having that happen to my wife.

'I took two breadsticks from the table and stuffed them up his nose. I was amazed by the accuracy of my aim. One went up each nostril. I couldn't believe it. Doug had just recovered from laughing at the tong incident when this started him off again. I was a bit worried that the breadsticks might enter his brain and kill him. But then he had just raped my wife. The world would be a better place without that little worm. Good riddance, I thought.'

Inspector, 'Do you plan to press rape charges?'

Ken, 'I don't think so, but it's up to her.'

Inspector, 'Is that the end of it?'

Ken, 'It's coming to an end. As you know, Sheila's clothes were somehow ripped off. What a sight — she was stunning. I wanted to fight off the men taking photographs, but then the man who flew through the air started calling Sheila a whore. I wasn't having that, and I jumped on his back. He kept screaming, "Not my nose". I was shocked when my wife hit me with a religious icon. Its head got stuck in my ear. I'm not sure why she did it.'

'Then I heard Charlotte screaming as the dark-haired girl pushed a tiramisu up her arse. She has never really been a coffee fan. Clearly, the dark-haired girl has got a thing for arses. If that wasn't enough, she then followed it up with some sort of berry panna cotta. Then, to cap it all, the weirdo started eating the contents of her arse.'

Inspector, 'That must be it?'

Ken, 'Not quite; this man with a tall, white chef's hat came running out with a cleaver, saw Sheila and fell on the floor, professing his undying love. The few men who were cleaning her up did a rapid exit.'

The moral of the story is:

I cook with wine, sometimes I even add it to the food.

— W.C. Fields.

The Great Cake Story: Part 5

Anna wondered why Inspector Knight wanted to see her. She had done nothing wrong. She was innocent, apart from the fighting, the cake abuse, possibly the prostitution, and sneaking into Jack's flat. She could explain all of the above, but she was still nervous.

Her parents had accused her of being a prostitute. She never found out who told them. Now she could be facing criminal charges. Why is life so difficult? She just wanted to get a law degree, or did she? What she really wanted was love, security, and more love. She wanted Jack to love her.

Inspector Knight seemed quite a nice man.

Inspector, 'Now, let's talk about the services you offer.'

Anna, 'You mean the personal services?'

Inspector, 'Yes.'

Anna, 'Should I start at the beginning?'

Inspector, 'If you want to.'

Anna, 'I joined the restaurant as a part-time kitchen hand a couple of years ago. In the summer it got sweltering, so I came to work in hot pants and a skimpy top. It was one of those tops that left your midriff free. The boys always complimented me on my looks. They constantly teased me regarding my boyfriends. In fact, I've never had a boyfriend, or really any other friends. I was still a virgin. My parents never allowed strangers in the house. To be honest, I didn't have the social skills to build relationships.

'I enjoyed the attention from the boys. It seemed to satisfy a deep need inside of me. One day I came to work without a bra. My nipples soon stiffened when I was with the boys. I guess that I was sexually attracted to them. John, one of the older boys who I had a particular crush on, walked up to me and pulled the bow apart that was holding my top together. Out fell both boobies. He licked and kissed them. I loved it, but panicked when he tried to put his hand down my pants.

'The following day, Nick tried the same trick. I wanted to stop him, but he was too strong, and out they popped again. This became the ritual for the next few weeks.'

Inspector, 'What was the management view?'

Anna, 'No one said a thing; it became normal that I wandered around the kitchen topless. To me, it seemed natural, but then things moved on.

'One Sunday morning, both boys started playing with me. They had a breast each. John said, "We have had enough of your teasing", and pulled my shorts down. I stood there, totally naked. I had no idea what to do next. I was a bit embarrassed regarding my bush, as it had never been trimmed. This didn't seem to worry the boys. John picked me up and carried me upstairs. Nick followed. Both took turns sucking my clit and the outside of my fanny.

'John removed his clothes, and I saw a prick for the first time in my life. He surprised me by trying to stick it in my mouth. I wasn't having any of that, so he went to the other end and prodded my fanny. I don't think he was very experienced, and I had no experience whatsoever, as they soon found out. I bled profusely as I became a woman. I was pleased it happened. I could now look at the other girls at uni in the eye.

'John was surprised and uttered, "I didn't know that you were a virgin. I'm so sorry".

I replied, "It's not a problem; it's just a bit of skin". John asked if he could continue, and I nodded. After some huffing and puffing, he came. I thought young lads came almost immediately. Nick looked at me with pleading eyes. I said, "Go on, you might as well have a go". I was surprised how nonchalant I was concerning my first encounter with sex. Nick followed the rules about young men and came after three strokes. Both of them thanked me profusely. It was a bit like me rewarding them at prize-giving.

'The next day, they asked if they could repeat the experience. I wasn't sure. I enjoyed the skin-to-skin contact, but in all honesty, I got very little out of it. I thought I would put them off by saying that if they wanted any more, they would have to pay. Rather than put them off, it went down really well. A figure of fifty pounds a time was agreed. A rota was soon organised, and I was fucked twice a week. The money was very handy.

'I organised contraception, and gradually increased my client base. It was usually new starters who I fancied. Then the head chef booked a few days, and then eventually, Jack had me twice a week. The older men were much more satisfying, but I've never had an orgasm. I guess what I've never had, I've never missed, but I would still like to experience it. At one stage, I was also doing lunchtime sessions, and two or three at weekends. 'My customers were always restaurant staff, so in many ways, it seemed like a family affair.' Anna suddenly realised that she was pouring her heart out. It was quite cathartic.'

Inspector, 'You realise that this is prostitution?'

Anna, 'It's my body. I can do what I like with it.'

Inspector, 'That is true, prostitution is not illegal, but you have not paid the tax on the income received. Anyway, I'm not a tax collector, but as a father of two girls, I do think you should consider your position. It can't be good for you.'

Anna, 'At least you care about your children; I have disowned my parents. To be honest, I have been thinking about things, and I want to live with Jack. I want to be his woman.'

Inspector, 'Jack seems to have a lot of women in his life, but moving on, can you explain why you were fighting, please?'

Anna, 'I had just told my parents that I was never going to see them again. I needed some love and attention. To be honest, I just needed some company. I couldn't face spending a night on my own. I had just returned from holiday and went straight to Garibaldi's. I stripped, showered, pampered myself, and got into Jack's bed. I was naked, and I was going to give him the best night of his life. He would want me forever after that.'

'I was just lying there, listening to the noise of the restaurant below. I was gently rubbing my fanny in anticipation when I heard someone climbing up the stairs. I hid under the covers. I didn't want to be disturbed. Suddenly, the bed covers were thrown off, and a body landed on top of me. It seemed to weigh a ton. The air in my lungs decided to do a runner.

'I was frightened of being raped, or worse. It dawned on me that the intruder had to be a woman, as she was looking for a penis under the covers. I then noticed that there was a large pair of dangling breasts present. Apart from my own, these were the first breasts I have ever touched. It was quite a nice

115

feeling.

'I decided to punch her; it was just one of those days. I hit her with a left jab, as taught to me at the Sea Cadets. She responded with a right hook. I suspected that she was also in the Sea Cadets as well. It was a good punch, and I ended up on the floor. I'm not the sort of person to avoid a fight. I stood up, ready for action, and she suddenly kicked me hard. She must have been taught kick-boxing at the Sea Cadets as well.

'I landed at the bottom of the stairs, as naked as the day I was born. Before I could protect my modesty, this attractive blonde was on top of me. Her fanny was on my face. At one stage, I was trying to get the hairs out of my mouth. I used my legs to grab her shoulders and managed to pull her backwards. I pulled my body from under hers and laid on top of her. I bit her nose, and she bit my boobs.

'After a fair amount of enjoyable wriggling, we both stood up, and the punching continued. Neither of us was too sure what we were fighting for. In some ways, we were just pleasing the crowd, who seemed to enjoy every punch. I was a bit worried about the photos; where would they end up?

'Without any warning, we were interrupted by this tottering old man holding his bum. Tears were running down his face. I asked if I could help. He was mumbling and laughing at the same time, and wildly gesticulating towards his rear end. He bent over and beckoned me to have a look. It wasn't the most impressive sight in the world. It certainly wasn't that romantic.

'I bent down and gently parted his buttocks. I could just about see a broken glass object up his rectum. Clearly, it must have hurt. I asked him how it got there, and he said, "Bouncers or bouncing". Obviously, this was some sort of fetish. I wasn't sure if he wanted it removed or not. Perhaps he just liked showing it to young women.

'Through his hand gestures and the intermittent grunting noises, I gathered that he wanted it removed. A crowd was now gathering to watch the latest developments. After fingering his arse for a while, I decided that some sort of extraction tool was needed. I dashed off to the kitchen to find a suitable implement and grabbed a spatula. The kitchen staff were a bit surprised to see me naked outside the agreed schedule.

'It was soon apparent that the spatula would not work. Wormy's anus was far too small. I couldn't help noticing that his erect penis was also rather small. In my mind, his name was now "Little Dick". I dashed back to the kitchen, with my boobs flying everywhere, to find an alternative. The kitchen staff cheered as I came back in; they really appreciated my nudity. I didn't want to say it, but I was rather enjoying it. It was liberating.

'The kitchen staff gave me a robot arm. I knew it wasn't going to work, but I thought that I'd better show some willingness. I dashed back. Little Dick didn't like the look of it and backed away from me, back to the kitchen. I wondered why I was doing this. He wasn't my problem. But then we found a winner. The staff had found some kitchen tongs. I returned to find Little Dick crouching in the corner.

'I pulled him out by the leg, forcibly putting him into a bent position, spat on the tongs, and forced them up his arse in a slightly open position. He had a few tears before. Now they were really flowing. More lubrication was needed. I was given some oil which I squirted up his arse. That seemed to help, but I needed more lubrication. I should have thought more carefully before using chilli sauce. He screamed in agony as it went up, but it did the trick. I managed to pull the offending item out of his bum. You will never guess what it was?'

Inspector, 'A pepper pot.'

Anna, 'You obviously knew, but I can tell you, I never expected that in a thousand years.'

Inspector, 'Was that the end of that?'

Anna, 'No, Little Dick indicated that there was another item travelling up his rectum, and suggested that I should have another look. I mentioned before that it wasn't a pleasant sight. Well, it was much worse now, as there was a gaping hole where the pepper pot came out. I didn't want to put my finger up there — who would?

'I grabbed a knife from the table. I'm not sure what happened, but a huge man was rolling on the floor laughing away. You know how someone laughing makes you laugh, well I got the giggles. I was laughing so much that I struggled to get the knife up Little Dick's arse. What made it even funnier, I was trying to get some traction, and without thinking, I inadvertently held his todger by mistake. It was the smallest one I have ever seen, a quarter of a chipolata.'

'Anyway, using the knife, I found another object deep in the bowels of his rectum. I spat on the tongs again, and up they went. I probably wasn't being that gentle as the laughing was getting to me. I caused him some pain. I don't pretend to be a qualified proctologist, although I'm pretty good with plasters. In response to my actions, he jumped up. This was not a good move, as now I couldn't remove the kitchen utensil. I'm sure that he was grateful in his way for all the care I had administered, but by then, I had had enough.

'I was feeling quite knackered when the blonde attacked me again. Charlotte had discovered that I was also after Jack.

It was now outright war. She used her kickboxing skills again and sent me sprawling for a second time. I literally grabbed at anything to stop me from sliding across the floor. It just happened to be Jack's leg. I'm not sure how, but it sent him flying across the room. He hit the table with the cake on it. The cake then spiralled into the air and then landed on Sheila's lap. It was just unbelievable. I felt sorry for poor Sheila. It was a big cake.'

Inspector, 'I know, I've seen the remains.'

Anna, 'I had been through enough. I gave the blonde an uppercut, and then a left hook. I then grabbed her by her golden locks and threw her. I couldn't believe my own strength. She landed head first in the cake. There was no point in her being modest now. Everything was on show. I felt sorry for Sheila for a second time, as somehow her clothes were ripped off in the process. I had my suspicions that the blonde had a hand in it.

'The man with the tongs up his arse appeared again, and either helped the blonde get out of the cake, or he raped her. Very hard to tell. I'm not sure if you could call it rape, probably more a touching of genitals. This other bloke then stuck breadsticks up his nose. I've no idea why he did it. Perhaps he was trying to get something into every one of his orifices.

'This unknown bloke then jumped on Jack's back. The blonde then tried to win Jack's affection by attacking the bloke with a candlestick, or something like it. I thought that was really sneaky, and decided to slow her down. I hit her hard with the only thing easily available — a tiramisu. It did surprise her, and it did slow her down, but I needed more ammunition. In went a raspberry panna cotta. It was all a bit pointless, but I enjoyed doing it. I was then surprised to see Little Dick sampling the delights of the blonde's' bottom with a breadstick.'

Inspector, 'Is that it?'

Anna, 'I could go on, but let's call it a day.'

The moral of the story is, "Little dicks can be right pricks".

The Great Cake Story: Part 6

Charlotte couldn't see any reason why Inspector Knight wanted to see her. She was very much a bit player, but when she thought about it she did have a fight with Anna and it was her husband who started the fight. She was stuck in the cake, and she attacked Ken. Charlotte wasn't as innocent as she first thought.

Inspector Knight started the questioning by asking her about her relationship with Ken. She wasn't sure what to say, but she then said a lot, 'He is a really nice man, caring, thoughtful, loving, intelligent, etc. You couldn't ask for a better husband, a fabulous house, a villa in Spain, a new car, no financial problems, etc. He is good in bed. He is spontaneous. He buys me lovely gifts.'

Inspector, 'Tell me what the problem is.'

Charlotte, 'He is too damn nice. I'm attracted to nasty bastards. I want to be used, abused, taken, mistreated. I want adventure, danger, risks. I want everything and nothing. I'm a wreck. I cause trouble wherever I go.'

Inspector,' 'Do you love Ken?'

Charlotte, 'No.'

Inspector, 'Did you love Ken when you got married?'

Charlotte, 'No.'

Inspector, 'Why did you get married?'

Charlotte, 'To spite Sheila. I was Ken's secretary — all he

went on about was Sheila. I had enough. I told him that I was pregnant with his child. I was lying. He agreed to marry me. At least I will get some money out of the old fart.'

Inspector, 'He could fight you, as the pregnancy was a deliberate fabrication.'

Charlotte, 'He will settle, he is far too nice to fight it in court.'

Inspector, 'That doesn't paint a very nice picture.'

Charlotte, 'Fuck you.'

Inspector, 'Tell me how you came to be fighting with Anna.'

Charlotte, 'I took a taxi to 'Garibaldi's, dressed only in a fur coat and shoes. I planned to fuck Jack senseless. He could then do what he liked with me. He could fuck me twice a day for ten weeks, or just throw me out. I wanted to be his toy. I wanted to be his fuck-buddy. No restrictions, no agreements. His friends could have me if that is what he wanted. I was going to be his property.'

'I snuck into Jack's bedroom to find that there was a bitch already in his bed. That's OK with me. He could have two bitches. I quite like a bit of fanny occasionally. I prefer a hard cock, but cunt will do. Then the bitch hit me. I hit her. She hit me. I kicked her arse down the stairs. I was going to kill her by suffocating her with my pussy. Then she used trickery to upend me, and then she bit my nose. I bit her boob back in revenge. We did some simulated sex, which seemed to please the onlookers. I made sure that they had a good look at my fanny. If that's what they want to see, then it's fine with me. I tried to expose Anna's fanny more, but this old geezer interrupted us. I told him to fuck off, but Anna is the compassionate sort.'

'While Anna was trying to sort the old bloke out, I thought: 'there are three of us trying to get our hands on Jack — me, Anna, and Sheila.' As far as I was concerned, there were no rules. I would do what I had to do to get the man.'

'I'm not sure why, but Anna was sticking a whole range of kitchen implements up the old man's arse. I didn't get the impression that he was enjoying it. I wasn't sure why Anna was holding his erect penis. I could understand it if it was a decent todger, but this was pygmy size. It was like comparing a chicken breast with a chicken nugget. In fact, it was probably worse. If it were flaccid, it would be undetectable. Anyway, why was it erect? Was he getting some kind of thrill out of this? Clearly, he was an evil little shit.

'I'm still not sure why Anna squirted chilli sauce up his arse. Perhaps she has got a mean streak after all. And why all the giggles? It was a funny situation, but the poor man was in agony. And why did she leave him with those tongs dangling? Some mysteries will probably remain as mysteries forever.

'As soon as Anna was finished with Turd Face, I was going to hit her hard. I will get that man, no matter what. She finished, and I kickboxed her across the room. She went sprawling. I saw her grab Jack's leg, which sent him spinning. Isn't life funny — he hit the cake and covered Sheila in cake mixture. She really was covered. Served her right, she is far too pretty for her own good.

'While I was admiring my handiwork, I hadn't expected an uppercut and a left hook from Anna. That woman is a mean hombre. I was still staggering around when she grabbed me by my blonde extensions and threw me across the room. For such a small frame, she was remarkably strong. Into the cake I went, head first. It's a big cake, you know.'

Inspector, 'Yes it is. I've seen the remains.'

Charlotte, 'As I landed, I grabbed the clip holding Sheila's dress together. That way, all three of us would be stark naked, and Jack could take the one he fancied most. Of course, Sheila was totally covered in cake. I really enjoyed that.

'I was sticking out of the cake, with my fanny on full show. I was hoping that my cunt was being appreciated. Then Turd Face grabbed me. I'm not sure if it was his little finger or his even smaller cock that entered my fanny. I can't say it matters anyway. As I struggled to get out, I saw my husband jump on Jack's back. I thought I would get my own back on hubby, and threw Jesus's mother at him. It looks like Mary lost her head in the process. I'm probably not going to heaven now.

'I was then surprised to find Anna rubbing a tiramisu into my fanny. She was doing an outstanding job. I wasn't far off from having an orgasm. She stopped, but then hit me with what looked like a strawberry panna cotta. This time her delicate fingers pushed me over the edge. It was an incredible orgasm; the mixture of Italian patisserie and sensitive fingers was just too much for me. Perhaps Anna was the one.

'I thought that my surprises for the day had finished, but then I found that Turd Face was removing the breadsticks from his nose. I've no idea how they got there. He was then using them to remove the pastries from my fanny. What a day!'

Inspector Knight, 'Is there anything else you want to add?'

Charlotte, 'Not today.'

The moral of the story is, "The party was so bad that even the cake was in tiers, and remember that the reverse of stressed is desserts".

The Great Cake Story: Part 7

Jerry was surprised that he was called upon to make a statement. He never really saw what happened in the restaurant, but he was happy to contribute.

Inspector Knight, 'I would like to start by talking about the thrusting event. I understand that your penis entered Sheila's vagina one thousand times?'

Jerry, 'That's correct, I withdrew and entered her exactly one thousand times.'

Inspector, 'Did you have her permission?'

Jerry, 'I'm not sure. I found her bottom sticking out by the side of the sink. I rubbed my finger up and down the crack of her arse. There was no reaction. I then put my finger in her fanny. Still, there was no reaction. I then rubbed my penis up and down the crack of her arse. There was no reaction whatsoever. I then put my penis into her vagina. Total silence.'

Inspector, 'I gather that you have construed that Sheila's silence was permission to continue?'

Jerry, 'I did.'

Inspector, 'You realise that this could be technically classed as rape. The Director of Public Prosecutions could take action against you, whether Sheila wants to or not.'

Jerry, 'Sheila had every opportunity to stop me.'

Inspector, 'Then once you were in her vagina, you thrust into her one thousand times. Did you not consider that excessive and inhumane?'

Jerry, 'I can see where you are coming from, but I meant no harm.'

Inspector, 'Have you considered what damage you may have done to Sheila? Not just physical damage but psychological damage.'

Jerry, 'I agree that looking back it was foolhardy. Is Sheila considering any action against me?'

Inspector, 'Not that I know of. I also understand that you did not know the identity of the woman you were fucking?'

Jerry, 'That is correct, I had no idea who she was.'

Inspector. 'Isn't that a bit strange?'

Jerry, 'I guess that it is, but that was the situation. I struggled to think of a way of tracking her down. Then, I thought about the footage from the security camera. From that, I managed to get a good likeness, and what a beauty. I became obsessed with finding out who she was.'

Inspector, 'So you demanded that Jack came to the kitchen?'

Jerry, 'Yes, as I said, I was obsessed.'

Inspector, 'Then, Jack identified her as the woman he was going to propose to? He identified her as the woman you made the cake for, and you did not make the connection?'

Jerry, 'How could I? I fucked the rear of a woman I had never actually seen properly. I had never met Sheila before. It's strange that I know her fanny so well, but not her.'

Inspector, 'Were you surprised when Jack ran out?'

Jerry, 'Not really, he is quite an impulsive chap.'

Inspector, 'How did you feel that you both wanted the same woman?

Jerry, 'I felt sorry for Jack, I would do anything for him,

but pleased for me, as there is now a chance that she could be mine.'

Inspector, 'You knew that there was a crisis in the restaurant, but you stayed in the kitchen?'

Jerry, 'Yes, I had meals to cook. Jack can handle things, he doesn't need my help in the restaurant. I did provide a series of kitchen implements for Anna. I was surprised that she was naked, but then I've seen her naked many times before.'

Inspector, 'Have you slept with Anna?'

Jerry, 'You know I have; it's not a crime.'

Inspector, 'We will see about that. I understand that you did enter the restaurant with a dangerous weapon in your hand?'

Jerry, 'I heard that Jack was in danger and I went to his rescue, armed with a cleaver. Then I saw the light of my life. There was Sheila in all her naked glory. I immediately fell on my knees and swore my undying love.'

Inspector, 'Is there anything else you want to add?'

Jerry, 'I don't think any harm has been done; can't we just forget the whole thing, and just move on?'

Inspector, 'It is not my decision, what will be, will be.'

The moral of the story is, "Jack and Jerry went up the hill, they met Sheila for a thrill, sod the water".

The Great Cake Story: Part 8

Wormy was very nervous about meeting Inspector Knight. He knew that he wasn't good with authoritarian figures. He wasn't good at interviews. He didn't really understand what had been going on. He wasn't really good at anything.

Inspector Knight, 'I need to warn you that there are several witnesses that are blaming you for this debacle. I also need to warn you that anything you say could be used against you. I also need to point out that there are suspicions that you are a drug dealer. Do you want your solicitor present?'

Wormy, 'I'm innocent, I have not committed any crimes.' Wormy was trying to stop his hand from shaking, but it was challenging.'

Inspector, 'We will see. Can I ask you how you happened to be at the restaurant?'

Wormy, 'I was trying to fix a date with my ex-wife. I booked the restaurant and had to pay a deposit. I failed to make contact with Sheila, and decided to have a meal there anyway.'

Inspector, 'Are you saying that you had no idea that Sheila was going to be there?'

Wormy, 'Yes, it was just a coincidence.'

Inspector, 'In my world, coincidences are not very likely. I put it to you that you were stalking Sheila.'

Wormy, 'I wasn't.'

Inspector, 'Yes, you were, you are a pervert. Do you admit

that you were walking around the restaurant naked from the waist down? Do you admit that you were exposing your penis?'

Wormy, 'I can explain.'

Inspector, 'It's too late for explanations; was your penis on show? Was a member of the restaurant staff holding it in public view; yes, or no?'

Wormy, 'Well, technically yes, but…'

Inspector, 'So we have established that you are a pervert, and possibly a stalker.' It's not looking good. I want you to describe the events of the evening in your own words.'

Wormy, 'I was planning to rekindle my relationship with Sheila by inviting her to a swanky restaurant.'

Inspector, 'So you turn up in tracksuit bottoms, and a T-shirt with the logo "My other woman is much prettier than this one" on it. Your duffle coat needs to be exterminated, and your shoes were not matching. Is this how you were going to charm Sheila?'

Wormy, 'As I couldn't get through to Sheila, I decided not to bother dressing up.'

Inspector, 'Or shaving? Were you trying to disguise yourself by painting your hair orange? Are you a drug dealer? Lots of drug dealers have orange hair.'

Wormy was now stuttering, shaking, and dribbling slightly. 'I'm not a drug dealer.'

Inspector, 'Have you taken any Class A drugs in the last year? We can test you. These drugs linger in your body for some time.'

Wormy, 'LSD, I tried LSD.'

Inspector, 'You know that possession can mean imprisonment for up to seven years, and an unlimited fine, or both. If you are a dealer, it can mean imprisonment for life.'

'So, we established that you are a pervert, a stalker and you take class A drugs.'

Wormy was finding it difficult to get his words out, but he managed to say that he arrived at the restaurant about seven thirty p.m. 'I wasn't sure what to order, so I pointed at the other table and said, "I will have that one".

Inspector, 'You pointed at a particular woman, and said you wanted that one?' That sounds like procurement to me. Did you think that Garibaldi's was a brothel?'

Wormy, 'No, of course not, but I don't know my vermercelles from my reatalleys, it all looks like spaghetti to me. What's wrong with old spaggy on toast? You add a dollop of cheese and some chokyarts, and, hey presto, you got a dish for a queen.'

Inspector, 'Talking about queens, have you had surgery to reduce the size of your penis? A number of the witnesses stated that you could get a mention in the Guinness Book of Records for the smallest penis in the world.'

Wormy, 'I've never had any complaints about its size. Anyway, it's not the size that matters. It's your technique that is important.'

Inspector, 'Is that why you raped Charlotte?'

Wormy, 'I didn't rape her!'

Inspector, 'Did you obtain permission from Charlotte before you put your penis in her vagina?'

Wormy, 'It was accidental.'

Inspector, 'We don't have a category of accidental rape. It was either mutually agreed sexual intercourse, or it was sexual penetration without permission. What was it here?'

Wormy, 'I only just entered her.'

Inspector, 'Did you seek her permission?'

Wormy, 'Not really.'

Inspector, 'Then it was rape. I need to warn you, once again, that you are facing some serious charges: rape, stalking, attempted procurement, possible possession of class A drugs, multiple counts of indecent exposure. The list just goes on. Do you want your solicitor present?'

Wormy, 'Look, I've done nothing wrong.'

Inspector, 'Please continue with your statement.'

Wormy, 'Where had I got to?'

Inspector, 'You were trying to procure the woman on the table next to you.'

Wormy, 'I only wanted to have what she was eating.'

Inspector, 'You have to order your own food, that was hers.'

Wormy, 'What I meant was, I just wanted the same as what she was eating.'

Inspector, 'I understand that the restaurant manager had to pacify them by offering free drinks.'

Wormy, 'That wasn't my fault.'

Inspector, 'Who's fault was it then? There were also complaints about the smell.'

Wormy, 'What smell?'

Inspector, 'I will just check my records, here we are: "a mixture of stale farts, cabbage, paint, motorcycle oil and beans, lots of beans". How do you explain that?'

Wormy, 'What can I say — that's me trying to be healthy.'

Inspector, 'It's more like a health risk. Please continue.'

Wormy was now sweating profusely. The pressure was getting to him, but he knew that he could prove his innocence. 'The meal arrived, but it was a bit tasteless. I called over a waiter and told him that I needed more spice.'

Inspector, 'Can you confirm who he was?'

Wormy, 'He was a really big guy, I mean big. He didn't seem to understand what I meant by more spice. So I shouted at him, "more spice". I wondered if he was deaf, so I shouted louder. I then decided to use my arrogant voice. He wasn't functioning correctly as a waiter.'

Inspector, 'Was he a waiter?'

Wormy, 'Of course he was; I then hit him with my ventriloquism act. I could see that it made a big impression on him.'

Inspector, 'What happened next?'

Wormy, 'I was going to complain to the management, but before I could, the waiter grabbed the spaghetti and rubbed it all over my head. I was surprised. He acted like a man provoked.'

Inspector, 'Did you say anything?'

Wormy, 'I said, "Good man, I think you dropped the spaggy on my head by mistake".

Inspector, 'What did he say?'

Wormy, 'He said, "Now listen here, you little shit, this is going to hurt". He picked me up with one hand, pulled my clothes down, grabbed the entire contents of the table, and stuck it up my arse. He then took one of those cheese grinders and used it to ram everything in as far as he could. Not a pleasant experience, I can tell you.'

Inspector, 'Are you a mule?'

Wormy had no idea what he was talking about. 'Do you mean Muffin the Mule?' The inspector wondered if it was some sort of code and nodded. 'I know that mule really well — I sometimes have my hand up his arse to please the young

132

children. They just can't get enough, and I don't charge them much. I think it's best to get them hooked when they are young. Sometimes, they are so quiet I think they are drugged, and then they start laughing. The parents aren't always happy about it, but they often ask me to come back, it's so addictive.'

Inspector, 'You fucking bastard, how can you be so calm about it?' He stormed off, saying that he would be back shortly.

The Inspector returned, and said, 'Apologies, I find it so hard when I'm up against such a hardened criminal.' Wormy agreed, which mystified the Inspector.

Wormy, 'It was extremely painful, I can tell you. I took my trousers and pants off and wandered around, looking for someone to help me. No one was interested. I just couldn't find any help. Then, I saw two naked girls fighting. One of them asked if she could help. I tried to answer, and although I'm normally quite good with pain, the tears were rolling down my face, and I found it difficult to talk. I vigorously pointed at my arse. She was a bit slow, as she kept asking me what I wanted.'

'I shouted, "There is something up my arse. There is an alien object up my bum". I bent over and walked back towards her. I almost pinned her up against the wall. I sensed that she was getting turned on. My cock started to harden to its full length of fifteen centimetres. That was going to impress her, but I needed her to check on my bum first. She bent down so that her nose was almost touching my posterior. She had little choice, as I had her pinned up against the wall.

'I suspect it was love at first sight, as she peered into my anus. Few women have had that privilege. She gently parted my buttocks. I could feel the warmth of her hands on my cheeks. Then I felt one finger entering my most private part. She identified that a glass jar was wedged up there. It reminded me of the time the hoover end got stuck up there, and also that terrible day I sat on a champagne bottle. That brought tears to my eyes.

'The naked girl asked if I wanted the glass item removed. I wanted to say, "For fuck's sake, do you think I'm some sort of fucking pervert", but I said, "Yes please". The girl asked the surrounding crowd if anyone wanted to put their finger up my arse to ascertain the exact position. There were no volunteers. The naked girl then held her breath, closed her eyes and wiggled her finger up there.' She jumped up and ran to the kitchen. I couldn't help noticing that her tits were bouncing all over the place.

'She was soon back with a spatula. I couldn't see that working. I heard her say that my anus was far too small. I heard someone else say, "Well, at least it matches the penis". She then came back with a robot arm. There was no way that it was coming near me. There is one thing having a glass object up your arse, but a robot arm is totally out of the question. I decided to hide until it was put away.

'The crowd seemed to be enjoying the spectacle, or maybe they enjoyed seeing a pretty young thing running backwards and forwards in the nude. I was enjoying it myself and started to consider the amorous opportunity that might be presented here. She finally came back with something that might work — some kitchen tongs.

'The naked girl pulled me back from the edge of the room and put me into a foetal-like position. She was much stronger than she looked. I enjoyed her naked body rubbing against me. I guess that she was experiencing the same thrill. She tried to spit on the tongs, but her mouth was a bit too dry. As she couldn't get much saliva, she asked for volunteers. Spit was flying all over the place. The level of accuracy was appalling, or perhaps they just enjoyed spitting at me.

'Some bright spark drowned the tongs in oil, which was probably a blessing. Up the tongs went. They were in a slightly open position so that they could grab the alien object. The further the tongs climbed, the more water came out of my eyes. In my circle of friends, I'm known to be a bit of a hard man, but this was beyond any pain I had experienced before. It got worse as she opened and shut the tongs. More oil was squirted up my arse. I got the feeling that progress was being made, but we weren't quite there yet.

'Some further lubrication was squirted up there. It was excruciatingly painful. I later discovered that it was hot chilli sauce. It felt like an Australian bush fire in your bowel. It was the worst possible combination of a vindaloo and toxic waste. I will never complain about spicy food again.

'Anyway, it seemed to do the trick. I screamed in agony, and the naked girl retrieved the offending item. You will never guess what it was.'

Inspector, 'A pepper pot.'

Wormy, 'OK, you knew. What a relief, but I could tell that there were other objects up there. I asked the naked girl to continue with the investigation. She said that she had done her bit. As I looked around the room, everyone looked away.'

'I felt my bum; there was a big hole where my tight little anus was supposed to be. I'm sure that it will return to normal one day.' The Inspector thought that it wouldn't happen in prison.'

Wormy, 'Obviously for me, this was a grave matter, but some of the others were laughing outrageously. One man was on the floor rolling about. I don't think they appreciated the gravity of the situation. The naked girl was giggling like mad. I kept saying, "Stop that", but it seemed to provoke even more laughter.

'The naked girl settled down and used a knife to search for the second item. At this stage, she grabbed my cock. I guess the erotism of the situation was getting to her. I couldn't really blame her for losing control. You don't see many todgers like that. To be honest, she wasn't that erotic or even sensitive. She seemed to be using it to steady her hand. She dropped my todger without even a thank you and put the tongs back up my arse.

'I'm not sure what happened, but the pain was beyond belief. I jumped up in agony, which bent the tongs. Then we couldn't get them out. The naked girl left me to continue her fight, and I wandered around with a kitchen utensil dragging behind me, wondering what to do. Well, at least things couldn't get any worse. Later, I spotted a naked girl sticking out of a cake. It was certainly a big cake.'

Inspector, 'I know. I've seen the remains.'

Wormy, 'It was clearly a good day for naked girls. Despite my pain, I dragged the girl out of the cake, but in the process, my todger may have accidentally entered her fanny. There was lots of cake around, so it was hard to tell.

'Then, without any warning, two breadsticks were shoved up my nostrils. I hadn't expected that. It caused me to feel quite faint. Someone shouted, "Eat some cake; that might make you feel better". There were loads of cakes about, but I was surprised to see my naked girl was then shoving tiramisu and panna cotta up the rescued girl's fanny. I took my breadsticks and used them to grab some of the tiramisu. I love anything that is coffee-based. I did get a few strange looks.

'Looking around, I spotted another naked girl. It was my Sheila. What was she doing here? Was she stalking me? Before I could approach her, a man with a tall white hat was professing his undying love. It's all beyond me. I decided that it was probably safer to stay single.'

The moral of the story is, "You can let the salt of the Earth get in your rectum, but keep the chilli sauce out".

The Great Cake Story: Part 9

Sheila arrived at Ken's office for a chat, nothing more. The last few days had been fraught, to put it mildly. There was no one in reception as Charlotte had left Ken for good. Sheila organised some coffees and sat down opposite Ken.

Ken looked to be depressed. Sheila ran through a few descriptive words in her head to sum him up: dejected, disappointed, doleful, demoralised, disheartened, they all seemed to start with the letter "D", but then she thought of glum.

Sheila, who was wearing a short mini-skirt and a colourful Desigual top, said, 'I know how to cheer you up.' She walked around the desk, pulled his chair out, and sat on his lap so that their heads were facing each other. She slowly kissed him on the lips and wiggled her bottom against his crotch. She could already feel movement down below. The trouser snake was on the move. She thought to herself, *'Men are so weak; I love it.'*

Sheila lifted herself slightly, unzipped Ken's flies, freed the raging beast, pulled her knickers to one side and introduced his todger to her love nest. Ken was impressed with the slickness of the whole operation. Within seconds, Ken was enjoying the silky softness of her cunt. Ken started to move his groin, but Sheila stopped; she took control.

Sheila very slowly used her vaginal muscles to tease Ken's cock. It was like an orchestral movement. Sheila could already feel Ken's temperature increasing. She suspected that he had not been laid for a while. His cock was certainly larger than average, and very stiff. Ken made another attempt to start fucking her, but Sheila restrained him.

Sheila's vagina continued to tease his rod. Sheila slowly raised and lowered herself. To Ken, it was pure heaven. Sheila gradually increased both the up and down movement, and the actual pressure on his cock. Ken wanted to come, but when he got near, Sheila stopped. His throbbing stopped in unison with Sheila. She started the rhythmic movement again, adding a slight twist. One of her hands scratched the side of his cock every now and then. Ken desperately wanted to come.

Sheila said to Ken, 'Do you want to come?' Ken tried to speak but could only just about master a nod. Sheila said, 'You have to say, "Yes please, my Queen". Ken tried to say it, but then Sheila decided to let him come by dropping herself onto him with some force.

Torrents of love juice flowed from Ken's loins. Both of them were surprised. Neither of them made any attempt to tidy up. They just hugged each other. Ken felt love. Sheila felt wet knickers.

Sheila said. 'What happened to you?' Ken replied that he got off with a warning. His two bouncers received the same. Ken asked if she had any come back. Sheila said, 'I imagined that it would be like Agatha Christie. All of those involved would sit in a room, and Inspector Knight would deliberate his views, but nothing. I got no comeback whatsoever.

'I did meet Anna in the town. You will be pleased to hear that she is no longer with Charlotte. She said that she was a two-timing, egotistical, selfish brat, that needed to get a life. She was quite venomous about her.

'Anna is back in the restaurant, maintaining her schedule and spending more time with Jack. Garibaldi's has problems as Jerry has left "to ponder the meaning of life". Apparently, Jack compensated a lot of his patrons, but the bookings have increased dramatically. A lot of the punters thought that the whole thing was just a show, and simply want more, a bit like Fawlty Towers. Anna is going to do some waitressing in the nude. I warned her about getting her tits in the soup. There is nothing more painful than a burnt nipple.'

Ken asked if she knew the whereabouts of Charlotte.

Sheila said, 'Anna mentioned Thailand as they like white girls there. Garibaldi's had a health and safety check, along with a food hygiene investigation. They passed with flying colours. They are still trying to get some of the cake mixture off the walls.'

Ken laughed and said, 'It was a big cake.'

Sheila said, 'It was challenging getting the cake marks off her dress.'

Sheila felt Ken's cock stirring again. She looked him in the eyes and said, 'What are you doing?'

He said, 'Any chance of sloppy seconds?'

Sheila said, 'No,' with a huge grin on her face.

Ken said, 'Do you think we should get together?'

Sheila said, 'I really like you. I've always really liked you, but I still feel that I'm finding myself. I had a terrible marriage with Wormy. It's still too early to put roots down again.'

Ken said, 'So, there is hope for me in the future?'

Sheila nodded, and said, 'But I'm always up for the odd shag.' They both laughed.

Ken, 'So what happened to Wormy?'

Sheila replied, 'Poor man, he was probably the most

innocent of us all, but he got arrested for indecent behaviour, attempted rape, actual rape, possession of class A drugs, propositioning, drug dealing, attempted bribery of a police officer and resisting arrest.'

Ken, 'But that's all nonsense.'

Sheila said, 'I know, but that is Wormy for you.'

Ken, 'So, what actually happened?'

Sheila, 'He was taken off to a prison cell where he experienced bleeding from the bowel. He was then rushed off to A&E. A scan showed that there were still some objects up there.'

Ken said, 'I felt a bit guilty about that, as it was one of my bouncers that did the damage.'

Sheila said, 'I'm sure that he brought it upon himself. Anyway, he needed emergency surgery. They removed a salt pot, a packet of matches, a tablespoon, two teaspoons, half a napkin, a bottle of Fanta, the lid from a vinegar bottle and a condom.'

Ken said, 'Where did the condom come from?'

Sheila, 'He denies all knowledge of the condom. To make things worse, the salt pot contained traces of weed. The police then searched his retirement flat to discover traces of LSD. However, there wasn't enough evidence to convict him, but he has received a police warning. Regarding his rectum, they are not sure if it will ever be fully functional again.'

Ken said, 'What does that mean?'

Sheila said, 'Nappy wearing.' Ken couldn't' help laughing.

'Apparently, Charlotte is not pressing any rape charges against him. They are not sure if it was his todger or his finger that entered her. However, he has been placed on the sex offenders register. The police have dropped all charges regarding his indecent exposure, as they felt that he had justifiable medical reasons for being in an undressed state. He is, however, being prosecuted for the attempted bribery of a police officer.'

Ken, 'What did he do?'

Sheila, 'It's all a bit unclear, but apparently he offered the officer the use of my body. The officer could have me five times a month for a year.'

Ken, 'That is disgusting, totally unacceptable; why did Wormy do it?'

Sheila, 'In the past I've got him out of many, many scrapes. He just assumed that I would help him again.'

Ken, 'And did he resist arrest?'

Sheila, 'Well it seems that Wormy did a runner. He kicked the officer in the groin, and just skipped off. However, Wormy struggled to run with a full cutlery set up his arse. You would, wouldn't you? Inspector Knight soon nabbed him and, in response, Wormy bit the officer's penis. As you know, those police uniforms can be quite thick, but Wormy made contact. The officer responded with his truncheon, and Wormy has lost his two front teeth. Wormy has asked me to appear in court as a character witness.'

Ken said, 'He certainly is a character. I couldn't believe the clothes he was wearing.'

Anyway, Sheila disentangled herself from Ken's nether regions, removed her wet knickers, kissed Ken on the cheek and departed.

The moral of the story is, "The police are not here to create disorder, they're here to preserve disorder".

Adventures in Spain: Part 1

After all the recent events, Sheila decided that she needed a break. She needed to get away from everybody and everything. Sheila had been to Alicante several times, but she thought she would go for something different, and booked five days in Benidorm. She just wanted to forget everything, and have a good laugh.

Sheila booked the Sol Peliconcs Ocas Hotel in Benidorm, where the TV series was filmed. She was looking forward to spending some time in the pool. She arrived in Alicante and caught the tram to Benidorm. She was surprised how slow and uncomfortable the tram was. After a taxi ride, she arrived at the hotel. It didn't look a bit like the hotel in the TV series.

After checking out her bedroom, Sheila went straight down to the pool. It was indeed the pool in the series. It even had the poolside bar! She could imagine Mateo serving some cocktails, and Madge dashing by in her scooter. Every time she turned a corner, she expected to see Donald or Jacqueline on a lounger, and it was sunny. Sheila loved the heat. It was also an ideal opportunity to get a bit of a tan.

She spotted three young lads looking at her. They were sitting around the bar with their feet dangling in the water. One of them beckoned her over, and they introduced themselves as Josh, Andy, and Glenmore. They were here to celebrate their twenty-first birthdays. They were all born in the same year.

They asked how long she had been there, and Sheila explained that she had just arrived. Glenmore asked if she was on a modelling assignment as she was so beautiful. Sheila laughed and explained that she was on a short break between assignments.

Josh asked if' she was going to be in the new Benidorm series? Was she going to be Johnny Vegas' new fling?' Apparently, all three boys, sorry young men, were huge fans of the series and were even members of the fan club. They had spent most evenings in Neptune's bar (Morgan Tavern) and the days by the pool, or on the Levante Beach.

Sheila said 'she wasn't going to be in the show, but that she was a fan. She had also heard that they were working on a stage show.' They all got on rather well, although Sheila thought that they were treating her a bit like a goddess.

The boys invited her to a party in their room that night. Sheila found herself accepting the invitation. That was one problem of being a deity. She arrived at seven p.m. to discover that the party consisted of her and the three boys, along with a large bottle of vodka, a cheap bottle of plonk, and a can of coke. She sat on the edge of the bed, with all three boys being nervously attentive. She kept pulling the hem of her dress down as the boys kept staring at her legs. Sheila was conscious that she was only wearing the briefest pair of panties.

They offered her a drink, and she politely asked for a vodka and coke. The old cracked glass contained three fingers of vodka and a dash of coke. If she didn't know better, she thought that they might be trying to get in her knickers. She rudely thought to herself, *'It's not usually that difficult.'* Conversation proved to be challenging, as the boys were so nervous, which encouraged Sheila to be a bit naughty.

Sheila leant back, exposing both of her legs, and eventually the crotch of her knickers. She didn't think that eyeballs could stick out that far. She asked if one of them could scratch her back. Andy was immediately on the case, but he was a useless scratcher. She told him to undo her zip slightly, and really scratch. He obeyed, but he lacked focus as he was captivated by her twin orbs of delight, which were now more exposed.

Sheila could see that Glenmore's erection was starting to cause him problems. He was a Jamaican lad who seemed to have more go about him than the other two. Sheila jokingly said, 'I will show you mine if you show me yours.' Sheila didn't know that shorts could be removed that quickly. Standing in front of her was a large, fully erect todger, clearly ready for action. Sheila stood up, slipped her dress off, and slowly pulled her knickers down.

There was total silence in the room as the boys just stared. Here was a girl, no a woman, who was clearly out of their league, stark naked in their bedroom. Sheila was loving this. She loved male attention. She loved men, even boys, admiring her body. Sheila sat down and slowly opened her legs. Everything was revealed. She was sure that she saw Glenmore wiping dribble from his face. There was a palpable air of excitement in the room.

Glenmore uttered something meaningless. He attempted a second phrase. Sheila managed to interpret it as "Can I touch your fanny, please". Sheila nodded. Glenmore prodded her vaginal area in much the same way as someone approached a dangerous, wild animal. Sheila said, 'It doesn't bite.' Glenmore ignored her and carried on prodding. Josh suggested that he should try separating the lippy bits. Sheila decided to help by lifting her legs up and apart. This tended to open up the vagina.

Josh said, 'There it is,' pointing to the hole that had appeared.' Meanwhile, Andy seemed somewhat fixated with her breasts. He had moved on from caressing to licking, which was all rather lovely.

Glenmore then stuttered out another comment. Sheila said, 'Pardon,' twice.

Then Josh said, 'Glenmore wants to know if he can put his finger in your fanny.' Sheila nodded. Glenmore was a bit rough. Sheila told him to be more gentle, as it was a very delicate organ. Josh replaced Glenmore's finger with his own. He gently inserted his finger and softly rubbed the side walls of her cunt. He asked if it was OK, and Sheila nodded. Sheila thought about how amateurish the whole thing was, but they had to learn.

Andy progressed to sucking her nipples, but he was starting to get a bit frisky. Then he started biting, and Sheila told him to stop. Meanwhile, Glenmore practised his fingering technique. Sheila was starting to feel a bit aroused and thought that she better move things along a bit. Sheila said to Glenmore, 'Is there anything else you would like to do?'

Glenmore said, 'I'm really happy doing what I'm doing.'

Sheila said, 'Really, are you sure?' Sheila wiggled her bottom in an enticing way.

Glenmore said, 'I'm happy, thanks.'

Sheila said, 'Stop being silly, put your cock in my fanny.' Sheila knew that was what his cock wanted to do.

Glenmore said, 'My Mummy said that I had to be careful. Some girls put razor blades in their fannies. Others are just trying to capture a man by getting pregnant. You might even have infectious diseases.'

Sheila said, 'For God's sake, get that cock in my fanny now, or I'm going.'

Josh said, 'I could take over if you want.' On hearing that, Glenmore rammed his engorged cock into Sheila's fanny and came straight away.

Glenmore pulled out quickly to "avoid pregnancy". Spunk went everywhere. He apologised profusely that he had lost control. Apparently, it wasn't his fault. He wanted to know if he had hurt Sheila. Sheila said, 'Everything is fine, although it's the quickest fuck I've ever experienced.'

He said, 'It will be better next time.' Sheila thought, *'The chances of a second time are pretty slim, in fact non-existent.'*

Sheila wasn't sure what was happening next, as the boys were just pathetic. Sheila said, 'Is the party over?'

Josh said, 'I would like a go, but I'm worried about my spunk getting contaminated.'

Sheila said, 'What do you mean?'

Josh, 'Well, I'm English, and Glenmore is Jamaican. Surely if we mix the spunk, we will get half-breeds.'

Sheila said, 'I thought Glenmore was your best mate.'

Josh, 'He is, without any doubt.'

Sheila said, 'You are just talking nonsense; I will not tolerate any racial discrimination. I' will not get pregnant. If you don't fuck me now, I'm going.'

It's amazing how quickly a young man can function in an emergency. Josh's pants were down, and his cock was inside Sheila's fanny remarkably quickly. There was no attempt at foreplay, just a few quick thrusts, and an ejaculation. Josh was a very happy man.

Sheila looked at Andy, who was still fondling her breasts.

He was definitely a tit man. *'Good luck to him,'* Sheila thought. She was asking him with her eyes if he wanted to fuck her.

Andy said, 'I'm not into that fucking business. I'm happy with a pair of breasts.' Sheila started to get up.

Glenmore and Josh both said to him, 'Here is your opportunity to lose your virginity, with a gorgeous woman.' After some badgering, Andy agreed to perform.

Sheila thought, *'What a cheek; Andy is being bullied into fucking me like I'm just a plaything.'*

Andy removed his shorts to expose a tiny penis. Sheila thought, *'That's small, but not as small as Wormy's.* It was also remarkably thin.' Andy entered Sheila, although she could not tell. Andy fucked Sheila, although she could not tell. Andy ejaculated inside Sheila, although she could not tell. Andy thanked Sheila.

Sheila cleaned herself up and put her dress back on. She told them that they could keep her knickers as a souvenir. The boys, now men, said that it was the best party they had ever had. They wanted to know when they could repeat the experience. Sheila didn't answer, as she was off to do some serious partying.

The moral of the story is, "Keep your knickers on if you don't want to be a Sticky Vicky".

Adventures in Spain: Part 2

Sheila wished that she had kept her knickers on, as a lot of women do, as it was starting to get a bit chilly. She thought that it would soon begin to warm up when she hit the clubs. Things were pretty busy at Morgan's Tavern as Sticky Vicky was performing that night.

You could usually catch Vicky fairly easily in Benidorm, as she often performed half a dozen times a night, at several different locations. She was now in her sixties and had been considering retirement for several years. Her daughter, Demaria Leyton, was planning to take over, but she would never have the fame of Sticky.

Sheila was keen to see a professional at work. Someone who had been performing naked for nearly twenty-five odd years. On that basis, Sheila had many years to go, but she doubted that she would have Vicky's stamina.

The Tavern was heaving. Vicky was a legend, especially amongst the British, and she even appeared in the Benidorm TV series. Sheila had managed to get a good seat near the front. Vicky arrived on stage to a massive round of applause. In all honesty, she was a short, dumpy little woman wearing far too much make-up. She was finding it harder and harder to disguise her age, but then time is rarely a good friend to any of us.

Vicky launched into her set by doing a slow strip. Sheila

thought that her body had a strange, shiny appearance, probably due to an over-abundance of moisturiser. Parts of her body had definitely moved south, but she showed a considerable amount of bravery. She was a genuine professional, showing no signs of modesty at all.

Vicky started by pulling literally metres of red material from her vagina. When I say metres, I mean metres. Sheila wondered how she got it all up there. She wondered if she had bundles already prepared, or was it the same material packed in over and over again? Then she wondered how often it was washed. Sheila found the display interesting, but not erotic. If you had never seen a fanny before it might have been slightly titillating, but she couldn't see how young men could get the horn from this. But then her show is packed most nights.

Out came the ping-pong balls to much applause. Her fanny had the capacity to hold a large variety of objects, including handkerchiefs, eggs, and even sausages. Sheila started getting squeamish when Vicky started extracting razor blades. Sheila got even more squeamish when a machete appeared from her lady parts. Sheila wondered if she had been capable of childbirth, and did some googling. Vicky had never married, but she had two children: a boy, and a girl. Her daughter's real name was Maria, and she first saw her mother performing when she was thirteen, and then decided that she would join the act at a later date. It was good to have ambition.

While Sheila was playing with her phone, the lights dimmed. What appeared on stage was a dancing light. Vicky then removed a lit light bulb from her fanny. Sheila decided that it was not for her. She would worry that it might get stuck in there. On the other hand, she knew that fannies have fantastic elasticity. If they didn't, then no child would ever be born.

Vicky finished by opening a beer bottle with her fanny. She then poured out the beer on stage. As far as Sheila was concerned, it all looked a bit painful. Then Vicky announced, in a solid Spanish accent, that there was a famous adult entertainer in the audience. She said, 'I would like to introduce you to Sheila, a rising star in the UK.' Sheila had no choice but to stand up.

Sheila felt that she had effectively been bullied into this, but what could she do? Sheila stood up and accepted the applause, and then kissed Vicky on each cheek. Vicky had assumed that Sheila came to Benidorm to work and that she had a stage act like her. She was effectively competition, not that it worried her. Vicky shouted out, 'Do you want to see Sheila perform?' There was an immediate positive response from the audience.

Sheila wanted to run, but she had to defend her professional reputation. She didn't want to appear wimpy in front of this Benidorm legend. She desperately tried to think of something, and then she heard herself shout, 'The man with the biggest todger can have me.' There have been times when one part of her personality has done something totally alien to the rest of her. This was one of those times, but it was "game-on".

There were a dozen volunteers who stood on the small stage. Sheila said, 'Gentlemen, I would like you all to strip.' There were lots of 'ooh's and aah's, and three of the men disappeared back to their beers. The rest stripped as requested, to much applause and merriment, from the audience. A female member of the audience came and took "her man" back, shouting, 'While I'm here, you are not going to fuck a little whore on stage, no matter how pretty she is.'

Everyone heard her man say, 'She's not my type at all.' Clearly, his type verged on the twenty stone.

Sheila said, 'I'm going to dance for you, which will undoubtedly cause your penises to erect themselves to their full level of magnificence. Vicki will then measure you all, and select the three largest cocks. Are you ready?' Looking around, it looked like some of the cocks had jumped the gun. It was also apparent that two or three of them were not in the race. Sheila thought that she might as well be hard, and walked up to the first little fella and said, 'You must be joking.' He just left the stage.

A second man did a runner before Sheila could abuse him, which she found annoying as Sheila was going to say, 'Well, where is it?' Sheila thought to herself that a few minutes ago, she would have done anything not to be here, but now she was enjoying it. She liked the power of the situation, she liked having an audience and, what was worse, her fanny was looking forward to having a new visitor.

There were now only five men on stage. One or two of the cocks were erect. The rest were partially hard, or totally limp. Sheila was often surprised how sometimes the smallest cocks turned into raging monsters. It was going to be interesting to see what was going to happen. Sheila could tell that the women in the audience were enjoying this much more than the men. In some ways, it was a total reverse of the typical shows put on in Benidorm.

A drum rolled, and Sheila removed the only piece of clothing she was wearing. Off came the dress, and Sheila was stark naked. There was a lot of clapping and a considerable number of wolf whistles. Sheila started gyrating in front of the five men. It wasn't dancing. It was sex. Sheila oozed sex. Sheila was sex! All five members of the five members on stage erected themselves to their full level of magnificence.

Vicky was going to measure them, but no one had a ruler. Vicky shouted, 'It's up to the audience to decide which member will penetrate Sheila's bahheenah.' Sheila hoped that it was the same place she was thinking of. Vicky lifted each erect cock one at a time and asked for an audience response. While this was going on, a large bean bag was brought on stage. Clearly, they were prepared for any eventuality.

The audience managed to narrow the cocks down to two. It was difficult to determine which one of these monsters was the winner. The obvious answer was for Sheila to service them both, but she wasn't getting paid, so why should she?

Vicky had the answer. She came back on stage with a huge red dildo. She decided the man who could take most of the dildo was the winner. Both of the contestants looked at each other. One was smiling. The other did a runner, with his extended cock dangling between his legs. So, the winner was Melvin from Darlington. Sheila didn't think she had ever had a Melvin before.

Sheila positioned herself on the bean bag with her bum in the air. The audience admired her body; it was a beautiful sight, especially under the spotlight. Vicky moisturised Sheila's fanny. She seemed to moisturise everywhere. Perhaps it was the hot weather. The drum rolled, and Melvin had the joy of entering Sheila's tight little cunt. Sheila thought, *'Thank god for the moisturiser. Otherwise, it would have been a difficult entry.'*

Melvin was a star. He knew how to fuck. His beast of a cock rammed home. He had the habit of almost departing and then ramming back in again. Sheila could feel his cock hit her cervix regularly. He took her entire fanny. She had nothing else to give him, but she knew that few men could resist her vaginal contractions. It was a war between a huge cock and a muscular fanny. Sheila knew that she always won.

The next time he departed, Sheila went for a severe contraction. Effectively, the circumference of the fanny had shrunk, and it would be harder for him to re-enter. This increased difficulty generated more friction as the piston came flying in. Melvin was shocked as he prided himself on being the boss. As he came with a roar, his wife came running out of the audience. She said, 'I went to the loo for a few minutes to come back and find you shagging a floozie on stage. You are a very naughty boy.' She turned to Sheila and said, 'I'm sorry about this. He is worse than a child.'

Sheila thought, *'Who is the boss now?'*

Sheila was left on stage, taking even more applause. There was no doubt that she was a star. She looked fabulous; those boobs and legs were just stunning. Sheila and Vicky hugged and kissed. Vicky was very impressed with Sheila's performance.

Sheila managed to retrieve her dress. She had contemplated borrowing some knickers from Vicky, but on reflection, she thought not. Probably just too sticky.

The moral of the story is that "a 'fanny is a fanny in any language". It turns out that the Spanish for the vagina is vagina, but it is pronounced bah-hee-nah. Well, you live and learn.

Adventures in Spain: Part 3

Sheila had a good sleep after her Sticky Vicky experience. Now, it was a day by the pool, and then a night out on the tiles. She had already appeared totally naked in Benidorm, but she was a bit nervous about coming out of the changing room locker.

It was going to be the first time ever. She was slightly afraid to come out in the open, so a blanket covering her, she wore. She considered covering up and sitting by the shore. But the time had come to show the world her itsy bitsy, teenie weenie, yellow polka-dot bikini. If she wanted to avoid attention, then this wasn't the outfit to wear, as she had so many admirers as she walked to the pool.

If Mateo really existed, then Sheila would be in his arms by now. Instead, she had Glenmore asking for more. He had seen her at the Tavern and desperately wanted to taste her charms again. In the end, she had to be fairly rude and tell him to go. She had got to an exciting part in Dune, the sci-fi novel by Frank Herbert. House Atreides was in serious trouble.

The sun was shining, and she had managed to knock back a couple of Pina Coladas. She thought 'the mixture of coconut cream, white rum, and tangy pineapple was the perfect combination.' She had put sun cream on her stomach and legs and was attempting to reach her back, when a good-looking coloured man, in a boater, just appeared from nowhere, and volunteered to assist. She turned over; the middle-aged man covered his hands in sun cream and started massaging her shoulders. It felt good, really good.

He re-stocked and continued to rub her back. She was a bit surprised when he unclipped her bra, but everything was decent as she was on her stomach, although he did manage to massage the side of her breasts. Still, it felt good, really good.

He rubbed the back of her legs and spent a fair amount of time on her adorable feet. He massaged her thighs, gradually moving towards the knicker line. She wondered when he was going to stop, but it felt good, really good.

His other hand was rubbing the small of her back. She realised that she needed a good rub. The two-handed rubbing was pure heaven. She wondered if he was a professional. The hands were strong but sensitive. It was just great, but both hands were at the knicker line. It was now the right moment to tell him to stop, but it felt good, really good.

One hand was under the knicker line, rubbing her bottom. To be honest, there wasn't much material protecting it. She wanted to say no, but he really knew what he was doing. Both buttocks were being thoroughly massaged, with the odd flick against her anus. It did feel good, it was brilliant, but she knew she was going to stop him now.

His other hand crept between her thighs and gently massaged her labia. It was amazing what he could do with just touch alone. His fingers followed the line of her cunt and attacked her clit. She jumped in a nice way. He knew just the right amount of pressure that was needed. She could sense her orgasm growing, but she was determined to stop him. It was difficult because it felt so good, really good.

Sheila was just about to say stop, when one finger

forcefully entered her fanny, and another entered her bum. To say that the orgasm was mind-blowing would be an understatement. Sheila had no idea why, but it was a fabulous orgasm, one of the best she had ever encountered.

The stranger in a boater turned to his grandson and said, 'That's how you do it.'

Glenmore said, 'I told you that she was a real beauty.'

The stranger said to Sheila, 'Thank you for making my grandson a man. The first one is so important. Have a good day.' Then she thought that he strolled off. Sheila decided that she needed a stiff drink.

The sun went in, and Sheila decided to get ready for the night's entertainment. This time, she was going to wear knickers, and had every intention of keeping them on. Tonight, Sheila decided to go to the Star Wars show. She heard that it was rather naughty.

When she got there, she found the venue slightly tacky. In fact, most of the Benidorm nightclubs are on the tacky side — glorified sheds with broken toilets, dirty beer-stained carpets, furniture from the dark ages, and very suspect burgers. It was perfect for many British holidaymakers who wanted sun, sex and booze. To be fair, the old town is a fabulous place to have a stroll, and the beaches cannot be criticised. Going inland, the mountain ranges are very picturesque, and Guadalest is a hidden gem. Sheila had always enjoyed going there.

The show was worse than she anticipated. It was basically an imperial trooper chasing Princess Leia around the room on motorised scooters. Leia gradually loses her clothes, and then they fuck in a somewhat regimented manner. The music was great, the food was crap, and there was absolutely no eroticism. Sheila imagined how she would do it, but then the crowd comes back every night to see the rebels lose to the mighty cock of the empire.

As she left, she felt a tap on her shoulder. It was her gentleman friend from this morning. The one who provided the sun cream extravaganza. He asked if she fancied a drink. He said that he was staying at Hotel Canfali by the Santa Anna church. He said that it was a bit of a walk, but the views are well worth it. She accepted, and they began their trek through the nightlife of Benidorm, and then through the old town.

The views up by the church were delightful. You could see the full extent of both well-manicured beaches and the mountains beyond. She wanted to stay in the skyscraper with the rectangular hole in the middle, but it turned out to be residential only. Without thinking, they held hands as if they had been lovers forever. He had the magical skill of natural charm. You were the only person in the world. Well, you were the only person in the world that mattered.

As they lent against the balcony by Hotel Canfali, he lifted Sheila's dress, pulled her knickers to one side and entered her. Sheila thought she was going to get a drink, and possibly a stay in a luxurious bed, but no, he slowly, so very slowly fucked her. There may have been onlookers, there may have been worshippers in the church, but none of that mattered. He was there to fuck Sheila.

There was no hurry. There was no rush. The fucking just went on and on. Sheila could feel the tension increasing in her. It was both exciting and frightening. She had never felt her body react in this way before. Where was it going? The fucking continued relentlessly onwards. Sheila wasn't sure if she could cope with the increasing tension. She might explode. She wanted release, her fanny wanted it to stop, but it had to go on. Then he suddenly shouted, 'Now,' and Sheila exploded. There was no other word for it. She felt herself crumble on the ground. There was darkness and light everywhere. She wasn't sure if she was still breathing or even alive.

Minutes or even hours later, she woke up. In reality, it was a few seconds, but he was gone. Nowhere to be seen. He was not in either of the two hotels nearby. He wasn't in the church. Would she ever see him again? She slowly walked back to her hotel in a very happy and contented state. She wasn't entirely sure what happened to her, but she would like some more. She also laughed to herself, *'Well, technically I did keep my knickers on.'*

Anyway, she had to pack to go home, not that it was a big job. The next day she saw Glenmore in reception. Sheila went up to him and kissed him passionately on the cheek. She said, 'Can you give that to your grandfather, please?'

Glenmore said, 'What grandfather?'

Sheila said, 'You know — the one who rubbed sun cream on my back yesterday.'

Glenmore said, 'I've no idea what you are talking about. My grandfather died ten years ago.'

The moral of the story is, "Avoid balconies if you have a ghost of a chance".

Garibaldi's: Part 1

Sheila had got home from an unusual break in Benidorm. She enjoyed it, but there were some strange moments with Sticky Vicky, Star Wars and some ghostly encounters.

On her return, she found a letter from Jack. He was offering her another business opportunity. The "events of that day" had been turned into a business. There were now four naked waiters, two of each sex, one of which was Anna. There were planned fights, deliberate poor service, organised accidents, angry staff members and other spontaneous acts of chaos. It was a bit like Fawlty Towers, except that there was always a sexual twist. It was working brilliantly, but they were struggling to cope with the new business.

Jack was looking for someone to handle a "meet and greet" service. From his perspective, it should be a beautiful, naked woman. Obviously, the first person he thought of was Sheila. He promised that he would respect her. There would be no hanky panky. A line would be drawn on the past. He promised that he had got over his obsession, and he would not make any attempt to propose to her.

Sheila was tempted, as it would be regular work, and she knew the place well. She wasn't so sure about Jack — had he got over his obsession with her? On the other hand, had she got over him? She decided that it was probably worth a chat, particularly as Ken had failed to find her any new business.

She suspected that his heart was still not really in his job. He was still trying to sort out the divorce with Charlotte.

Anna was enjoying her work at Garibaldi's. She had realised that she was a natural exhibitionist. Anna liked looking at the faces of the diners, as she delivered their food in the nude. She loved the look of lust in the men, and the look of contempt in most of the women. If the women were particularly unpleasant, she would make a point of bending over, so that her fanny was totally on display. The men always appreciated that. It was so much fun. In fact, the fun was interfering with her university work.

Jerry was back in the kitchen, providing some of the best culinary experiences in Croydon. He was still giving Anna a regular work-out, but he still had the hots for Sheila. He was occasionally allowed out into the restaurant, especially when things got a bit saucy.

Wormy was in prison serving a six-month sentence. Wormy wasn't really sure why he was there. He wasn't really sure how long he was going to be there. He wasn't sure why he kept nodding off. He got an extra month in prison for contempt of court, as he fell asleep during the sentencing. He was determined to go back to Garibaldi's to sort them out. They had been his downfall.

Actually, he was quite enjoying prison. They fed you three times a day. He could watch TV as much as he wanted. The cell was warm. He didn't have to make any decisions. The bed could have been a bit softer, but he got used to it. The only downside was the communal shower. Whenever he went there, he was interfered with. He wasn't sure if it was mandatory or not, but they seemed to like him.

They would say things like, 'Come here, you little lamb,'

play with his todger, and then stick a rod up his arse.' Since the Garibaldi incident, he hadn't felt much in that area. Anyway, it was all amicable, and he looked forward to it, although he often felt dirtier coming out of the shower than going in.

Inspector Knight was still digging for dirt on the Wormy pervert. He was convinced that he should be put down for life. There were things in Wormy's cupboard that needed to be exposed. He wondered if Sheila was involved in his criminal activities, and decided to keep an eye on her.

Sheila turned up for her meeting with Jack. It was somewhat surprising seeing naked waiters and waitresses. Sheila thought that Anna looked radiant — the job obviously suited her. Jack arrived in a very smart three-piece suit, with a white shirt and a colourful tie. They kissed, and Sheila asked if he had just returned from a funeral. 'Very droll,' 'he said, 'How are you?' Sheila explained that she had just had a proper break in Benidorm.

Jack explained what he was looking for in a "hostess". He wanted her to have fun, and he wanted her to take part in some of the planned antics. As far as he was concerned, he was evolving a new type of dining experience — a sexeventmeal. Jack hadn't thought of a proper name for it yet, but it was working. He wanted her to wear a cloak that didn't do up. She wouldn't wear anything else. As and when she wanted, she would expose herself. It would add surprise and suspense to the evening. He knew that in this way, her personality would shine through.

Sheila said 'she was very interested, but she was still concerned about his behaviour.'

Jack said, 'What do you mean?'

Sheila said, 'Well, you have more or less raped me on two

162

occasions.'

Jack responded, 'I've already apologised for those indiscretions. My behaviour was unacceptable, although I was provoked. I'm a changed man, but let's say that in future if I put a foot wrong, then I will give you one thousand pounds.' Jack knew how Sheila's mind worked. Sheila agreed to start this coming Saturday.

Jerry was excited that Sheila was returning. He decided to go out and buy a video camera so he could film her and watch Sheila's charms as often as he wanted. Jerry wondered if she would be interested in helping him beat his thrusting record. On reflection, he thought it was unlikely.

Anna was also pleased that Sheila was returning, but also annoyed. Up to then, she was easily the prettiest girl in town. Now she was going to be outclassed. At least she would have a friend to talk to.

Ken was agitated by these developments. He saw Jack as competition for getting Sheila's hand, and hopefully, the rest of her. Now, Jack would be in a position to press home his advantage. Besides, he would be able to see her glorious body, in all its naked glory, almost every day. What was he going to do?

Charlotte's state of mind was a bit suspect. She hated Ken with a passion. She decided that the love of her life was Jack. It was those two evil cows that were stopping her from getting what she wanted. She tried to remember their names. She thought it was Hanna and Stella, probably the two most evil people in the universe.

Sheila started work on Saturday night. The cloak didn't cover that much, but at least she could make a pretence of protecting her modesty. She usually flashed the punters as they entered, and once again when they were seated. Sheila also liked displaying her charms as she walked back to the door. She loved the way it stopped the men from talking to their partners.

She cuddled Anna and was introduced to the other three: Jane, Ellis and Mark. Jane was a pretty girl with a particularly cute arse. She had big brown eyes, long slender legs, and a 36C rack. The two lads were good looking, but what attracted her attention most was their semi-erect cocks. Sheila said to the boys, 'I can see that you like working here.'

Mark said, 'It's not easy, watching naked girls all of the time, and you are not helping. What makes it worse is that I get touched up all evening.'

Ellis jumped in, 'He's right, you bend over to put a plate down, and you either find someone grabbing your todger or a finger up your arse.'

Sheila said, 'I've never experienced that.' Both of the waitresses agreed that they hadn't either, perhaps the odd grope or a pat on the bum, but little else. Sheila asked who was doing this. The lads said that it was the women diners.

Ellis said that on one occasion this woman wouldn't let go of his cock, and he had to call for the manager.'

Sheila said, 'Did she let go then?'

Ellis said, 'Only after the manager offered his cock as a replacement. The woman said that she was here for cock, and cock is what she was going to have.'

Sheila said, 'What happened next?'

Ellis, 'The manager gave her cock.'

Sheila said, 'That was very good of him.'

Ellis said, 'I don't think the manager minded that much; she was a pretty little thing.'

Sheila said, 'I guess that's one of the sacrifices, management has to make.'

While this conversation was going on, she noticed that Mark had been staring at her fanny. Mark's cock was now fully erect and quite impressive. Sheila secretly asked Anna if she had sampled the delights of Mark's cock. Anna said that she had, but that both Mark and Ellis were still boys, even though they were both over twenty-one. Sheila was feeling a bit sorry for the lads.

An hour later, Sheila followed Mark down the stairs to the wine cellar. Sheila laid her cloak over one of the low-lying barrels and said, 'I see that you like what you see.'

Mark said, 'Yes, mam.' It made Sheila feel old, but she bent over the barrel and made herself available for him to enter her. Without her knowing, Jack had quietly followed them down the stairs. He waved Mark away.

Jack positioned himself behind Sheila, grabbed her hips, and entered her. He was forceful, manly, energetic, enthusiastic, robust, and considerate. As he approached his orgasm, he was strenuous, vigorous, exuberant, dynamic, and caring. Sheila wasn't sure what Anna was on about — this was not the todgering of an inexperienced lad. He came with a roar. Sheila recognised that roar. It was Jack.

She turned to find Jack with his todger hanging out of his nicely pressed suit trousers. Sheila said, 'You bastard.'

Jack said, 'What do you mean?'

Sheila, 'You know, what happened to Mark?'

Jack said, 'I was protecting my business. I don't want him wandering around the restaurant with a limp cock. Our female diners want to see a real todger — the more erect, the better.'

Sheila said, 'You are right, I just felt sorry for him.'

Jack said, 'I wouldn't worry that much, Anna often helps him out. Anyway, I owe you one thousand pounds.'

Sheila said, 'So you do, but I normally charge more for rape.'

Jack said, 'From my point of view it was well worth it.'

The moral of the story is, "A cask of wine works more miracles than a church full of saints, but always be careful that you are not followed into the cellar".

Garibaldi's: Part 2

Sheila had enjoyed her first three months at Garibaldi's. It was great meeting new people. The restaurant was thriving. There was a real buzz about the place. Apart from the sexual activity in the cellar, Jack had left her alone. In fact, she was starting to get quite horny. She might have to go and see Ken.

Jack was amazed just how well the restaurant was going. They were struggling to cope with the demand. He was also impressed with Sheila's performance. She had made an enormous difference. The online media was full of compliments about her. Customers enjoyed her warm, welcoming manner. They were amazed that she remembered them from previous visits. They also admired the subtle way that she exposed herself. Both men and women simply admired her natural beauty.

On the other hand, he was getting more and more frustrated. He pretended that he had got over Sheila, but in reality, whenever he saw her, he just wanted to take her. Jack was finding it harder and harder to resist. This was surprising, considering just how congested his love life was. He was fucking Anna two or three times a week. He was very fond of the girl, but there was no real emotion there. He wouldn't mind it coming to an end, but then that wouldn't necessarily give him Sheila.

To complicate things even further, Charlotte was back on

the scene. She was a real woman. She was up for anything, but dangerous with it. Charlotte could easily fuck a man to death. Again, he had no genuine desire for her, apart from the natural mating instinct. He made it clear to her that he was only available one day a week. Jane, the new waitress, also made it obvious that she would be up for the odd tumble. Jack thought that she had an adorable arse, and he would like to get his teeth into it. If Sheila was available, how would he fit her in?

Anna had more or less given up on university. She knew that she would regret it later. At first, she had given up uni to spend more time with Jack, but slowly she found that her affections were gradually switching to Jerry. Jack was simply using her. She knew that she just satisfied his needs. He just laid on his back and let her do all the work. She went to his room, screwed him into the ground, kissed him good night, and left.

Jerry treated her like a human being. He was interested in her. They made love in many different positions. Jerry usually took charge, which meant that there was lots of variety. Anna was also starting to get her first glimpse of an orgasm. It wasn't there yet, but the journey had begun. This was only happening with Jerry. Was it because she was falling in love with him?

Jerry shared his love of films with her. They had worked their way through all eight seasons of Game of Thrones, and ten seasons of the Walking Dead. It was great sharing life with a man who cared about her. He had even asked her out on a date, which wasn't easy with their restaurant responsibilities. She needed to reduce her time with Jack so that she could spend more time with Jerry. Would Jack be OK with that?

Jerry was enjoying Sheila's nudity in the restaurant, but he found that his affections were now mostly directed at Anna.

She was always willing to try new things. He admired her dedication. He was impressed with her intelligence. He loved the fact that they cuddled up to watch films together. Sometimes, they woke up in the mornings in each other's arms. But he hated the sex rota, and he particularly hated the fact that Jack was fucking her two or three times a week. Should he have a word with him?

Wormy had just been released from prison. It was a close thing because you only served half your sentence if your behaviour was acceptable. The riot nearly stopped that.

Wormy started as a "fish" as he didn't understand the prison process. He was also obviously "fresh meat" to be consumed by the old lags. He was "funky" for a while, as he tried to resist having showers, but once he gave in, he became a "June Bug" — that is, a prisoner that is considered to be a slave to others. The main problem was that Wormy was a slave to almost everyone.

He was quite a valuable asset, as his arse was very accommodating. Because of his cruet set experience, he could take almost any attachment, no matter the size. He was the best June bug ever experienced in a British correctional institution. Consequently, the prisoners didn't want to lose him. He was blamed for every misdemeanour in the prison service. He was even blamed for crimes in other prisons. He became a bit of a celebrity.

A riot was organised in his honour. There is no point going into the detail, but two prisons were burnt down, thirty other cells were lost, several prison officers were hurt, and fifty-two prisoners had their prison sentences extended. Her Majesty's Prison Service was very keen to see the back of such a hardened criminal. They felt sorry for the Probation Service.

Wormy wondered how he was going to get home, as he had no idea where he was. He was happy to get a bus or train, but he still found the sitting down process very painful. He wasn't too sure if his arse would ever truly recover from the attention it had received over the last few months. He did know that a visit to Garibaldi's was still on the cards. Revenge would be so sweet.

Inspector Knight had been informed that Wormy had been released from prison, despite organising a major riot. The inspector was now on guard. He would be waiting for him in Croydon. He had been anticipating a crime wave on his return.

Ken hadn't seen Sheila for a while. He suspected that Jack was having his wicked way with her, although he had also heard that Charlotte was back with him. He needed to check with Sheila to see if this was true.

Charlotte was sharing Jack's bed one day a week. She was giving him the full works. It won't be long before Anna is out of the way. She wondered why she had changed her name from Hanna. Charlotte didn't see Sheila as a threat. She was far too old for him. It looked like she changed her name as well. Stella suited her far better.

Between entertaining Jack, she was giving Mark a good seeing to. He was a bit young, but he had a great todger, and he was keen to learn. She hadn't got her hands on Ellis yet.

Ken phoned Sheila and asked if she fancied a quick one. She did and had her coat and hat on in no time at all. It was very quiet in Ken's office, which was quite handy, as Sheila was stripping almost on arrival. Ken said, 'Slow down, old girl, it's not that urgent.'

Sheila didn't like the "old girl" comment, but said, 'It might not be for you, but it is this end.'

She was down to her underwear when Ken said, 'I have to admit it, you are looking more gorgeous than ever.'

Sheila said, 'Stop admiring me, and get your cock out.'

The bra was off and down came the knickers. Sheila said, 'Where do you want me?'

Ken said, 'Across the street.'

Sheila said, 'There is no time for joviality, get that cock in me.' Ken felt a bit intimidated, but took his trousers and pants off. Sheila was lying on the sofa, on her back. She was holding her legs up and out. This was one of her favourite positions, as it gave the man full and easy access to her fanny, and she could see what was going on. Sheila said, 'Ride me, cowboy, and don't spare the horses.'

Ken wasn't the sort to hang around when a good thing was on offer. He grabbed Sheila's legs and decided to plough straight in. What a beautiful velvety feeling. What softness. What a silky texture. His cock was in heaven. He wanted to take his time, but he could see that she was in a hurry. She wanted, no demanded, her climax now.

He began a series of steady thrusts. His cock could sense her urgency. His cock could sense her hunger. She responded with a musky bouquet. She responded with liberal quantities of fanny juice. She responded with grunts, the grunts of a woman preparing to come. She responded with the look of love. She came, he followed shortly afterwards.

They wallowed in their orgasms. They wallowed in the intertwining of their bodies. They wallowed as his cock shrank in her cunt. They wallowed in the semen that ran down both their legs. Sheila told him that she loved him. Ken told her that he loved her. Ken immediately proposed marriage and Sheila said, 'No.' Ken immediately suggested that they lived together, and Sheila said,' 'No.'

Sheila said, 'You need to know that Charlotte is back with Jack.' Ken asked if Jack was fucking her. Sheila said, 'No.'

Ken said, 'Do you want to fuck Jack?'

Sheila said, 'No.' Sheila still didn't know where life was taking her. She had no explanations to give Ken, explanations on why she said, 'No.' Anyway, life goes on.

The moral of the story, "If you can't be with the one you love, fuck the one you are with".

Garibaldi's: Part 3

Sheila wondered why she told Ken that she loved him. Was it because she loved him, or was it the heat of the moment? It was clear that Ken wanted her. Anyway, Ken was still married to Charlotte. It could be some time before there was a divorce settlement. Sheila felt that she had never really shaken Jack off. If he called, she would come running, even though they had never been lovers. Does that mean she loves Jack? Would it be better to draw a line and start again?

Jack was still happy with the way the restaurant was going, but the staff were revolting. Actually, the revolt suited him. Jerry confronted him about his relationship with Anna. He demanded that the sex rota was scrapped and that he should stop fucking his woman. Jerry threatened to resign if his demands were not met. It was worse than that. Jerry was all geared up to fight with Jack if necessary.

Jerry was astounded when Jack said, 'That is all fine with me. I will agree to your proposal if that is what Anna wants.' The problem that Jerry had was that he had not even discussed this with Anna. Would she be happy with this? He wasn't sure. Should he propose marriage? Two wages are better than one.

From Jack's' point of view, dumping Anna would solve his other problems. Charlotte was giving him the best sex of his life. Anna was now a side-show, and he had almost forgotten about Sheila. It's funny how amazing sex can dominate a man's whole world. And to top it all, he was screwing Jane's adorable little arse, on Charlotte's day off. She was a totally different experience to that of Charlotte, a sweet, innocent, almost shy fuck. In some ways, it was a demure, secretive, almost naughty fuck. It was a fuck where an older man was taking advantage of a young girl, and the girl was grateful. Actually, that was the attraction. The girl was grateful.

An angry Anna stormed into Jack's room. She said, 'I have been fucking you two or three times a week, for nearly three years, and you have the audacity just to end it.'

Jack said, 'Calm down.'

Anna said, 'Calm down, I want to kill you.'

Jack said, 'Let's take this slowly. What did Jerry say to you? He doesn't always listen that well.'

Anna, 'So, now you are criticising your head chef?'

Jack, 'Sorry, but please tell me what Jerry said.'

Anna calmed down a bit and said, 'Tell me what Jerry asked you to do.'

Jack, 'OK, he stormed into my room and demanded that the sex rota should be scrapped, and that I should stop fucking his woman. He threatened to resign if I did not meet his demands. I simply said that it would be fine with me if that is what Anna wants.'

Anna, 'He called me "his" woman?'

Jack, 'That is exactly what he said. I have seen that you two were getting closer, and I wouldn't want to stand in your way if that is what you want.'

Anna said, 'What do I want?'

Jack said, 'Don't ask me I barely know what I want myself.'

Jack, always being the optimist, said, 'Are we having our session tonight?' Anna just looked at Jack and saw him for what he was. However, she was keeping "what he was" to herself. She turned and slowly walked away.

Like any good movie, Jack said to himself, *'I will take that as a no.'*

Anna confronted Jerry with, 'Am I your woman?'

Jerry had been practising his speech all afternoon, 'I, Jerry Clark, love you and want you to be my wife. Will you marry me?'

Anna said, 'Does that mean that I'm your woman? Does that mean that I can watch your box sets?'

Jerry said, 'Yes and yes.'

Anna said, 'I will accept your love, and I will live with you, but I don't believe in marriage. I would like to sit down with you and agree on the terms of our relationship.'

Jerry wasn't sure what she meant, but he said, 'I do.'

Charlotte had almost manoeuvred Anna out of the scene. Sheila was not an issue. That slut, Jane, needs to be eliminated. She knew exactly what she was up to with her shy little smile, and her puffy little breasts, and her shaved fanny, and her legs that go on forever, and her perfect teeth, and her sickening sneaky voice, and her "You can fuck me, Mr Jack, if you want to" attitude, and her constant desire to please, and that's enough.

Ken decided to go to Garibaldi's to tackle both of his women. He had to know that Jack was not fucking his woman and that he was fucking his other woman. In other words, he needed to know that Sheila was available, and then get evidence for his divorce petition. He needed to catch Jack fucking Charlotte. Later, the divorce could be finalised as adultery. Jack would then be named as the other party.

Ken arrived at Garibaldi's to find Sheila waiting at the door. She asked what he was doing there. He was frank; he wanted to see who was fucking who. Sheila said that her job was to be a naked hostess, and she undid her cloak to expose her nude body. She looked stunning with her nudity encapsulated by a black cloak with a light shining behind. Ken thought that she looked like an angel.

Ken asked again. 'Are you sleeping with Jack?'

Sheila said, 'Firstly, it's not your business, but I can definitely confirm that I'm not sleeping with Jack. If you have to know, Jack is sleeping with Anna two or three times a week, he is sleeping with Jane one day a week, and the rest of the time he is sleeping with your missus, or possibly ex-missus. I don't know.' This was the first time that he had seen Sheila angry. Ken believed her and apologised.

Ken asked again, 'Why won't you live with me?' He promised her the best of everything.

Sheila said, 'I've had one terrible marriage in which I did everything. I've had three children who have left home. This is the first time in my life that I've had Sheila-time. I can do what I like, to whom I like and when I like. At this moment in time, I like to be alone. I admit that I love you, but not enough to change my life.'

Sheila was going to walk off, but she turned and said, 'You can find Jack and your missus up those stairs. If my timing is right, he should have his cock in her fanny just about now.'

Ken stealthily walked up the stairs to see Jack lying on the bed with Charlotte on top of him. As far as he was concerned, they could not see him or his camera. Charlotte was rubbing Jack's cock against her breasts, first one, then the other. She then moved into a sitting position and rubbed his cock against her clit. She teased his cock against the entrance of her fanny, but never put it in.

Charlotte had seen her husband's image in one of the mirrors. Her back was facing Ken. Charlotte then bent forward so that her husband could see her exposed fanny. She used her fingers to expose it as much as possible. She wiggled her bum like a cat on heat. In some ways, she wanted Ken to burst in and cause a scene. Charlotte would love it. She continued wiggling her bum and stretching her fanny. She didn't want to hide anything from her ex. Ken thought that the woman was a tart, but he was transfixed.

Charlotte grabbed Jack's cock and rubbed it up and down. First slowly, and then more vigorously. She played with his foreskin and put her fingernail into the penal opening. She continued to play with Jack's cock until it was absolutely hard. Ken had to admit that it was a fine specimen, but it was a bit odd looking at another man's anatomy, especially his private parts. Jack was also displaying a fine set of balls. If Ken was a more revengeful man, he could have removed Jack's private parts in no time at all. That would certainly change the tone of his voice.

The Charlotte show, continued. She took Jack's engorged cock and stuffed it up her fanny. She was far from being gentle. She rode him like a woman possessed. She made sure that Ken could see his cock ploughing her furrow. Jack wondered what had got into her. She was certainly much more active than Anna. The speed increased dramatically, and Jack wondered if she was trying to castrate him. The tip of his penis was being bruised as he collided with her cervix, and the base of his cock was being crushed against her pelvic bone. The speed and force were of an order that Jack had never experienced before.

Charlotte was totally in control. Jack's only chance of freedom was to come, but the carnal pain was stopping that. He was expecting blood to appear at any moment. Ken was glad that they were getting a divorce. He wasn't sure that he could watch much more of this. Ken didn't think it was possible, but Charlotte upped a gear. Jack was now suffering extreme pain, and was shouting, 'Please stop.'

Charlotte shouted back, 'Don't tell me to stop, you wimp.' She leapt off him, and then unexpectedly jumped back on again, with her full weight landing on his private parts. Ken wasn't sure what damage had been done, but Jack had probably dislocated everything. Charlotte shouted out, 'Have you got the photos you want, you waster?' Ken did a runner, and Charlotte then attacked Jack's cock. She realised that it was all over and tried to bite his cock off. She decided that if she can't have him, then nobody can. Jack managed to push her away before his favourite body part was severed off. Jack ended it there and then, and Charlotte ran off into the night.

Jane was grounded. Her parents would not let her leave the house. Someone had sent them photos of her and Jack in very compromising positions. Her mum wanted them destroyed, but her dad thought that they should keep them in case they needed evidence in the future. It was strange that her dad checked the evidence almost every day.

Sheila was somewhat surprised by the day's events. It seemed that it was going to be a quite normal day, but then Jerry had a go at Jack. Anna had a go at Jack. Jerry proposed to Anna. Ken got his photos. Charlotte tried to bite Jack's cock off, and then got the old heave-ho. Jane resigned. Sheila thought that it was unlikely to get any worse.

But then Wormy was planning his revenge, but that's another story.

The moral of the story is, "At first, it would appear to be just another cock and bull story, but fate favours those who wake before the cock crows".

St. Valentine's Day Massacre: Part 1

This was the busiest day of the year for the restaurant: St. Valentine's Day. The dressers had been in overnight, and the dining area was a mixture of red, pink and white. There were large drapes across the ceiling and down the walls. Red roses were in abundance. There was an Eros fountain, and a temporary Juliet balcony had been installed.

There were bright red tablecloths, with bunting behind each chair. The stage had been enlarged, and two large screens with video projectors had been installed. The cutlery, crockery and table displays had been laid out. Two large nets were containing red, pink and white balloons. There were huge boxes of carnival masks, the type you see in Venice. In the past, they found that masks reduced people's inhibitions.

Sheila had to admit that the restaurant looked the part. It was starting to get her excited. She wondered if the cost could be justified, with all the fittings and the additional staff. On the other hand, the event was a sell-out; it was the place to be on Valentine's Day, especially with the entertainment that had been booked.

The extra staff were needed to handle the additional bookings. Sheila was a bit concerned that both a hen party and a stag group were coming. One is often a problem, but two on the same day could be a nightmare. But then, she was only a hostess. It's not her job to question management.

Talking about management, Jack was still receiving medical treatment for his testicular injuries. The stitches in his penis were still hurting, but the scarring should be minimal. He had been lucky, but that was not how it felt at the time. He still had his concerns, as things had not been adequately tested yet. That was why he was feeling pretty grumpy. Anyway, he was looking forward to the night's events. It should be fun.

Charlotte had not been seen at the restaurant since the fateful day. She was staying in Mark's dingy little flat. It was dingy before Charlotte arrived; it was even dingier now. Mark was generally too knackered to object to any of her demands. He wasn't sure what was worse — no sex, or too much sex. Charlotte had decided that she was going to the "ball". She was not going to miss it. She would be naked and was planning to fuck as many blokes as possible.

Jerry and Anna were now living together. They still hadn't sorted out the agreement. Things were going pretty well, except for one thing. Anna wasn't getting enough sex. She had been used to having sex every day, sometimes even two or three times a day. Of course, this was with multiple partners. Poor Jerry was a great lover. His thrusting techniques were world-class, but he just couldn't keep up with her demands. She had thought of sneaking back into Jack's bed for a quickie, but he had his own problems. She couldn't resist sniggering about it.

Anna was looking forward to the evening's festivities. Last year, she ended up fucking three of the diners. It was that sort of event. She couldn't see that happening this year, but then she knew that she couldn't trust herself. Jerry was going to be very, very busy in the kitchens.

Jerry was a bit worried about Anna. Living with her was just brilliant. She satisfied all of his emotional needs. It was sex that was worrying him. It was obvious that he was asking too much of her. Her poor little fanny probably needs a rest. She wasn't used to the demands of a real man. Without telling her, he decided to reduce their sexual encounters to just twice a week.

Anyway, he didn't have time to worry about that. Today was the busiest day of the year. He thought he had everything organised, and if there was a crisis, there was always late-night shopping. Some of the desserts from Waitrose would have to do.

Ken had received a free ticket from Sheila to the Valentine's event at Garibaldi's. He wasn't sure if he wanted to go or not. He wasn't sure if Sheila wanted him to go, but it was an excellent chance to see more of her. Ken laughed to himself that he had seen all of her quite a few times. At the same time, he was very frustrated with her; why won't she accept his offers? Ken thought that he was good with women, but recent events suggested the opposite. Anyway, after a lot of internal debate, he decided to go.

Despite her parent's wishes, Jane decided that she was going to Garibaldi's, no matter what. They will need all the help they can get. She was sure that she could find a handsome customer to fuck. She still couldn't understand why Mark was not returning her calls. If he is still there, she was going to make sure that he sees her fucking someone else. That will show him.

Wormy was still planning his revenge in between bouts of sleeping. This planning malarkey was arduous work. He made sure that his van was full of petrol. It was the first time in his life that he had put more than ten pounds of petrol in his car in one go. It just shows you how times have changed.

Inspector Knight decided that he needed to relax more. Wormy's return had not caused the massive crime wave in the Croydon area that he expected. He was pleased that he managed to get one of the last tickets to the Valentine event at Garibaldi's. He was looking forward to some mild titillation. He might even see that gorgeous bit of crumpet again, the nude lass holding the cake. What was her name? He checked his records. It was Sheila. He really wouldn't mind seeing her tits again. Sometimes, he was surprised just how naughty his thoughts could be.

Sheila decided that she wasn't going to wear her cloak tonight. There was no point being subtle when you have two pre-marital groups. She would greet her guests in her birthday suit, and a mask. She wasn't sure if Ken was going to be there or not, but she had every intention of getting some action. She really fancied being laid.

Jack had decided to start tonight's event with a quick speech. He was hoping to collect money for a charity that repairs men's bits. He knew that it was a very specialised area, but they needed money, and he had been very grateful for their assistance. Without them, his trousers would not fit properly.

Jack called a meeting with the key staff to make sure that everything was ready. Jerry was on schedule with catering. There were no real problems. He made a point that they decided not to have a large cake this year. Anna explained that there were six additional waiting staff, three of each sex. Two of them were not keen on stripping off, even though they knew that it was a requirement. She said, 'Don't worry, I will sort it.' Anna said that the waiting task was easy as everyone was having the same, apart from drinks. Even there, we are providing free wine on the table, as part of the ticket price. Sexy, but not pornographic, films had been loaded on the projectors; they would run all night.

Sheila had a friend helping her at reception. Sheila had also organised some of the special events. So far, no problems had been reported. She asked who was going to let the balloons down and when. No one seemed to know, but Jack agreed to sort it. She was also a bit concerned about the lack of bouncers. Jack told her to organise a couple. The head barman said that he was ready. They all agreed that it was unlikely that anything significant would go wrong.

The guests started to arrive. Some were dressed in all their finery. Others were more casual. There was a general air of excitement. They were even more excited when a stark-naked Sheila greeted them. Sheila always enjoyed looking at the men's eyes. You knew exactly where they were going to look: face, fanny, boobs, fanny, fanny, fanny. The eye movements of the women were more difficult to ascertain, usually face, body, surroundings, other guests. Sheila greeted them and one of her friends, Linda, took them to their seats. She had never been naked in public before. In fact, Sheila had never seen Linda naked before. She had quite a trim figure, petite boobs, and a big smile. She kept complaining that her fanny was producing too much lubrication. Sheila said, 'Don't worry, you might need it later.'

Her friend said, 'When does the orgy start?'

Sheila looked at the car park and thought, *It's just about to start*. Both of the big parties arrived at the same time, one was full of nurses, the other one mostly contained football players. Of the bus load of nurses, only two or three, including the bride, were actually nurses. The rest were simply dressed in a variety of medical costumes. They were already reasonably drunk as they had stopped at two pubs on the way to Garibaldi's. Sheila was anticipating trouble.

The troop of nurses fell out of the bus and managed to stagger to the entrance hall. A rather mature chief bridesmaid led them. The girls immediately abused Sheila. They fondled her nipples and fingered her fanny. Sheila tried to stop them, but there were just too many hands. Lots of banter, bordering on abuse, was thrown about. Sheila didn't think she was a big-breasted, two-timing, sex-mad, manhunting, perverted tart with a fanny the size of a tube station. Linda got even more abuse, but living with George, her husband, gave her the skills to handle it.

The arrival of the nurses changed the whole atmosphere of the restaurant. Sheila thought, *'It is going to be a night of romance and good fun, so let the party begin.'* The footballers — it looked like a complete team with their coaching staff — and some of the reserves were piling out of the old Routemaster bus. It looked like the best man was dressed as a referee, except that his black outfit was edged in pink silk.

Sheila said to Linda, 'Prepare to protect your girlie bits.'

Linda said, 'They can play with mine if they like; George hasn't touched them in years.'

Most of the footballers were milling about outside. Some were having a final puff. One of them was trying to sober up the bridegroom. Others were knocking back a bottle of vodka. Sheila opened the door and said, 'Are you coming in?'

They turned towards Sheila, had an almighty ogle, shouted, 'We will be coming soon,' and then stampeded. Sheila was literally bowled over and lifted by a dozen men. It was impossible to protect oneself — the nurses were bad, but this was ridiculous. Hands were investigating every orifice. Sheila could tell that these men had serious, amorous intentions.

Linda was trying to save her, but there were too many of them, and she had to continue her work as a hostess. She was actually rather jealous, but she knew that her time would come.

While Ken was queuing to get in, he thought he saw Sheila being carried off by a group of footballers. He felt his chances of giving her one, were starting to look slim. He also wondered if she really was the marrying sort. Linda welcomed him with a great smile. Ken couldn't help noticing that her fanny appeared to be very moist. He considered petting it, but he was too much of a gentleman, so he patted her bum instead.

The guests continued to arrive ready for the event to start at seven thirty p.m. Charlotte had smuggled herself in and was soon stark naked. She was enjoying the attention of the goalkeeper, who wasn't keeping his hands to himself. In fact, he wasn't far away from scoring the first goal of the evening.

Jerry was making good progress, when Sheila arrived in the kitchen with half a dozen footballers. To be strictly accurate, half a dozen footballers arrived, carrying Sheila. At first, he thought she might be in trouble, but she was laughing and giggling away, so he just decided to watch. He noticed that there were fingers where there shouldn't be. He even wondered if there would be an opportunity to beat his thrusting record, but then he remembered Anna.

Anna was already in the corner of the restaurant being propositioned by two men dressed as policemen. It was hard to resist the long arm of the law, especially when you have needs.

Wormy was sitting outside the restaurant in his car. He was feeling a bit reckless, so he left the engine running. He wondered if he would get another month in prison for doing that. He was still feeling extremely bitter, very bitter indeed. He was determined to get revenge. He was determined that tonight was the night for action. Then he fell asleep.

Jane stripped off in the car park. She just loved being naked in public. It made her feel so alive. She stood in the queue, waiting to go in. She didn't want to use the staff entrance in case they turned her away. She knew that Sheila would let her in. A couple of the men in the queue were trying to look at her without their wives noticing. She could have told them that the wives always notice and that they will be punished for their crimes later.

Jane was reasonably confident that her parents would turn up eventually to reclaim her. It would be an excellent opportunity to embarrass them.

Inspector Knight was sitting at his table, observing the scene. Normally he would be taking notes, but here he was off-duty, although, in reality, you are never off-duty. He anticipated that there would be criminal activity tonight; a policeman's lot is never done.

He noticed the two fake policemen in the corner caressing Anna. Would she never learn? He noticed Sheila, with the great boobs, being carried off into the kitchen by a group of footballers. He noticed that the goalkeeper's cock was deeply entrenched in Charlotte. He saw that three very busty nurses were molesting one of the waiters. He noticed the petite girl in reception having her bottom patted. He smelt smoke.

He noticed that Jack had taken to the stage. Jack grabbed the microphone and welcomed everyone to a night of romance, passion, and titillation. Jack said, 'Before the festivities begin, I would like you to think about those less fortunate than us. We are all strong, healthy, sexually active adults. Our equipment does the job it is supposed to do; it is fully operational.' There were quite a few sniggers, but Jack continued, 'But there are those out there who can't get it up. They need our help.'

There was a considerable amount of laughter. Ken thought, *'What is he on about? I'm not helping anyone get it up.'* Jack continued, 'Firstly, I want your compassion. Secondly, I want your money, and thirdly I want your underwear. It's all for a good cause. Your underwear will be sold to raise monies to help the unfortunate to get it up.' Jack removed his trousers and pants on stage and waved them in the air.

The head bridesmaid stood up and said, 'Girls, this is our chance to shine, this is our chance to show the world. Off with your knickers!' The entire troop of nurses stood up and, without any hesitation, de-knickered themselves. Inspector Knight had never seen anything like it. He had never seen so many naked pussies before. In a couple of cases, he would have preferred the knickers on.

Jane went around collecting the knickers up. Both the Inspector and Ken admired her cute arse. Ken was convinced that she was deliberately displaying herself, but he wasn't objecting. The best man stood up and said, 'Are we going to be beaten by a group of NHS workers? No, I demand that all members should be free.' Down went his shorts and pants to much applause.

The captain and centre half dashed into the kitchen and said, 'You must free your members.' They all obeyed and whipped off their undergarments. Sheila now felt much more vulnerable. Jerry thought, *'Now things are getting interesting.'*

Lots of things were happening. On the big screens, two films were showing: Last Tango in Paris, and Eyes Wide Shut. Masks were being distributed. A couple of naked girls were on the Juliet balcony. The first course was being served by three naked waiters and two nude waitresses. The remaining waitress was topless, but had a picture of Boris covering her fanny. A selection of Motown songs were playing in the background.

Jane and Mark spotted each other. Jane ran up to the nearest man and said, 'Quick, fuck me now.' Inspector Knight wasn't sure what to do. He really wanted to fuck that cute little arse. *But photos could get in the press. But she is so cute. I could lose my job. Should I stop her undoing my flies? I might lose my pension. She is just so cute, and her mouth feels so warm.*

The scene was set. The night was young.

The moral of this scene-setting is "hard to tell at this stage".

St Valentine's Day Massacre: Part 2

Sheila was lying on her back on the kitchen table, surrounded by four or five half-naked footballers, with Jerry looking on attentively. Both breasts were being suckled, and her fanny was getting a considerable amount of attention. Sheila wondered if this was in the job description for a hostess.

The footballers couldn't decide what the best tactic going forward was. They agreed that Sheila was "in play", but should they go straight up the middle, or come in from the blindside? It was essential to maintain the team balance, but also to disguise one's intentions. Here, the plan was reasonably clear, and Bob entered the centre circle. Sheila thought, '*At last, one of the footballers is tackling me.*' He started with a half-volley, then made a couple of feints, and then followed up with some neat work near the penalty area. He was nearing his goal.

Things then started to go wrong — there was no obstruction, but there was a serious deflection. As he panicked, he gave Sheila a bit of a shoulder charge. I guess that his natural instincts had taken over. He was immediately red-carded for ungentlemanly behaviour. He tried to break away, but was soon knocked out of bounds.

So far, no one had scored, but Bill, a resolute defender, decided to pitch in. He was good at turning his opponent and soon had Sheila on her side. He had to admire the passing skill of his opponent, and after deciding that her defences were down, he went for a very manly sliding tackle, and he was in. He decided that her fanny was on-site, and consequently, the goal was in-sight. With just one-touch, he rammed his balls home. He dribbled, and then he scored. The away team was ecstatic. Sheila thought that there had been some foul play.

The next footballer went for a dive and was soon sucking away at her fanny. It looked like she had another ball carrier on her hands, or rather her fanny. He started biting, which Sheila regarded as dangerous play. He was still near the goal area when Jerry decided that he was off-side. Jerry hit the offender with his hat a few times. Sheila decided that it was a hat trick. The footballer ran off, having missed out on a great goal scoring opportunity.

There was a substitution request from another footballer, but Jerry pushed him away. He wanted to "sweeper" away, and decided to go for a restart himself. There was no referee, so he could do what he liked. He wanted to take possession of this exceptional player.

Anna was determined to stay loyal to Jerry. It was her first genuine relationship. It was the first time that a man was treating her like a woman, and not just a fuck-toy. He respected her. She respected him. She knew in her heart of hearts that Jerry would never cheat on her. It would be impossible. He loved her that much. She realised that she must have the same high principles, partly for her own peace of mind. The fake policeman's truncheon entered her fanny.

Anna thought to herself, *'That feels good. I really need that.'* The second truncheon entered Anna's mouth. At first, she thought it might have been an unlawful entry, but then she remembered that she had effectively given permission for everything. It wasn't a breach of the peace. The two officers of the law had got a good rhythm going. Anna was pretty sure that they had done this before.

She knew that she was being used. That was the official statement describing her life. But with Jerry, she could escape from her own prison. The rhythm of life was increasing, and she could feel the start of a possible orgasm. It was so elusive during her time with Jerry, but she started to realise that an orgasm was possible. Possible, but not probable. She wondered if she was subconsciously stopping it. Was she somehow punishing herself? Was it her parent's' fault? It is so easy to blame others.

She had worked out that the orgasm was somehow related to her state of mind. With Jerry, she was more relaxed. Could she teach herself to relax with these two? It wasn't fair — the fake coppers were clearly enjoying themselves, and she knew that they would get their orgasms soon. As so often during her sexual encounters, her body was there, doing its stuff, but her mind was humming. Hum-drumming around the universe, looking for an orgasmic release. Well, it wasn't going to happen this time; the two plods came together.

Both her fanny and her mouth were full of cum, and not for the first time. She had been used. They were satisfied customers. What next? She decided that she needed to cheer up, but her guilt was now catching up with her.

Jack hadn't expected such a positive response to his speech. Half of the diners were either bottomless or totally naked. There was laughter and happiness everywhere. The masks seemed to be having their effect in several cases. The bride looked to be entertaining a large number of footballers. He considered whether he should join the queue or not, as his stable of women had seemed to disappear: Sheila was never his, Anna was with Jerry, Charlotte was clearly not welcome, and Jane had done a runner. He quite liked the idea of fucking the bride before her wedding night. Looking at the size of the queue, so did many other men.

Talking about forbidden fruit, he couldn't see Sheila anywhere, but he did spot Anna. She had tears in her eyes, so he beckoned her over. As she approached, his cock hardened. Not surprising really, as his cock knew her well — it was like meeting an old friend. Anna laughed and said, 'Looks like there is still some life in the old fellow.'

Jack asked, 'Why are you crying?'

Anna said, 'Can I trust you?'

Jack said, 'No.'

Anna continued, 'I've just cheated on Jerry.'

Jack said, 'Does Jerry know?' Anna shook her head, and Jack responded, 'Then you haven't.'

Anna said, 'But I know.' While this was going on, Anna was fondling Jack's cock. Somehow it was second nature. It was what she did.

Without really thinking about it, she turned around, bent over and gently put Jack's cock in her fanny. She was worried about hurting him. She could actually feel some of his stitches in her fanny. In fact, the stitches were rubbing against her G Spot. She was getting hotter and hotter. Her heart rate was increasing. She increased the rhythm. She was ignoring Jack. She was just using his stitches. She could feel this primaeval force building up in her. She could sense that satisfaction would soon be hers. Yes, it came, a small nuclear explosion in her groin. She had been waiting twenty-four years for this. It was a minor miracle. Her whole body felt warm, no hot. There was calmness and joy. Thank you, universe.

Jack just wondered what had happened. It was clear that it was nothing to do with him. At least he could get a hard-on, but could he come? Before anything was said, Anna joyfully skipped off to the kitchen. In the background, she could hear "Tracks of My Tears", and laughed. Then she laughed again.

Jane and Mark were shouting at each other. Jane, who was bending over a chair, said, 'You never returned my calls?'

Mark, 'It wasn't easy with Charlotte in the room.'

Jane, 'I bet you were fucking that trollop.'

Mark, 'I was actually, and it was very nice too.'

Jane, 'So, you are saying that she is a better fuck than me?'

Mark, 'She is a better fuck than you; she really knows how to please a man.' Tears were running down Jane's face.

She turned around and said, 'What do you think?'

Inspector Knight had his cock deeply entrenched in Jane's pussy. He wasn't sure if he had ever seen a prettier arse. In a solemn voice, Inspector Knight said, 'We have got a fine arse on our hands here; if you are waiting for a turn, I should be finished soon.' and he upped his humping.

The first course was being cleared, and the main course was being served. Both the male and female waiting staff were being regularly abused, but that was part of the deal. That was why they were being paid a significant bonus. It was interesting that the waitress with the Boris picture on her fanny was getting the most attention. Apparently, the diners wanted to fuck him before he got a chance to fuck them. The naked girls on the balcony were carrying out some acrobatics. From that angle, it was challenging for them to maintain their modesty. Ken didn't know where to look. Actually, he did. Without asking, Linda came over and sat on his lap.

It was Wednesday evening at about five o'clock when they noticed that Jane wasn't there. Where had our baby gone? They had sacrificed everything for her. Why would she treat us so thoughtlessly? How could she do that to us? We never ever gave a thought for ourselves. We had struggled all our lives to get by.

Jane's parents silently closed the front door. Her dad said, 'I bet she was keeping the appointment she made with that Mark from the pub trade. What did we do wrong? I bet she's having fun, the one thing that money can't buy. Let's get her back.' They got in their Morris Minor, which they bought from a man in the motor trade, and checked their A-Z of London. They would get to Garibaldi's somehow.

Jack noticed that the queue for the bride was getting shorter. Perhaps they were running out of men. One of the tradesmen was preparing the indoor fireworks. Another had just got the line ready so that the acrobats could do their tightrope walk. "Dancing in the Street" was coming across the sound system. The wine was flowing. The bar was busy, what could go wrong?

Then Wormy entered the scene. He had been asleep in his car. The heating wasn't working correctly. In fact, it had never worked. Well, it used to work, but stopped after Wormy repaired it. Anyway, Wormy was cold, so he wore a very thick bubble jacket, motorcycle gloves, and a balaclava. No one had ever accused Wormy of being a good driver. In fact, no one was brave enough to get in the car with him driving. Sometimes, he even forgot how to drive a car. It was that bad. This was one of those days.

He knew that he was in reverse when he put his foot down. The car back-fired loudly, and the vehicle shot forwards and smashed into a parked vehicle. Then, both cars continued their journey straight into the front of the restaurant, and then they continued straight through the dining room, hit the back wall, and then they went their separate ways. Wormy's car veered into the kitchen, leaving the other car in the dining room. Wormy hadn't expected that, nor had the kitchen staff, nor had the diners, and nor had Jack.

Sheila was still on the kitchen table, but this time she had Jerry's cock up her fanny. Jerry had got to two hundred and twenty-six. Sheila welcomed the distraction, as the thrusting process had lost its allure. Sheila tried to get up, but couldn't because Jerry, who was on top of her, had been knocked unconscious.

In the kitchen, the maniac driver managed to push open the door of the wrecked car. It was amazing that he hadn't been killed. The car was a total write-off. The kitchen was also a write-off. Sheila was struggling to work out how the car had found its way into the kitchen. Sheila was terrified when the terrorist walked towards her. He was covered in dust. He clearly had a bomb under his coat. You could just about see two beady eyes behind his balaclava. It looked like an automatic weapon in his hands. What was most surprising was that he was on fire. What was especially frightening was that there was leaking petrol everywhere.

Sheila prepared to meet her maker, not that she believed in God. Her time had come. There was no way she could defend herself with Jerry on top of her. It was amazing that his cock was still in her fanny. Ignoring that, there was nothing she could do. This was probably the most frightening thing she had ever experienced.

The killer said, 'It's only me,' in a childish, pathetic way.' She could almost hear a smirk. She thought she recognised the voice, but couldn't pin it down.

Then the kitchen door was smashed open, and in ran Jack and Anna. Anna looked at Sheila and said, 'How could you? I leave Jerry alone for a few minutes, and you fuck him at the earliest opportunity.' Before the conversation could continue, they spotted the masked marauder walking towards them. They were a bit surprised to see that he was on fire. Wormy pointed his weapon towards them, and Anna and Jack retreated behind Sheila.

Wormy wasn't too sure what was going on. Why was Sheila lying naked on the kitchen table with a man on top of her? Since their divorce, she has been fucking everything in sight. Why did a nude woman and a man with no underwear rush in, and then hide behind Sheila? Why were they so frightened of him?

Inspector Knight was just reaching his climax when two elderly people arrived and shouted at Jane, 'What the hell do you think you are doing?' Jane thought that they couldn't have timed it better.

Her father pointed at the Inspector and said, 'Is that Mark? You will have to marry him now.'

Jane said, 'No, that's Mark,' pointing at him.

Her father said, 'What's he doing?'

Jane said, 'He is watching that gentleman fuck me.'

Her mother said, 'Language!'

Her father said, 'Who is that man?'

Jane said, 'I've no idea, ask him.' Inspector Knight wiped his cock on the tablecloth and moved away without saying a word.

Jane's father looked horrified, although he was rather admiring his daughter's nudity. At that moment, there was a huge crashing noise, and the front of the restaurant caved in.

Then he saw his prized Morris Minor enter the premises. He hadn't expected that, nor had his wife and daughter. A beige people carrier closely followed it. Later, the cars went their separate ways. It was all a bit strange, to put it mildly.

It is not every day that a naked lady comes and sits on your lap. Ken was enjoying getting to know Linda. He had got to know her boobs quite well. He had got to know her legs quite well. He was just at the stage where he was getting to know her fanny. She was helping the process by undoing his flies. Linda had never cheated on her husband before. She was so excited about the possibility of a new prick in her cunt when she was knocked flying by a Morris Minor wing mirror. She hadn't expected that. Ken hadn't expected it either.

Linda wasn't hurt, but it ruined the moment. It was amazing how quickly these things happened. Ken was just about to put his finger in Linda's little garden when there was an almighty bang, followed by a mighty crash. He wasn't sure if it was an act of terrorism or a police raid. He considered doing a runner, but then he had a job to finish. He picked Linda up, brushed the dust off her breasts, and entered her holy of holies. Linda swooned.

A war had broken out between the nurses and the footballers. It was much more than a food fight, as anything that was not screwed down was in the air. Luckily, the bride was still being screwed down. Otherwise, she would have been used as ammunition. The waiting staff were trying to serve the desserts, but most of the diners just saw them as additional munitions. The strawberry trifles were particularly prized. They made a very satisfying "plop" when they landed. Charlotte had led a group of footballers behind the bar to attack the nurses from the rear, but this diversionary tactic was soon repulsed.

The advent of road vehicles in the restaurant soon put an end to the food fight. The noise, the dust, and the smoke quietened things down quite a bit. Both opposing armies were finding it hard to adjust to what had just happened. Neither army had expected that. The acrobats hadn't expected that either. It was fortunate for one of them that she landed on top of Charlotte. That seemed to quieten Charlotte down quite a bit. The other acrobat bounced off the Morris Minor and crashed onto the table that Inspector Knight was hiding under.

The Inspector was brought up listening to the war stories of his father. His dad was clearly as heroic as they came; his gallantry was legendary. His one medal was regularly polished. The Inspector had often wondered how brave he would be in a real crisis. That is why he had made a strategic retreat. Under the table, he could assess the situation and make his plans. He hadn't expected a naked acrobat landing on the table and crushing it. He hadn't expected a table leg up his rectum. He had reprimanded that Wormy character, but now he was a victim too.

Mark told Jane that he was sorry for the way he had treated her. Mark and Jane cuddled. Jane whispered in his ear, 'Is she a better fuck than me?' Mark nodded his head, and Jane slapped him. Mark wasn't sure if it was a real angry-type slap or a friendly admonishing tap. Either way, it hurt. He wasn't sure if he would ever understand women, but then he was part of a much larger club, as far as that was concerned. Jane's parents put their coats around them.

Jane's father went to ascertain the damage to his beloved Morris Minor when a very exhausted looking bride approached him. She asked if he had fucked her yet. At that moment, the front of the building collapsed, and of their own accord, all the balloons were released. You could criticise the bride for some of her behaviour, but she was a kindly soul. Jane's father had been knocked down and, clearly, medical treatment was required. The bride quickly ascertained that his trousers and pants needed to be removed, and she gave him fanny to cock resuscitation. He liked it, he liked it a lot, but he hadn't expected it.

No one was expecting the front of the building to collapse, but none of them expected the next move. The Morris Minor simply burst into flames.

It was certain that no one had expected the front of the building to collapse, or the Morris Minor to explode, but then they weren't expecting what happened next.

The kitchen doors were thrown open, and there stood an armed killer. They were surprised to see that he was on fire.

Jack and Anna had managed to get the unconscious Jerry off Sheila. The hardest part was disentangling their genitals. It appeared that the juices had set, or it might have been the icing sugar that was originally on the table. They then debated whether they should tackle the armed assassin or not. Sheila said, 'Some of these fanatic extremists would kill you with the blink of an eye. They are ruthless trained killers. They are radical murderers. We need to leave it to the professionals.' They all agreed that inaction was the best way forward.

A burning Wormy walked into the dining room. He was a truly terrifying sight. Wormy looked around. The half-naked footballers started retreating. Some of them managed to make their way out of the war zone. The nurses were a tougher lot, but even they didn't like the look of Wormy. The police outside were warned that there was a vicious looking terrorist inside. Jane's dad and the bride were oblivious to the impending danger. His cock had never had such a workout before. He wondered how often she got a migraine, and there was no sign of multiple bellies.

Wormy shouted out, 'Do not be frightened, no one will be hurt if you follow the right path.' Wormy was referring to the path beside the restaurant. The people in the dining room assumed he was a religious nutter. They were confident that the bomb was going to go off shortly.

Wormy looked around the room. He wondered what had caused all of this? There was a wrecked Morris Minor on fire by the stage. The front of the building and the balcony had collapsed. There was food everywhere, literally everywhere, including the walls and ceiling. Charlotte was lying unconscious on the floor. Inspector Knight was under a table with a large wooden object up his arse. He knew how that felt. There were police sirens outside, and lots of flashing lights. An older man was fucking a woman in a bride's head-dress. A young couple was cuddling. There were balloons everywhere. In the background, Edwin Starr's "War" was playing. Wormy thought, *'It looks a bit like a war zone; who could have done this?'*

Wormy thought he could smell burning, and things were getting hot. He took off his balaclava to see that he was on fire. He took off his coat and his trousers. At that moment, the man who was preparing the indoor fireworks set them off. Three rockets hit him hard, and as he turned to flee, the next barrage hit him in the arse. As you know, this was not the strongest part of his anatomy. Wormy didn't experience too much pain until it exploded.

The police soon apprehended Wormy. Everyone was shocked by the turn of events. Sheila could just not believe that it was Wormy.

The moral of the story is, "All you need is Love".

St Valentine's Day Massacre Aftermath: Part 1

Sometimes an aftermath is just an aftermath. Other times it is world-changing. For Sheila, this aftermath was the latter. Almost everything changed.

Firstly, the restaurant was condemned. The foundations were never that good, and the force of two vehicles crashing into it was just too much for this Grade 2 listed building. The fire caused by the Morris Minor exploding put the building almost beyond repair. The asbestos found in the ceiling and wall cavities made the site quite hazardous, but the severe damage was caused by the Second World War bomb exploding.

Second World War bombs exploding are quite rare, but apparently Wormy triggered it off when the door of his car was ripped open. The bottom of the door smashed against the exposed bomb's trigger mechanism. If it hadn't been a delayed-action bomb, then a lot of people would have been killed. Sheila thought, *'I bet the Germans hadn't expected the delay to be over seventy years, but then they hadn't made any allowances for the bloody disaster called Wormy.'*

Jack had made several suggestions that they should get together, but Sheila had ignored all requests for a meeting. She was now even more confused about the future. She was then a bit saddened to hear that Jack and Anna had emigrated to

Barbados.

Jack had received a substantial windfall from the insurance company. He wondered if he should use his millions to re-build Garibaldi's or should he retire? He wanted to discuss it with Sheila. What he wanted to do was to whisk Sheila off her feet, and take her to a desert island, where they would live for happily ever after. As he got no response, he did the second-best thing.

Anna's whole life seemed to be about achieving an orgasm. Pathetic really, but that was just the way it was. It's strange that the orgasm happened during the St. Valentine Day's massacre. Even stranger that it happened with Jack. Even stranger that it was Jack's stitches that did the trick. When Jack asked her to go to Barbados with him, she thought, *'Why not — it doesn't have to be forever. And it would piss my parents off, and it would be nice not to have to worry about money, and... there are many other reasons.'* She was worried that she would have to find ways of putting stitches in Jack's cock.

Anyway, from Sheila's perspective, she had lost a good friend, and possibly the man she loved. Then things got worse: Ken and Linda had hit it off. Linda realised what she had been missing for all these years. She enjoyed a real man teaching her how some parts of a woman's body worked. She hadn't realised how much fun sex could be. She now looked forward to the long winter nights. Linda's husband hadn't noticed that she had gone.

Ken had decided that he couldn't cope with the way Sheila was. He wanted her, but she had turned him down so many times, and to be honest, she was too much woman for him. He realised that he was suffering from loneliness. Well, he was suffering until he met Linda. She was a bundle of fun. She was happy to be his meek, pliable partner. Her innocent docility was just what he needed. He sold his business to his partner, and they decided to move to Barcelona.

From Sheila's perspective, this was devastating news. She had lost Linda, her best friend, but what was worse, she had lost her manager. She knew that he was far more than that. He was someone she could turn to. He was someone who would cuddle her when she needed it. He was often her lover. What was happening to the world?

Jerry woke up from unconsciousness to find that the restaurant had gone. His job had gone, and then Anna was gone. He couldn't really blame her. She did find him in the kitchen with his cock in Sheila's fanny. There were no excuses. His guilt would have been a lot less if he knew what Anna had been up to, but then Anna was happy to keep him in that state. As far as she was concerned, it served him right. She did often wonder what her life would have been like if she had stayed with him. She doubted that she would be in Bridgetown, knocking back cocktails. Jerry had tried contacting Sheila, but there was no response.

Jane wasn't too sure if she wanted any more valentines. Her relationship with Mark never prospered, and they lost contact. He kept saying things like, 'That's nice, but Charlotte would have done it this way, Charlotte never said that she wasn't in the mood, Charlotte never said that her bottom was just for pooing.' She forgot the number of times that Charlotte was mentioned. It was almost impossible to ignore the elephant in the room.

Then came the fatal day when she said, 'If you fucking like Charlotte so much, then fuck off, and go and fuck her.'

Mark packed his bag and fucked off, never to be seen again.

It took some time for Mark to track Charlotte down. The acrobat falling on her head seemed to have done her some good. She had settled down with a fisherman in Plymouth. She didn't want to see Mark, but she did want some babies.

And talking about babies, Jane thought she might be pregnant. She was pretty sure that it was not Mark's. She had a sneaky suspicion that it was Inspector Knight's. Well, they were the only two options. Should she bring another officer of the law into the world?

And, as if things couldn't get worse, her father had run off with that tart, the bride from the party. Her husband to be had heard about her shenanigans and disowned her. The bride thought that it was for the best. She wondered if she had deliberately engineered it, as she wasn't usually that promiscuous. Then, she met Albert with the Morris Minor. How could you not love someone who had one of those cars?

Well, technically he didn't have a Morris Minor, but he would when the insurance money came through. Then, they would move into a lovely little townhouse in Peckham. Jane's mother had turned to alcohol. She always had leanings in that direction, but now there were no excuses to resist. "It was something inside, that was always denied for so many years. He was leaving home. Bye, bye".

Jane thought, *'Mum has lost her husband, but she might soon get a grandchild. What should she do?'*

The Inspector required extensive anal surgery. It wasn't so much the table leg in his anus that was the problem, but the splinters. The splinters were a problem because they entered the intestine in the opposite direction to faecal matter. He managed to cope, but he had a grudging respect for Wormy's previous problems. The pain was beyond the pale.

On a brighter note, the Inspector had been awarded a police medal for bravery. He realised now that hiding under the table was indeed an act of courage. He was also struggling to get Jane out of his mind. He was at least twice her age. It was easily the best fuck of his life. The other two happened nearly thirty years ago, and the memory had been somewhat lost in the mists of time.

The ARU, Armed Response Unit, had arrested Wormy. SOCIT, The Serious and Organised Crime Investigation Team, also turned up. There was an argument about who was going to get the glory of capturing this armed villain. It was known that he had a track record for this type of crime. It was the second time that he had attacked this particular establishment.

It was fortunate that Inspector Knight was there to provide evidence against Wormy. The Inspector's statement was quite damming: 'The accused was dressed in protective clothing, in preparation for the night's attack on the Garibaldi Italian Restaurant. He had previously reconnoitred the property and chose Valentine's Day to achieve maximum effect. He arrived at the premises quite early and pretended to sleep in the vehicle. In reality, he was waiting to choose the best moment to storm the building.

'His car had a full tank of petrol to fuel his planned arson attack. He deliberately rammed a private car into the front of the restaurant, to do as much damage as possible. Both vehicles entered the building at considerable speed, damaging property, and putting lives at risk. He knocked some acrobats off their tight rope and crashed one of the cars into the stage.

'He cleverly manoeuvred the car he was driving into the kitchen to terrorise his ex-wife. The kitchen staff and the restaurant manager were threatened with a high-powered rifle. The accused rushed into the dining area to assault some of the dedicated NHS workers. He threatened the occupants with a home-made bomb attached to his body, causing them to flee. The fact that he was on fire didn't seem to slow him down in any way.

'He showed no remorse for triggering the bomb in the kitchen. He was clearly a hardened criminal. The Armed Response Unit was called. I would have done more, but I had been severely injured, which limited my capability to assist.'

Sheila found it all somewhat hard to take in. Wormy was taking the divorce harder than she thought. You live with a man for years, and still, they surprise you.

The moral of the story is, "The only constant is change".

St Valentine's Day Massacre Aftermath: Part 2

Sometimes, the aftermath of an aftermath is worse than the aftermath. Sheila had just received the terrible news.

Jack had been killed in an improbable accident. He was sitting on a beautiful sandy beach waiting for his lover to turn up. The locals had made a fire to cook some seafood that had been caught. Either deliberately, or accidentally, some manchineel wood had been put on the fire.

The manchineel trees are extremely dangerous. The trees produce small green apple-like fruits that are highly toxic if ingested. When the bark of the tree burns, the smoke causes blindness. Even the sap causes skin blisters and burns. Apparently, Jack had no idea what was going on. He was suddenly blind. In his blindness, he tripped over a loggerhead turtle and hit his head on a rock. He was unconscious when the tide came in, and he drowned.

The local police were suspicious about the way he died. The locals know that the manchineel tree should be avoided at all costs. The wood of the tree is never, ever, used in fires. Usually, the tree is marked with red rings to highlight the danger. They were also concerned about the recently produced will, that left everything to Anna. There was no evidence against her, and frankly, they didn't have the resources to pursue the case. Anyway, Anna was going back to England.

She was now worth a few million.

Sheila was devastated. She would have gone to the funeral, but the cremation had already taken place. She wondered if a remembrance service would be organised in England. She wondered what Anna was going to do next. She wasn't envious of her millions, not a bit.

Jack wouldn't have liked to see his beloved restaurant turned into a block of flats. Work couldn't start until further Second World War bombs were removed. All that time, diners were sitting on a tinder box.

Anna felt sad about Jack's death, but it was true that they were not getting on. Jack was very demanding, partly because he was so bored. He just didn't have enough to do. Another constant source of irritation between them was Sheila. Barely a day went by when he did not mention her name. It was just Sheila, Sheila, Sheila! What magic spell did she have over him? But now he was gone.

Anna never thought it possible, but she was missing her parents. Strange how family ties seem to strengthen with distance. She decided to go home. A whole new world was opening up to her. She even contemplated seeing Jerry, but her newly acquired wealth might be a barrier. She still wasn't sure why Jack changed his will, but she thanked him.

Ken had never told Sheila that he had dementia. Away from work, he was deteriorating fast. He kept confusing Linda with Sheila. They were both merging into one. Linda contacted Sheila to see if she wanted to see him. Linda also explained that he was still technically married to Charlotte. If he died, she would inherit everything, and she would be broke, and homeless. Sheila wasn't sure if she wanted to see Ken, her old friend, in that state. She thought, *'Life can just be shit sometimes.'*

Jerry was very saddened to hear of Jack's death. He wondered if Anna might be willing to share his bed again.

Jane decided to have the child, partly to please her mother, but in reality, she realised that she was letting a life-changing decision just happen. She wanted a child herself, but she expected to have one with a life-partner. Should she approach Inspector Knight? To be fair, it wasn't really his fault, although it was his cock and his semen.

Her mother had agreed to help with the child's upbringing, but she would have to go dry first. She was pleased that her father was so happy. She enjoyed her visits to Peckham, but she was dreading telling him about her pregnancy. It turned out that he was thrilled. This was now a typical day in her life. Funny how things change.

Things were looking up. It appeared that every splinter had been removed from Inspector Knight's rectum. Purely by chance, he met Jane in the bank. He thought that she was putting weight on.

Wormy did a deal with the Crown Prosecution Service. He had never good at deals. Wormy explained that he was at the restaurant to confront the management. He made it clear that he had no intention of ramming the Morris Minor, or the restaurant. It was just an accident. He had no intention of deliberately knocking the acrobats off their rope. It was just an accident. He had no intention of smashing into the walls or the kitchen. It was just an accident. He had no intention of triggering the bomb in the kitchen. It was just an accident. He didn't threaten the restaurant staff with a gun. In fact, he didn't even have a weapon. He didn't have a bomb either. He wasn't wearing protective clothing. He didn't threaten the diners in any way. He said all of this while sobbing and protesting his innocence.

The CPS had a very different view. He admitted that he was there to confront the management. Only an idiot would drive that way by accident. Only an idiot would behave the way he did. Only an idiot would dress like that. They had their suspicions that they might have an idiot on their hands. But then there was Inspector Knight's statement and the video evidence. No, there was no doubt that he was guilty. Even if he wasn't, it would be a good idea to protect the public from someone like him.

The CPS was concerned that he did not have a solicitor. Apparently, he was more than capable of defending himself. Wormy accepted a five-year sentence with parole after two years. Wormy was quite looking forward to a free lunch, but he was a bit worried, as his bottom was just getting back to normal.

The moral of the story is, "Avoid Loggerhead turtles, Second World War Bombs, and the CPS, to live a long and prosperous life".

The Interviews: Part 1

It was past ten o'clock in the morning, and Sheila was still in bed. This was unheard of. She was usually up early, doing her housework, and then off to earn her daily crust. When she had to get up early, she would be happy to kill to get an extra hour in bed. At weekends she rarely laid in. Today was an exception. She forced herself to turn over and get a couple of extra hours of sleep. The strange thing is that she never felt better for it. Anyway, a cup of coffee was calling.

Sheila had not experienced unemployment for a long time. She was self-employed, but through Ken or her other contacts, there had always been a steady stream of work. Garibaldi's had been a constant source of revenue. She had not been on the hunt for business for donkey's years. She wondered how long donkeys live.

Then it dawned on her that she needed to approach the agencies. She would need a CV. She needed a replacement for Ken. Suddenly, she saw the way forward. She decided that she was getting a bit slow, as she should have thought of this before. Perhaps her brain had become programmed to only think in one way. The good news was that she had a decent bank balance so that she could be choosy. But then she knew what she was like. She would panic and take the first thing on offer. This was a by-product of her father's legacy. He always told her that she would come to nothing.

It was tricky putting a CV together. In many ways, her work depended on her appearance and willingness to go that extra mile. It was difficult detailing the services she offered without coming across as a whore. It was a fine line between being an adult performer and a prostitute. She decided to put a photo portfolio together. She had a great collection, although some of them were not suitable.

Her next challenge was deciding which agencies to contact. Some of them looked very dodgy. Some were a cover for escort work. Another was an online brothel. After some serious googling, she identified about a dozen acceptable organisations, although only time will tell.

And time was kind to Sheila. An interview was organised for the following week. Their website suggested that most of their business revolved around upmarket porn films. This was a challenge for Sheila. Her mantra was that she never sold sex for money. How does a porn film fit into this? Technically she is being paid to act, although, with porn, she thought it wouldn't need that much acting. Logically, and Sheila was quite logical, it's what she does now, but it is on film. It's probably the connotations that worried her, but then the only commitment is an interview.

Sheila went through her regular interview routine of having a manicure, pedicure, hair styling, a little bit of tanning, and she even trimmed her bush slightly. Sheila had never been keen on tanning, but she needed a slight glow. She certainly didn't want the full orange treatment. The entire process just helped to improve her confidence levels. It took her a fair amount of time to select the best colour coordinating outfit.

Sheila was sitting in the potential employer's waiting room, early as usual. She was a bit surprised by some of the wall displays. It certainly wasn't the place that you could take young children to. There was a cabinet containing all of the awards they had won over the years. There seemed to be a large number of gold-painted phallic symbols. She tried to have a good look, as some of them appeared to be on the large size, but she was too embarrassed to get close.

The tart on reception had phoned through to say that Sheila was there. Sheila is not usually rude about other women, but "tart" was the word. No other name could so succinctly describe her attributes: badly dyed blonde hair, with black roots; very short mini-skirt with thong; cracked bright red nails; an over-indulgence in mascara; painted-on eyebrows; chewing gum; nipples trying to escape from her vest; shiny black stilettoes. The list just went on. Sheila wondered how she could type with those dangling eyelashes, but then she only typed with one finger.

The tart then asked Sheila to walk this way. Sheila wasn't sure if she had to wiggle her bum in the same way or trip on every third step. Sheila desperately wanted to steady her as her whole walking process just looked so dangerous.

Sheila entered the room to find two casually dressed men waiting for her, Josh and Target. Both were very good looking, but possibly a bit condescending. She immediately got the impression that they were in the meat trade, and that she was just more meat. It reminded her of a previous interview for the *Snow White* pantomime, where she had to strip off and effectively have sex with the owner. Well, she was determined that it wouldn't happen this time.

Josh said, 'Coffee, tea or a cold drink?' Sheila went for a cold drink as you couldn't rely on the coffee arriving in a cup and saucer. That was soon organised, and the interview started.

Josh said, 'Thank you for your extensive CV and portfolio of photos. We have been looking into your past. It would appear that you were the Sheila that was caught on stage having sex at the Croydon Theatre?' Sheila nodded. Josh, 'And you were the Sheila of *Snow White* fame, who had sex on stage with multiple dwarves?' Sheila nodded. Josh, 'And you played Lady Godiva on several occasions?' Sheila nodded. Josh, 'But you claim that you are not a porn star?'

Sheila explained that she had never made a film. Josh, 'But we have a video of you performing at a local museum, taken by an internationally well-known photographer.'

Sheila said, 'Well I've never made a film except for that one.'

Target said, 'It appears to us that you have had a very illustrious career.'

Sheila said, 'Not really — most of these happened by accident. Ken just got me the jobs, and I went along and performed.'

Target, 'Who is this, Ken?'

Sheila, 'He was my agent.'

Target, 'Did you have a contract with him?'

Sheila, 'No, anyway he has retired now with dementia.'

Target, 'If we go ahead, we will need to check that out.'

Josh said, 'Sheila, let's be clear. We make pornographic films. You will be required to have sex in front of a camera. Is that a problem?' Sheila shook her head.

Josh, 'I'm going to go through a list of topics; let me know which are a no, no.' He started the list: heterosexual sex, lesbianism, masturbation, fisting, orgies, sex with animals, anal sex, BDSM. Sheila stopped him.

She said, 'Sex with men or women is OK, orgies are OK,

215

but I'm a lady.' Josh and Target could tell that she was.

Target said, 'I think we understand, but we will have to detail your preferences and constraints later.'

Josh said, 'We are very interested in taking you on, but we have to see you naked, and we have to test that you have the right attitude for the porno industry. This will involve you in sexual activity.' This is where Sheila decided to be strong.

Sheila said, 'What type of sexual activity?'

Josh, 'We have a standard test where six men will have sex with you in an hour; they get ten minutes each. That way we can judge your performance.'

Sheila decided to say, 'No way,' but she actually said, 'Shall I strip off here?'

Josh said, 'That would be fine.'

The stripping didn't take long, as she was only wearing a dress and some skimpy underwear.

Target said, 'Very nice. I like the boobs and those legs, but I'm a bit surprised to see that you still have a muff.' Apparently, in today's porn industry, there is no beaver.

Target started fondling her boobs and said, 'Very nice, very nice indeed.' His hand moved to her fanny. 'That will do nicely,' 'he said. Sheila thought that he had done pretty well so far. Sheila was bent over, her fanny was opened up, and a finger was put up her anus.

Josh said, 'That's a fine body you have got there; are you ready for some fucking?' Sheila nodded, but it was all a bit clinical. Sheila followed Josh through the office. A few of the office workers looked up, but they were very used to seeing naked men and women wandering around. It was all in a day's work.

At the end of the office, there was a small room with a bed

and a cradle mechanism. The cradle held the woman in place with her legs spread apart to enable easy access to her cunt. She had been in one before. Josh said, 'I will go and find six volunteers; while I'm doing that, I will get you lubricated.'

An apprentice, who was over the age of eighteen, came into the room with some lubrication. He started rubbing it into Sheila's genitalia. Sheila said, 'Don't you normally spray it on?'

The lad said, 'Most people do, but I prefer to get my hands dirty.'

Sheila said, 'I bet you do.' However, he did an outstanding job of massaging all of the critical parts. It was a bit embarrassing, having a brat just out of school manipulating her fanny and fingering her anus. It was even more shameful that her body was reacting very positively.

Josh came back and spoke to the lad, 'Looks like you have done a good job there, but I think that fanny could do with just a bit more handling.'

The lad said, 'OK, boss,' and rammed two fingers up Sheila's cunt. It almost made her come. She certainly felt that she was well lubricated now.

Outside the door, six trouserless men were waiting. The first one jumped on board and did not come in the allotted ten-minute slot, so he was removed. The second one came far too quickly, so the third man was given fifteen minutes. He was a steady Eddy sort of guy. Sheila thought it was going to be touch or go if he came in time. He did it with seconds to spare. The next guy may have come. If he did, it was only a dribble. Number five was a star. He went straight in and gave Sheila two orgasms in five minutes, and then filled her up. Sheila later learnt he was a porn star. The last man standing was a pathetic shy creature, who shot his load over Sheila's stomach to much jeering. Apparently, he didn't like to get inside a woman's bits. Overall, there was a positive response from the testers.

Sheila walked back to the interview room with spunk running down her leg. She sat down, and Target said,' 'Things are looking good, but there is one problem — that muff. If you want to progress things with us, we need you shaved. It would be great if you could do that, and be back here tomorrow.'

Sheila cleaned herself up, got dressed, did her goodbyes, and went up the road to have a nice coffee in a china cup and saucer. She thought about what she had just been through. Effectively, she had been gang-banged. But it didn't worry her at all. Then she started worrying about the fact that she wasn't worried. It was strange how circumstances changed your attitude and principles. A few years ago, she would be protesting about female abuse. She would have burnt her bra. But who is exploiting who?

Anyway, the current challenge is: Does she remove her pubic hair? How does she do it? Could she get someone else to do it for her? She started thinking about possible volunteers. The potential candidates were a bit thin on the ground. The only person she could think of was Jerry. After some hesitation, she phoned him.

Sheila, 'Hello, Jerry.'

Jerry, 'Hi, Sheila, this is a surprise; long time no speak.'

Sheila, 'Sorry I haven't been in contact, but I've just been swamped lately.'

Jerry, 'I have the opposite situation — no work, nothing to do. I'm a bit bored really.'

Sheila, 'I'm sorry to hear that, but as you have some spare time I wonder if you could do me a favour?'

Jerry, 'I would be pleased to help.'

Sheila, 'Well, you know that you gave me one thousand thrusts.'

Jerry was suddenly very interested, and said, 'Did you want a repeat performance?'

Sheila, 'Not really; one thousand thrusts is enough for any lady, but I do want some help in that area. Could you remove my muff?'

Jerry, 'You want me to remove your gloves?'

Sheila, 'No, "muff" is another name for pubic hair.'

It all went silent. Then Jerry said, 'You want me to remove your bush?'

Sheila, 'That's right, are you happy to do it?'

Jerry said, 'Let me think about it.' Laughing, he said, 'I would love to do it. When?'

Sheila said, 'It must be tonight.'

Jerry, who has always been a bit cheeky, said, 'Can I fuck you as well?'

Sheila said, 'With the positions you will need to get me in, I don't see how I could stop you.' They agreed to meet later that night.

The moral of the story is, "No pubics in public".

The Interviews: Part 2

Jerry couldn't believe his good luck. How often do you get a call from a beautiful woman asking you to shave her bush off? He collected together his kitchen knives and his shaving kit, and caught a taxi to Sheila's flat.

Sheila opened the door with a radiant smile. She was genuinely pleased to see him. They talked about the final days of the Garibaldi Restaurant. They tried to piece together what happened. How did the two cars end up in the restaurant? Who started the food fight? Who would have thought that the bride would run off with Jane's father? Who got Jane pregnant? Did Wormy have a gun? Because Wormy pleaded guilty, there was no trial, so there was no need for a detailed investigation.

They talked about his thrusting record and laughed. Jerry never ever thought he would reach a thousand thrusts; Sheila admitted that her fanny was sore for a few days afterwards. She gladly admitted that it wasn't an experience she wanted to repeat. Jerry was secretly disappointed, as round two was top of his agenda.

They both felt sad when Jack's name came up. What a way to go, especially when he had so much money in the bank. They both wondered what Anna was going to do with it. Neither knew if Anna was back in the country yet or not.

Sheila explained why she needed to be shaved.

Jerry said, 'Have you shaved down there before?'

Sheila said, 'I haven't shaved down there myself, but the hospital did it before my children were being born.'

Jerry said, 'I've been wondering what would be the best position for the shave?'

Sheila said, 'I think the dental chair approach, but instead of focusing on teeth, we need to focus on my genitals.'

Jerry said, 'Have you got a dentist's chair?'

Sheila, 'Of course I haven't, I was just being conceptual.'

Jerry said, 'Taking that into account, I guess that the best way forward would be for you to be on your back, with your legs up in the air.'

Sheila said, 'They need to be spread apart so that you can remove every single hair.'

Jerry said, 'How are we going to stop you getting cramp? That position will certainly hurt after a while. I don't think the hair removal is going to be a quick process.'

Sheila said, 'I noticed that you brought your kitchen knives with you. I hope that you are not planning to use them.'

Jerry, 'I have a very delicate touch; it's amazing what I can do with them.'

Sheila said, 'I think we should just keep them for an emergency. I think a simple razor will do the job.'

Jerry said, 'I think I know what we can do. You need to lie on your back on your bed, with your bottom area right on the edge. I will tie ropes around your ankles, and then tie the other end to whatever is handy — a doorknob or window latch, for example. That way, your legs are stretched apart, but it shouldn't be that uncomfortable.'

Sheila said, 'It doesn't sound very ladylike, but it should do the job.'

Jerry asked if she had any rope. Strangely, she didn't, but

she had some bungee cords.

Sheila had a quick shower and presented herself to Jerry in all her naked glory. She thought about covering her boobs, but it seemed a bit prudish. To be honest, Sheila felt a bit shy; it's one thing fucking all and sundry, but it's totally different being shaved in your own bedroom, by a relatively new acquaintance. She had to admit that they had fucked a few times, but not in a romantic way.

Regardless, the job had to be done. Jerry laid some latex sheets on the bed to stop it from getting wet or damaged. Papers were put on the floor to protect the white carpet. Sheila put some thick socks on and laid on the bed as instructed. The latex was a bit chilly, but she knew that it would soon warm up. The bungee cords were tied around both ankles over the socks, and then a series of cords were strung together to form an extended rope. One end was attached to the bedroom door handle, the other to the en-suite bathroom door handle. From Sheila's perspective, it looked dangerous, to put it mildly.

She suggested to Jerry that it didn't appear to be safe. In a typically manly way, he said, 'Don't worry about it.' He was eager to get the job started.

Jerry admired what he saw before him. In some ways, it looked like a turkey ready to be plucked. On the other hand, it looked like a beautiful woman willing to be fucked. Either way, there was very little modesty on show. Sheila kept putting her hand down in a vague attempt to cover her exposed pussy. It was more than exposed — the lips were parted, and you could see deep into the passage. The passage that Jerry had thrust into a thousand times.

Putting on his professional hat, he surveyed the task in front of him. There was a fair amount of hair covering the mons. This was thick and dark and would need some serious surgery. There was hair on each side of the labia. He noticed that here, in particular, the hair was of varying lengths. There was also some hair around the anal area. This would all have to come off.

He had a selection of tools ready, mostly stainless steel. He had them neatly laid out, like a professional chef in a kitchen. I guess that's because he is a professional chef. He had Sheila's Ladyshave razor, which was Sheila's weapon of choice. There was a massive container of shaving cream, a bottle of baby oil, and a box of plasters.

Sheila pointed out that he needed to avoid getting alien substances in the vagina itself, as it could easily lead to infections. Jerry asked her how she usually cleaned her fanny. Sheila explained that it was self-cleaning. Jerry said, 'Neat,' but had no idea what she was talking about. It was almost certainly one of those strange female mysteries.

Jerry could see that Sheila was a bit tense, and consequently lit a few candles. He put the "Best of the Carpenters" on. It was far too loud, in Sheila's opinion. He took his shirt and trousers off, in case they got oily. Sheila noticed his grey Y-fronts; they looked hot. They were ready to start.

Jerry decided to massage Sheila first to help her relax. Oil was splashed on, and his hands went to work. No part of the target area was spared. Sheila was both relaxed and aroused. She could tell that Jerry was also excited, as his trouser snake was trying to slide out of his Y-front opening. Sheila wondered if she should let him fuck her first, to help calm him down.

Before she could decide, Jerry started laying on the shaving foam. She wondered how much he generally used on himself because he was spraying on prodigious amounts. It was as if his hand was stuck on the spray button. Her genitals were covered in a cumulous, cloud-like formation. If the MET Office had seen it, they would probably issue a yellow warning, a potential danger to life.

Sheila shouted at Jerry to stop, but the Carpenters were singing "Rainy Days and Mondays" too loudly. Jerry grabbed his kitchen knives. Sheila started screaming and kicked her legs violently. The bungee cords went wild. Most of them separated and spun around at high speed. Two landed around Jerry's neck, and two attacked his genitals. The en-suite bathroom door, which had always been a bit suspect, came crashing down on Jerry's head. This knocked him unconscious and pushed his head on to the mountain of shaving cream covering Sheila's vagina.

Sheila tried to move, but having Jerry's head and the bathroom door on top of her made things very difficult. However, the extensive use of massage oil, and the slippery nature of the latex sheet, made her struggling quite successful, and she managed to slip under Jerry's body. In the process, her knees smashed against Jerry's testicles. She thought she heard a crunching sound, which was entirely appropriate, as the Carpenters were singing "Close to You".

Sheila thought she could smell burning. Some of the bungee cords had knocked the candles over, and Jerry's socks were on fire. Sheila tried to reach them, but she was still trapped under the door. Sheila tried to kick the sock off Jerry, but in the process knocked a bottle of baby oil over, which started burning immediately. This was starting to get serious.

Fortunately, the neighbour in the adjoining flat heard the fire alarm going off, and having a spare key rushed into

Sheila's bedroom. He immediately put the fire out. He had heard rumours that Sheila might be slightly on the risqué side, but this was ridiculous.

Sheila was stark naked, apart from a pair of socks and a couple of bungee cords strapped around her ankles. Her private parts were covered in baby oil and a mountain of shaving cream. He had never seen so much cream before. There was a tray of surgical instruments, all laid out very neatly. What were the plasters for? There was a latex sheet covering the bed, and clearly, a semi-naked unconscious man had been laying on top of her, but why was there a door on top of him? And to cap it all, the man's socks were on fire.

The Carpenters were singing "Top of the World". It didn't look like Jerry was feeling top of the world at all. On a final note, the neighbour couldn't help but admire Sheila's boobs. He was also hoping to see her fanny, but the shed load of shaving cream was too hard to remove, although he tried.

The Emergency Services soon whisked Jerry off to A&E. Sheila followed in her car and waited by his side until they could assess the fall range of injuries he had acquired. Jerry was still unconscious, but the doctor was happy to share the prognosis with Sheila.

'Firstly, it is going to take some time to remove the bungee cords from his testicles. One of them has done an excellent job of giving him a vasectomy. We can't work out how they got pushed in so far. It's as if someone kicked them in. The bungee cords around his neck have cut some of the blood supply to his brain, but we are expecting a full recovery after a period of recuperation. The concussion obviously didn't help. The extensive bruising on his back will heal, but the cracked ribs will be very painful and will take months to get better. The burns on his feet will require some attention and may require some minor grafts.'

Sheila decided to leave and come back another day with some grapes.

Sheila decided to keep her dreadlocks; stuff the porno industry.

The moral of the story is, "Don't mix hair and bungee jumping".

One Hundred

Every now and then, Sheila found herself pontificating about the meaning of life. She had asked Jerry to carry out a small favour, one that he was eager to perform. The poor guy is now in hospital, wondering if he could ever father a child. He is probably lying in bed, at this very moment, desperate to get the bungee cords removed from his testicles. How did it happen, and why?

Sheila wasn't sure if a bunch of grapes would make his crown jewels feel any better, but it would ease her conscience. Anyway, she put a particular tick against Jerry's name in her little black book. Since her divorce, she kept a simple list of her sexual conquests, or rather men and women who had given her one, or rather anyone who had entered her fanny. She wasn't sure if she was proud of the list, or ashamed of it.

Actually, deep down, she was rather proud. She had stopped being a caterpillar and had blossomed into a flutterby, although given the right opportunity, she might settle down. I guess that she had to find the right bush, or the right person has to find hers. But she had hit a momentous moment. There were now ninety-nine names in her book. *'Ninety-nine,'* she thought. Some of them had no name. Some didn't even have a memory attached to them. Some were passing ships in the night. Some were dead. She remembered Jack's smile. Some were even in hospitals having their goolies operated on.

Sheila decided that she should choose who number one hundred should be. It has to be someone new, someone who has never sampled the delights of her fanny before, as the list does not contain any repeats. It was a list of names, not a list of encounters. She would definitely need a much larger black book for that!

So, where do you find a man? In her mind, she created a simple list: gym, library, supermarket, pub. It was not a problem she had encountered before, as the men found her. She considered advertising, but it was going to attract the wrong sort. What about friends and relations, or husbands of friends and relations? She decided to go to the gym.

Sheila had been to the gym a few times but found it rather dull. She selected a leotard that left little to the imagination. Almost transparent in water, it just about covered her crotch if she was careful, and she wasn't planning on being careful.

It was a very masculine gym. It smelt of used jockstraps, it smelt of ingrained sweat, it smelt of one of the by-products of overcooked sprouts. It wasn't the sort of gym an attractive young lady would go to, but it was perfect for Sheila's aspirations. It was a one hundred, type of gym.

Sheila used the running machine, where her unrestrained breasts beat a rhythm of their own. They seemed to acquire several admirers, especially when one escaped. The rowing machine caused even more excitement as the crotch of her leotard kept encroaching inwards, leaving her lips on full display. One admirer, called Peter, offered to assist her while she was rowing. He gently recovered her gusset and re-established her modesty, not without some investigation with his fingers.

Sheila thought, *'He will do.'* She was not generally

attracted to the brawny, muscular types, but he would do. Peter would have the honour of being Mr One Hundred.' Sheila whispered, 'Is there somewhere we could go for some privacy?'

Peter said, 'There is a coffee shop across the road.'

Sheila said, 'Somewhere even more private.'

Peter said, 'I could see if the manager's office is free.'

Sheila thought, *'Brawny but thick.'* She said, 'Is there a place where you can fuck me?'

Peter said, 'Are you saying that you want me to fuck you?'

Sheila said, 'That was the general idea.'

Peter, 'Are you saying that you want to be fucked now?'

Sheila, 'No, I was thinking of next Christmas.'

Peter, 'Oh, that should be OK then.'

Sheila, 'Of course, I'm talking about now, this very moment.'

Peter said, 'There is the old storeroom below the gym.'

Sheila said, 'Let's go for it,' although she had lost any real enthusiasm for the job in hand. Peter went and got the key from the manager of the gymnasium. He told him that he had to fuck this looker, who was on heat.

Sheila followed Peter down to this dirty, cobwebbed room that contained a stack of gym mats. She stripped off and helped Peter remove his clothes to find a magnificent, carved torso and a large, but limp, cock. Sheila thought, *'We will soon change that.'* She sucked his cock with great enthusiasm, but no reaction. She sucked his left testicle with great enthusiasm, but no response. She sucked his right testicle with great enthusiasm, but no response. She gave him a good rimming, but no reaction.

Sheila decided to move up a gear. She rubbed her breasts

over his cock with great enthusiasm, but no reaction. She rubbed her breasts over his head with great enthusiasm, but no response. She rubbed his cock against her fanny with great enthusiasm, but no reaction.

She stood there stark naked, with a blank look on her face. In front of her was a superb hunk of a man with a large, limp cock. While she was surveying the scenery, there was a knock on the door, and in walked the manager. He asked how things were going, but he could tell from Sheila's expression that she wasn't happy.

The manager said, 'Before you, is a classic case of steroid overdosing. The chances of you getting that cock hard, are as likely as Prince Andrew becoming a TV commentator.' Sheila looked at the manager with pure lust. The manager said, 'And it's no use looking at me, as I have the same problem.'

Sheila got dressed and went home, buying some grapes on the way.

The moral of the story is, "If you like steroids, you don't get your oats".

Grapes

Sheila was not the sort to be downhearted. She knew that she would find Mr One Hundred in the near future. Anyway, she was off to deliver some grapes. She was slightly nervous about seeing Jerry, as the entire episode could easily be blamed on her, either directly or indirectly.

He would have been OK if she hadn't asked him to shave her pussy. He would have been OK if she hadn't panicked when he picked up the knife. He would have been OK if the bungee cords had not been used. He would have been OK if the bathroom door had been fitted correctly. Anyway, why did he pick up the knife? And why did he use so much shaving cream?

There he was. Jerry was sitting up in bed with a big smile on his face. Sheila felt quite relieved, but a little bit perplexed. Surely, he shouldn't be that happy? They kissed each other's cheeks, and Sheila sat down by his bedside. Sheila asked how it was going.

Jerry said, 'As far as I'm concerned, everything is a blur. I turned up at your flat with my set of kitchen knives. I've no idea why I had them with me. Then I woke up in a hospital. At first, I thought I had just been concussed, but then I found several other injuries.' Sheila just nodded as Jerry continued.

Jerry said, 'I have quite a few bruises all over my back, and two or three badly cracked ribs. Apparently, they are going to take months to heal. I don't feel too bad, but the blood supply to my brain was restricted for a while, this is partly why I have memory loss. However, it has also affected my smile. It is stuck in place.'

Sheila said, 'So, it's not just because you are pleased to see me?'

Jerry said, 'I am pleased to see you, but I can't stop smiling. I'm even smiling in my sleep. It's not easy, you know, being miserable, and smiling all of the time.'

Sheila said, 'Are you miserable?'

Jerry said, 'Well, I've not got a lot to be happy about. Apart from the above injuries, my foot has been burnt. Not that badly, but badly enough to require a skin graft. They took the skin from my bum. That wouldn't have been too bad, but they put my skin on the wrong person. There is a young lady in another ward, that is wearing my bum skin on her face. They didn't have enough for her, so they came back for some more. I don't know how her face feels, but my bum is sore, really sore.'

Sheila said, 'I bet she is not smiling. What did the hospital say?'

Jerry, 'After they stopped laughing and making wise-cracks like: 'just bumming around, turn the other cheek, we will get to the bottom of it, I can't be arsed, rear-guard, etc., I will get some compensation. Then they took a graft off my other cheek for my use. I can hardly sit down.'

Sheila thought, *'At least he is smiling.'*

Jerry said, 'This is the part you won't believe. There are bungee cords stuck to my testicles.'

Sheila instinctively said, 'No, I can't believe that.' Jerry lifted the cover to expose his genitals. Before her were two black testicles that were the size of melons. Sheila hadn't expected that. The stomach, groin and thighs were a strange set of colours: black, blue and yellow. Sheila hadn't expected that either.

Sheila had never seen anything like it before. There was no way you could walk with goolies that size. Sheila was struggling not to laugh, as it was just so surreal, but she did manage to say, 'No sign of any bungee cords.' There was a slight titter, but she was holding back an outrageous laugh.

Jerry turned over to expose a black and blue bum, topped by extensive bruising all over his back. Strips of skin had been removed from both buttocks, and his lower left leg was all bandaged. However, the really distressing sight was two really massive bollocks, that were pushing his legs apart. If there were a competition for the biggest balls in the world, Jerry would be a contender. Sheila thought that she might contact the *Guinness Book of Records*.

The size of the balls was one thing, but from each testicle, a cut-off bungee cord was protruding. Sheila made a mental note to buy some more bungee cords. She also thought that the yellow and green colours of the cords made a nice contrast to the black and blue bruising, and the pink skin graft area. All in all, you don't usually see testicles that size, bursting out from a multi-colour posterior.

Sheila had no choice. The outrageous laugh arrived. There was no stopping it. You could see that Jerry was not amused. Sheila managed to say, 'Does it hurt?' And then she burst into another fit of raucous laughter.

Jerry said, 'What the fuck do you think?' But then he was still smiling.

Sheila managed to control herself after the ward sister

asked her to keep the noise down. Jerry went on to explain that they can't remove the bungee cords until the swelling has gone down, but it was the bungee cords that were causing the swelling.

Sheila said, '*Catch 22.*'

Jerry had no idea what she was talking about. Jerry said, 'It looks like I can still fire live rounds from one ball, but the other is kaput.' Sheila was starting to feel guilty, but it wasn't her balls-up.

Jerry said, 'Any idea how this happened?'

Sheila had always prided herself on her integrity and said, 'That's how I found you at my door. Clearly, there are some depraved sex maniacs out there.'

Jerry said, 'I assumed that might be the case, but why would they use bungee cords? Apparently, someone really hammered them into my testicles.'

Sheila said, 'Beats me. Anyway, you are still smiling. I brought you some grapes.'

Jerry said, 'Thank you, but I can't eat them until I wipe this smile off my face.' Sheila leant over to give him the grapes, but in doing so, leant on his left leg. Clearly, Jerry didn't like that, as he screamed in agony. His left hand shot up and knocked the drip over onto the floor. Sheila tried to grab it but caught the nurse that was rushing towards Jerry's bed to see what the problem was. The nurse landed on top of Jerry with terrific force.

There was good and bad news. The good news was that one of the bungee cords was not attached to Jerry's body any more. The bad news is that it was still attached to Jerry's testicle. Fortunately, the tubes were still in place, and there was every chance that the scrotum could be repaired.

The nurse was very apologetic as she removed her elbow from Jerry's eye. The bruising was terrible, but he won't lose his sight. The good news is that the smile has gone, perhaps forever.

Sheila grabbed some of the grapes and was nibbling them as she left. At least she had cheered Jerry up a bit.

The moral of the story is, "The grapes of wrath can lead to depression if you are not careful".

The Neighbour: Part 1

As far as Sheila was concerned, it was still early morning when there was a knock on the door. She peered through the little spy-hole to see that it was her handsome neighbour: the one that had saved her from the fire. She didn't really know him or his partner, but they shared door keys in case one of them was locked out.

Sheila gingerly opened the door, as she wasn't dressed. She was still in a tiny baby doll nightie with almost non-existent knickers. She gave him the once-over, and thought, *'Sometimes you have to go out hunting for Mr One Hundred, and other times they come to you.'*

He said, 'Is there any chance of borrowing some coffee?'

Sheila said, 'I could let you in, but I'm not properly dressed, do you mind?'

Elvis said, 'No, that would be fine. Anyway, there is not much of you that I haven't seen.' They both laughed as Sheila unbolted the front door. Elvis couldn't help but admire what he saw. A real beauty, in a semi-transparent nightie. Her boobs were clearly defined through the material. Her erect nipples were even more apparent. He could just about make out her little black triangle, and those legs were legs to die for. *'What a stunning package,* 'he thought.

Elvis introduced himself and said that he couldn't function in the morning without a coffee. Sheila put the kettle on to make him one. She gestured for him to sit down by the kitchen table. She noticed that he was fixated with her body. Her fanny was juicing up thinking about him entering her. She decided to make her move.

Sheila said, 'Do you mind if I do my exercises while we wait for the kettle?'

Elvis said, 'Of course not.' Sheila slowly took her nightie off, exposing her gorgeous breasts. Her nipples were even more erect now, something that Elvis couldn't help noticing. In fact, he had experienced several erotic dreams since seeing her boobs when he saved her from the fire. He couldn't believe that he would get a second chance of seeing them.

Sheila removed her knickers deliberately and provocatively, making sure that Elvis had a good view of her now juicy cunt. Elvis never saw her fanny last time. This certainly made up for it. His mouth went dry, and his cock went absolutely rigid.

Sheila loved it. She thought, *'I'm only a few minutes away from hitting the big one hundred.'* Sheila stood in front of him, with her arse about two feet away from his face. She bent down and touched her toes. She spread her legs further apart so that every facet of her fanny was on show. She could feel his hot breath. He could smell the intoxicating mixture of her smells, smells that had turned men on for thousands of years.

Sheila exercised by standing and bending. With every movement, she got slightly nearer to Elvis. His tongue was desperate to lick out her moist little cavity. Her boobs were dangling in a teasing and seductive manner. There was no way that any hot-blooded man could resist such enticement.

Elvis stood up, gently patted her bum, rubbed one finger over her pussy and said, 'I've got to go now.' Sheila had never seen a man move so quickly. He was soon out of the door, leaving the spare jar of coffee on the table.

Sheila accused herself of being a slut. Worse, a slut on heat. How could she ever look Elvis in the face again? She also started to wonder if she had lost it. How could a man resist such temptation?

Well, she had a second chance at temptation when she met Elvis in the supermarket. Sheila decided that she could either be shy and demure, or outrageous. She decided to go for the latter. Sheila was in the vegetable section when she saw Elvis pushing his trolley towards her. Sheila rushed to the scales, pulled her boobs out of their straight jacket, and placed them on the scales. She shouted out, 'You don't get many of these to the pound?'

Elvis wondered what was happening at first. You don't often see naked tits on a weighing device in the middle of the fruit and veg section. Elvis told Sheila to put them away, as his wife was close by. Sheila said, 'No, you do it.' Elvis, terrified that his wife would catch him, managed to return Sheila's boobs to their rightful home. It wasn't an easy task, as they seemed far too large for the bra. They kept bouncing against each other, and as you got one in, the other came out.

One of the shopkeepers saw his dilemma and agreed to hold one in place, while he attempted to secure the other one. It was tricky pushing the erect nipples in as they kept wanting to stick upwards. Both men congratulated each other on a job well done. Elvis's wife said, 'I thought I saw you fondling a woman's breast?'

Before he could answer, the storekeeper said, 'Actually, your husband is a hero; he just helped me with the Heimlich Manoeuvre.' Elvis was so relieved. He could stop sweating.

His wife accepted the explanation but said, 'I leave you alone for a few minutes, and you are at the first pair of boobs you come across; surely mine are enough for you?'

Elvis thought, *'Your boobs are more than enough for a small army.'* His wife was a fearsome woman. Over twenty stone and growing; her hair was thin and patchy. Her thighs rubbed together over bandy legs. Her sagging breasts rested on top of multiple bellies. She was at the doctor's so often that Elvis thought she might be having an affair with him, but no such luck. What was worse was her personality, or her lack of one. She was aggressive, argumentative, demanding, greedy, bellicose, uncompromising and hostile, and they were her more attractive characteristics.

She also tended towards violence. Elvis had picked up a brochure that offered services to "battered men" in case he needed it. He felt obligated to have sex with her. When she felt randy, it was like a giant, white rhinoceros heading towards you. You could only have her from behind because it took too long hunting through the bellies to find her fanny. Her titanic arse would press against you, and in a very husky voice she would say, 'You know where it is, now get on with it.'

Elvis' problem was that he wasn't always sure where it was. He was convinced that they moved around a fair bit. On one occasion, he had tried mating with her belly button. His wife couldn't assist as her fat chubby arms couldn't reach that far. Elvis often wondered how she wiped her bottom.

Elvis had managed to avoid sex by watching "Match of the Day". This meant that he went to bed an hour later than her. He would then sneak up the stairs to check out the situation. If the light was on, then it wasn't safe, and he would have to return. If you heard the regular rumble of her snoring, then it was reasonably safe to continue. But he had been caught out in the past. She never asked how come football was on every day.

Mornings were high risk. Fortunately, she started work earlier than him, but weekends could be treacherous. He understood that her job as a marriage guidance counsellor was quite demanding, but he was annoyed when she suggested that he should consider Viagra, 'as "clearly things were not right down there". Then, there was Sheila — how could he resist?

Sheila was still feeling very frisky. Elvis was coming towards the meat section. Sheila leant against the glass counter, pulled her knickers down, lifted her skirt and shouted out to Elvis, 'Is this meaty enough for you? Get your loins here. Nice bit of rump, sir?'

While Sheila was trying to gain Elvis' attention, a storekeeper came up to Sheila and said, 'Sorry, madam, we don't allow naked bottoms up against our counter glassware.' He tried to move her away. In doing so, Sheila slipped over as her knickers were still dangling around her ankles.

Elvis, like the gentleman he was, came straight to the rescue. He attempted to pick Sheila up, but in doing so, his thumb slipped straight into Sheila's fanny. She wasn't expecting that. Nor was he. But, of course, the inevitable happened — his wife turned up. In a very gruff voice, she said, 'What are you doing with your thumb in that woman's vagina?'

The shopkeeper explained that this woman had collapsed. 'As per our set procedures, I loosened her clothing, and your husband was checking for any internal injuries.'

The wife said, 'I've never heard of that before, but if it is company procedure, then who am I to argue.'

The wife turned to Elvis, 'When you have completed your check, make sure that you wash your hands properly. Use soap and wash the back of your hands. You don't know where that woman has been.' Elvis reluctantly removed his thumb and helped Sheila up. Sheila gave him the "look", and Elvis pulled her knickers up.

His wife said, 'Can't she pull her own knickers up?'

Elvis said, 'I was only being a gentleman; she is suffering from shock.'

His wife said, 'Well, in the future, you can help me with my knickers.'

Elvis said, 'Yes, dear.'

Sheila decided that she had done enough temptation for the day and went home.

The moral of the story is, "Why do women golfers wear two pairs of knickers? In case you get a hole in one".

St. Valentine's Day Massacre Aftermath: Part 3

One thing that Sheila knew was that "life just goes on". It has its ups and downs, but it just goes on. What is a total disaster one day, is suddenly history a few weeks later. Memories and emotions get distorted, but life just goes on. The river of time was presenting the next instalment in the St. Valentine's Day Massacre; the schemers and plotters were planning to get together around Jerry's bedside to wish him well.

Sheila, as we know, is still unemployed. Her relationship with Jerry is somewhat strained, but then he is suffering short-term amnesia. Not that he can remember he has got it.

A pregnant Anna was on her way home. This explained why Jack changed his will. She was distraught when she heard about Jerry's injuries; none of it made sense to her. Part of her wanted to re-kindle their relationship. Anna would be there.

Jane had confronted Inspector Knight about her pregnancy. She expected a major confrontation, but he said, 'If the child is mine, then I would be happy to marry you and look after both of you for the rest of my life.' It sounded too altruistic to be correct, but he was thinking of the upside — regular todgering. He had spent the last few months fantasising about Jane's pussy. He would do almost anything to get back in there.

Jane accepted his proposal, and they married quietly in a

registry office and honeymooned in Weymouth. They took a small room in a hotel that used to be a holiday camp. At least it had beautiful views over the bay. It wasn't particularly romantic, but neither were they. Gradually, Inspector Knight got the hang of it — his sexual intercourse techniques gradually improved. On the fourth day, he actually took his trousers off. Jane decided that it would be better if he kept them on; the thirty-year age difference was starting to show.

Jane found his constant need to pee a bit irritating. In fact, the smell of urine tended to follow him around, or was she just imagining it? His habit of flicking ear wax and bogies around was also a bit off-putting, or was she just being too fussy? His habit of shouting, 'There goes another one,' as a turd went down the toilet was also slightly annoying, or was she just being too particular? Or his habit of shouting, 'Big one coming,' 'during sex was a bit off-putting, or was she just being a bit too finicky? Perhaps it's just some of the joys of marriage.

Inspector Knight was enjoying himself. He had experienced more sex this week than in the rest of his fifty odd years put together. It was clear to him that Jane was enjoying his manly ways. She particularly liked some of his little sayings. "Big one coming" seemed to be going down really well. He wasn't too sure about exposing himself at first, as it might shatter her innocence. Also, the scars from his recent rectal accident were a bit frightening. He was also looking forward to having a son, someone he could pass his manly ways onto.

The name change, also amused him. Her maiden name was Day. She had now switched to Knight. He found "Knight and Day" amusing. Anyway, they would both be at the reunion. They weren't sure if her mother was going to attend or not. Inspector Knight decided that everything should be OK, as long as that hardened criminal doesn't turn up.

And talking about hardened criminals, it appeared that Wormy had been released from prison. Wormy contacted a solicitor to represent him, as he couldn't cope with the bottom encounters. For two nights in a row, he had to pleasure all of the inmates in D Wing. It was too much for any man, let alone an idiot like Wormy.

In fact, during the appeal, the solicitor argued fairly strongly that Wormy was an idiot. He hadn't planned to use that type of defence until he met him. He argued that Wormy's driving record proved that his driving was suspect. He had driven into a flood and lost his job. He had parked in the A&E ambulance drop-off area. He had confused the M4 with the M40. He had spent two hours driving around Bracknell, trying to escape.

The police forensic team couldn't find any evidence of a gun or anything that looked like a gun. The police couldn't find any bomb-making equipment in his flat, but they did find a very odd-looking stew. They found a room covered in paint and a black bathroom. A police psychologist suggested that he might be a Satanist, but after detailed searches, they could not find any human bones. They were, however, surprised to find some bags of cement.

The protective clothing argument was also dismissed, as a series of photos of Wormy proved that it was his usual dress. The judge said, 'If he wants to dress like an idiot, then it is up to him.' The judge then released Wormy on parole, but the police would be watching him. Wormy knew the police would be watching him, but he would be watching the Garibaldi staff.

As far as he was concerned, there were questions that needed to be answered.

According to Linda, Ken was on his last legs. Ken couldn't travel, but she would definitely come to the reunion. She was keen to get together with Sheila, her best friend.

Jane's dad and Blondie, the love of his life, we're also planning to attend, as it had brought them together. Blondie was a bit nervous about attending, as she was a bit of an outsider and also heavily pregnant. She wasn't sure who the father was. It could have been her jilted fiancée, or her new love, Horace. Part of her wished that he wasn't called Horace.

Charlotte hadn't decided whether or not she was going to attend. As far as she was concerned, it was all in the past.

Almost everything was in place for the grand reunion. Just a date and time needed to be confirmed. Sheila was wondering how things would work out when she got her regular barrage of wolf whistles from the local construction site.

Almost every day she got these whistles. Today, she was going to confront them. She walked into the site and shouted, 'Who wants me first?' She took her coat off, then her top and skirt. She stood there in her purple bra and panty set. She shouted, 'Who wants to fuck my little fanny?' There was total silence from their side. She knew that they would back down and went to pick her clothes up.

Suddenly, a hand went up, and the man said, 'I will.'

Sheila said, 'I will what?'

He said, 'I will fuck that juicy fanny of yours.' All the men cheered.

Sheila said, 'Where?' He pointed towards a shed. Sheila picked up her clothes and followed the man to the shed. Before she got inside, she was given a hard hat. He said that safe sex was important.

Inside the shed, the man drew the blinds and locked the door. Sheila said, 'I don't mind an audience — you can invite your friends in if you want.' Sheila was thinking that he was going to be Mr One Hundred. Without any warning, he burst into tears. Sheila wasn't expecting that.

Freddy, the builder, was gay. Sheila said, 'So what, some of my best friends are gay.'

Freddy said, 'On a building site, things are different. If I come out as gay, they will treat me differently. They won't let me use their showers for a start.'

Sheila said, 'You must be true to yourself.'

Freddy, 'It's easy saying that, but I would rather continue as I am. Will you help me, please?'

Sheila said, 'Of course, what do you want me to do?'

Freddy, 'I need you to pretend that you are having a good time.'

Sheila started screaming and shouting, 'More, Freddy, more.' She put on the best performance she could, shaking the shed and making lots of "oohs". She ruffled her hair and went outside. Sheila made a drama of handing over her knickers to him as a souvenir.

Another man came over and took the hard hat and walked her back to the main road. He said, 'Thank you.'

Sheila said, 'What do you mean?'

The builder said, 'We all know that Freddy is as gay as a new eiderdown, but we all love him. He has the heart of a lion and the soul of a saint. That was nice of you to maintain his cover. You will only get respect from us from now on.' Sheila was almost teary as she walked away.

The moral of the story is, "Most men need a shed".

The Hospital Visit: Part 1

Sheila wondered when Mr One Hundred would make his entrance. So far, we have had two impotent muscle-builders, a gay builder and an unhappily married man from next door. The campaign is not going well.

Anyway, she was looking forward to the reunion, although it might be seen as a pregnant mother's get-together. There was going to be a lot of hormones in one room. Sheila had purchased three sets of bibs and booties with "I'm a Miracle" printed on them.

Jerry's recuperation was proceeding slowly. The medical staff managed to re-unite his left testicle with his scrotum, and although things looked slightly odd, it was the best they could do. He would probably get used to his balls hanging down a lot further than they used to. He obviously couldn't wear shorts or swimming trunks any more, and he would have to be careful not to sit on them.

As the bruising around his eyes dissipated, his permanent smile returned. There was still a bungee cord stuck in his right testicle. A date had been scheduled for its removal, which was encouraging. Most other parts of his body were still very sore or bruised. The girl that had Jerry's bottom skin grafts on her face was making significant progress. He watched her boyfriend kiss her on the face. Jerry thought, *'Careful, you are kissing my arse.'*

It was now three o'clock, and the Garibaldi gang was about to make an appearance. In rushed Anna. It wasn't really rushing, more a fast waddle. She gave Jerry a big hug, which hurt him immensely. He didn't say anything, as it would have spoilt the moment. Anna asked him how he was. Jerry went through the full list of his injuries and ended up showing her the state of his pubic area. She had never seen anything like it before. She didn't think that balls could get that big. It was way beyond XXXXXXL. She commented on how pretty the various colours were. Anna said, 'Well, I am impressed; despite all of this, you just keep on smiling.'

Jerry said that he was devastated to hear about Jack. They had been bosom buddies for years. Anna said, 'At least I have an everlasting reminder of him,' and patted her tummy.' Jerry asked when it was due. Anna said, 'Now!'

Before he could answer, Mr and Mrs Knight arrived. Jane didn't know Jerry that well, but she still gave him a big hug, which hurt him immensely. He didn't say anything, as it would have spoilt the moment. Jane asked him how he was. Jerry went through his full list of injuries and ended up showing her the state of his pubic area. It was not something she ever wanted to see. She had never seen such enormous balls or so much bruising before. She asked what the thing sticking out of his massive testicle was. He calmly said that it was a bungee cord.

Jane did not know what a bungee cord was, and calmly asked, 'Why did you put it in there?'

Jerry said, 'I didn't, someone else did.'

Inspector Knight had a good close look. He said, 'It looks like someone has really hammered it home.'

Jerry said, 'That was the doctor's view.'

Inspector Knight went into detective mode, 'Do you know of anyone who had a grudge against you?' Jerry shook his head. Inspector, 'Is there a satanic cult working in your neighbourhood?' Jerry indicated that he had no idea. Inspector, 'Have the police been involved, as we need to get to the bottom of this.' Everyone laughed, except Jerry, who had heard it all before, but he just kept on smiling.

Jerry congratulated Jane on her wedding and asked when the baby was due. Inspector Knight said, 'Now!'

Linda and Sheila arrived together. Linda didn't know Jerry at all, but she still gave him a big hug, which hurt him immensely. He didn't say anything, as it would have spoilt the moment. Linda asked him how he was. Jerry went through his full list of injuries and ended up showing her the state of his pubic area. Linda was shocked. She had never seen men's bits properly in daylight before.

She asked what the melons were for. Why were they painted that colour? Why was a lead sticking out of one of the melons? Why was one hanging down a lot further than the other one? She got a pen out of her bag and started poking the whole area. With Ken, and now this, she realised that she was having a breakdown. Her only option was to bite one of the melons, and in she went. No one expected that, especially Jerry. Inspector Knight managed to pull her away before there was too much blood.

Sheila was damping down the blood when the first doctor arrived. They were all surprised when he fainted. Sheila carried on damping down and getting covered in blood for her efforts. A nurse soon got things under control by using pegs. Sheila wasn't expecting that. She assumed that Jerry wasn't that happy about it, but he was still smiling away.

When Horace and Blondie turned up, Jane was stunned to see her dad with his bit of stuff. Sheila used it as an excuse to change her clothes. In fact, she put the curtains around the bed next door and stripped off. Everything had to be removed, as it was one big, bloody mess.

Horace and Blondie had never met Jerry before. In their opinion, he didn't look well, especially with blood oozing from his genitalia. That didn't stop Blondie from giving him a big hug, which hurt him immensely. He didn't say anything, as it would have spoilt the moment. Blondie asked him how he was. Jerry went through his full list of injuries. His pubic area was already on show, so they could see the damage that had been inflicted on him.

Blondie asked what the thing was sticking out of his crown jewels. She grabbed it and pulled. She actually pulled it a bit harder than she should have, and Jerry followed her and landed on top of Anna. The shock of his arrival prompted another arrival. She was giving birth to Jack's son. As a group, they managed to get Jerry back onto the bed.

Unknown to Sheila, Wormy had followed her. He knew that there was going to be a reunion, but he hadn't expected it to happen in a hospital. Rightly or wrongly, he disguised himself as a doctor to investigate things further. Well, all he did was to put a white overall on.

Inspector Knight let go of Linda, as he needed to get help for Anna. Linda, who had started foaming at the mouth, bit Jerry's other testicle. Only she knows why. Jerry screamed in agony, and in his flight from Linda, managed to push Jane over, causing her to go into labour. Someone shouted, 'We need hot water.' Horace ran off to get some.

Sheila wondered what was going on, but she couldn't

help, as she was waiting for a dressing gown to arrive.

Inspector Knight returned with a doctor for Anna to find that his wife was also giving birth. He then spotted Wormy in his doctor's disguise, and more or less dragged him towards Jane. Linda was now chasing Jerry around the ward. It wasn't easy for him, as he was holding a testicle in each hand. He wondered what his testicles had ever done to receive this amount of agony.

Horace came back with two saucepans of boiling water. No one knew what they were for, but hot water was always needed during childbirth. Sheila said that she would like a cup of coffee. Wormy was struggling to get away, but the Inspector was holding him in place. Wormy had never really liked fannies that much, especially during childbirth. In his struggle to escape he knocked the Inspector over, who then knocked Horace over, causing the now cooling water to hit Blondie on her back. She quickly removed her coat, but the sudden exertion pushed her into labour.

Anna gave birth to a boy. There was clapping and cheering all around, except from Jerry who was still being chased by Linda, and Wormy who was trying to escape from Inspector Knight, and Jane and Blondie who were also in the process of giving birth. One of the doctors placed the baby in a cot while he looked after the mother.

The Inspector suddenly recognised Wormy, and screamed, 'It's that hardened criminal,' and immediately chased after him with a fire extinguisher.

Jane also had a baby boy. Horace wasn't sure who to comfort, his daughter or his girlfriend? At that moment, a drunken woman dashed into the ward with a huge pair of scissors. She bumped into the Inspector, which caused the extinguisher to explode. She said, 'Where is that horrid Horace? It's off with his balls!'

She suddenly saw Horace holding the hands of two different women, and she ran towards him, screaming. She hadn't taken into account how slippery the floor was with the extinguisher discharge, and fell over onto her bum, with the scissors sticking upwards. Wormy, who had been running away from the Inspector, also miscalculated and landed directly on top of the scissors. Once again, his anus saved him from serious injury.

Jane shouted out, 'Mum, you have a grandson,' and showed her a beautiful baby boy. At that moment, Blondie gave birth, so Jane had a new sister, and her daughter had an uncle that was younger than her. Both babies were then put into cots, while the doctor looked after the proud mums.

So where are we now? Anna was cuddling a baby boy. Jane and her mum were cuddling a baby boy. Inspector Knight had Linda under control. Horace and Blondie were cuddling a baby girl. Wormy was waiting for medical attention regarding the pair of scissors up his bum. Dr Mackerel was a bit concerned about which baby boy belonged to which parent, but it all seemed to work out. Jerry was not in a good state. His mental health was getting dangerously worrying.

Then suddenly Jerry cracked. He just sat in a chair holding his testicles and screamed and screamed. Jerry was put in a strait jacket for his own protection and moved to a more secure ward. Linda was similarly straight-jacketed to stop her biting testicles.

Inspector Knight left with his wife, his newborn son and his mother-in-law. There was an outbreak of happiness.

Horace and Blondie left with their newborn daughter.

They gave Anna and her newborn son a lift. There was another outbreak of happiness.

Wormy crept off to A&E, as wormy types do, leaving Sheila on her own. She was still waiting for a dressing gown.

Later, the curtains were pulled apart by a young doctor. He said, 'What have we got here?'

Sheila said, 'The girl of your dreams.' The curtains were pulled shut, and Sheila found Mr One Hundred.

The moral of the story is, "When do babies know when it is time to be born? When they run out of womb".

A Short Aftermath

Sheila pondered about the meaning of life. She thought that yesterday was a good day with the birth of three babies; three new souls to enjoy the wonders of this beautiful planet. However, it turned out to have a dark side as well. Ken passed away in the night on his own. Sheila shed a tear, well, quite a few tears. He was a good man, who really didn't deserve the horrors of Alzheimer's.

She remembered the good times that they had spent together. She remembered his wise words and constant encouragement. She remembered his daring, but caring, love making. She remembered his offers of marriage. She named a star after him because he was a star. She wondered if somehow Linda sensed his death. Perhaps it was that which pushed her over the edge?

This was bad enough, but then she learnt about the passing of Jerry. She was only with him yesterday. The hospital was not sure about the cause of his death. They won't know until the autopsy has taken place. Sheila cried some more, partly out of guilt. Was she responsible indirectly for his death? We are all just journeymen, interfacing with friends and family, occasionally doing good, or wrong, or more often something in between. We rarely encounter evil, but we tolerate indifference.

She named a star after him as well, because he was also a

star. A life cut short by stupidity, and to some extent, her recklessness. But then she knew that Jerry would not want her to punish herself. As she said before, Life goes on.

They say that things come in threes. Clearly, it's absolute nonsense, but Wormy was in the hospital fighting for his life. Sepsis is a secret killer. A pair of scissors up your rectum is not good for your health. Sheila planned to buy him some grapes.

She also needs to buy some grapes for Linda. Hopefully, she will recover from her breakdown. How will she feel about Jerry? Biting his testicles may have been a major contributing factor towards his death. Does she know about Ken yet?

She was not feeling particularly happy when there was a knock on the door. It was Elvis. She opened the door, and he presented her with a box of chocolates, and sang, "All because the Lady Loves Milk Tray".

Sheila abruptly said, 'What do you want?'

Elvis said, 'My wife is away on a course, so I'm here to take you up on that offer.'

Sheila said, 'What offer?'

Elvis said, 'You know, a night of passion.'

Sheila said, 'You had your chance; you let that cow of a wife dominate you, so you can take your chocolates, stuff them up your arse, and fuck off.' Sheila slammed the door. It may have been the first time in her life that she had slammed a door. She found it quite therapeutic, quite satisfying. She really wouldn't mind another go.

On a different note, Sheila was going to be invited to some christenings and even had the opportunity of being a godparent. Sheila had already decided to turn them down. She didn't believe in God — why should she, when good friends are taken away before their time?

She decided to have a Horlicks and go to bed early.

The moral of the story is, "Quite often a tray of chocolates leads to black magic. On a more serious note, you should appreciate your friends when you have them because, like chocolate, they don't last forever".

The Neighbour: Part 2

Sheila had a restless night. She kept dreaming of doors slamming. One would slam hard and then wake her up. She felt a bit guilty about the way she had treated Elvis. He clearly deserved it. He was just treating her as a sex object, but then wasn't she portraying herself as one? Sheila found it hard to be angry for long and decided to apologise.

She slipped a dressing gown over her nightie, cooked a full English breakfast, and knocked on his door. Elvis had a lay-in. He was enjoying the delights of a double bed on his own. It had been heaven — he could roll about, and kick out as much as he liked. He realised that, subconsciously, you must know that there is another person in the bed. You must accept it at quite a primitive level. Freedom was a double bed on your own.

For him, it was more freedom than most, as his wife took a high percentage of the bed. She was a fearsomely large woman who demanded bed space and took it. Her snoring kept him awake for hours. What was worse was her cramps. She would suddenly sit upright, screaming, 'Do something about it, do something now!'

Most of the time, she felt cold. Her feet and hands were literally like ice. Her feet, in particular, would come across and steal his heat. Sometimes, she felt like a cold leg of lamb. Something that had just left the freezer. Other times, she felt like a raging volcano. The heat that she could produce would satisfy the needs of a small town. She often had to turn the pillow over because it was soaked in sweat. He wondered if other men had enjoyed these marital delights. He was just going to have a sneaky wank when there was a knock on the door.

Elvis put his dressing gown on and then looked through the peep-hole to see the mad woman from next door. He wondered if her schizophrenia had got better. He thought Greta, his wife, had mood swings, but Sheila was something else. He gingerly opened the door.

Sheila said, 'Good morning, Elvis, I've cooked you breakfast as your wife is away.' Sheila pushed her way into the flat and put both breakfasts on the kitchen table. She got the knives and forks out of the drawer and sat down to eat as if she had been there for years. Sheila did a quick scan of the flat and came up with cold, austere, grim, sombre, colourless, soulless and Spartan, to describe the flat. She quite enjoyed playing with words.

Without saying much, they both tucked into a hearty breakfast. Sheila broke the silence by saying that two of her best friends died yesterday. Elvis sympathised. Sheila said, 'It's no excuse for the way I spoke to you. You just happened to catch me at a bad time.' As far as Elvis was concerned, it was no big deal. He had spent his whole life catching women at a wrong time. He explained that he even met his wife at a wrong time.

Sheila was desperate to find out how a good-looking man like Elvis met an evil dumpling. Sheila giggled at the image she had created in her mind, but she was trying not to be fattist. Elvis explained that she was a neighbour, who was being extradited for overstaying her welcome in this country. Elvis explained that he felt sorry for her and agreed to marry her so that she could stay. After the ceremony, she moved straight into his flat.

Sheila said, 'Didn't she have her own place?'

Elvis, 'No, she had nothing. We married, she moved in, and we have been together for more than a decade.'

Sheila, 'Why don't you just leave?'

Elvis, 'She has something over me, I can't just leave.' Sheila was all ears.

Sheila said, 'Go on.'

Elvis said, 'I would rather not.' The conversation ended.

Sheila said, 'Do you have sex together?'

Elvis, 'Only when football is not on the box. I do everything I can to avoid it.' Sheila noticed Elvis looking at her cleavage, and deliberately let her nightie fall apart slightly.

Sheila said, 'Was your sex life ever good?'

Elvis said, 'I had a great time in Hong Kong.' Once again, Sheila was all ears. She loved a good, sexy story and urged him to continue.

Elvis, 'In a different lifetime, I worked for Dennis, the fire engine and bus manufacturer. I was offered the chance of spending six months in Hong Kong, helping to build a local service centre and a sales organisation. I was reluctant at first, as I had only been "married" for a year. My boss urged me to go, as it would enhance my career, and would be a great "life-experience". He kept winking at me for some strange reason.

'My wife wasn't keen on the idea until I described the bonus package. She then quickly packed my case. So the decision had been made, and I was off to one of the jewels of South China, for six months. I soon found the company's two-bedroomed flat. It was compact, but kitted out with all of the necessary amenities of modern life, including a maid.

'She was a very pretty Filipino girl, with long dark hair. She was quite tiny, less than five feet tall. She couldn't speak a word of English and had no intention of learning it.

'After my journey, I was quite tired and decided to go to bed. Jet lag hit me hard, but I was awake enough to see Leelee get undressed and get into bed with me. She rubbed her naked body against mine, but I ignored her. She played with my cock, but I ignored her. I pretended to go to sleep, but it was difficult with this attractive oriental lying next to me. Every now and then, I lifted the sheets to observe her nudity.

'Her breasts were immature. I wondered how old she was. I was aggressively against any form of paedophilia or forced sex. I later learnt that she was twenty-four, but she could easily have been mistaken for being sixteen. She had an adorable bum, short but shapely legs, and a dark minge. The rest of her body was almost hairless. I later discovered that her breasts were not fully developed due to malnutrition in her teen years. Apparently, it was quite common.

'When I eventually woke up, I found her lying there crying. There were genuine sobs. I worked out that she thought I didn't like her. Apparently, if I didn't like her, then I would get another girl, which meant that her family would starve. If I didn't show affection, then I would be directly responsible for the death of an entire village. Civilisation as we know it would end.

'I had no choice. I pulled her legs apart, and I fucked her. The relief was immense. I had spent the night with a major hard-on. My balls were aching. I had no time to consider the implications of my action. I just fucked her. I had never seen such a happy girl. She kept bowing and thanking me. That differed greatly from the reactions I got from Greta. The best I ever got there was a snort.

'I continued fucking Leelee that day, and for the next forty-odd days. She seemed to enjoy it. She had the odd orgasm, which always embarrassed her. She used to apologise profusely. She seemed to think that it was wrong. I could have sex whenever I wanted, except Sundays, which was her day off. I've no idea where she went, but she often came back looking exhausted.

'Sometimes, I looked forward to Sundays for a rest. Other times, I couldn't wait for her to return. I think I was in love. This has always confused me. Do you love the woman? Or do you love her body? Are you in love with sex? Regardless, I got lots of fabulous sex. She woke me up most mornings by sucking my cock. It was strange waking up that way. She was the best alarm clock I ever had. When I got out of the shower, she was on her knees, waiting to suck me off. I don't think she realised that men needed a recovery period between bouts.

'I don't want to give you the impression that it was all sex. I went to work. We had a few meals together, but she didn't want to be seen as a couple. Was she ashamed? I don't know. I knew her body intimately. I investigated everywhere. Her body was mine to play with.

'Part of me was ashamed. Was I exploiting her? Was she a willing partner? Her wages were paid by the company directly to an agency, that then paid her parents. Was this simple prostitution? How would I feel if this was my daughter? Had she been programmed at an early age to just please men?

'All I know is that when I returned to the flat, she was always really pleased to see me. There was hardly any cleaning to do. There was only so much TV you could watch. She was bored silly. Fucking was a great diversion. Anyway, she couldn't wait to get my cock out of my trousers.

'Then she had a chance to prove her loyalty. My boss came over to check on progress. I let him have my room, as it was much larger, and I slept in the second bedroom. He asked if I liked the facilities. He asked if Leelee was looking after me. I nodded enthusiastically to both questions. He said 'that's great, and that he had been looking forward to sampling the charms of Leelee's cunt while he was here.'

'It was difficult lying in bed, listening to my boss screwing my girl. Leelee seemed to be making a lot more noise than she did with me. It was hard to sleep with the sound of a creaking bed, her screams, and his grunts. She was in the shower, waiting for his cock to enter her mouth. It was all unacceptable, and then he left.

'I was determined to show Leelee how disappointed I was. I fucked her hard and fast. I cared only about my needs. I simply used her. She loved it. She responded magnificently. She orgasmed almost continuously. At that moment, I think I stopped loving her.

'Then, one day, she stood by the front door with packed bags. She kissed me on the cheek and left. Not a word, not even a wave. She was gone. I'm not sure how I felt. Even now, I look back with confused emotions.

'The next day, there was a loud knock on the door. I opened it to what appeared to be Leelee. It was actually her younger sister. She walked in, unpacked her bags, and started cleaning the kitchen. Again, she could not speak a word of English.

'I got into bed that night and wondered what was going to

happen. She stripped off. She then leant over and started sucking my cock. She wasn't particularly good at it. Once my cock was hard, she climbed on top of me, and simply heaved up and down until I came. She got off, sucked my cock dry, and went to sleep. It was all somewhat robotic.

'The next night, she stripped off, leant over, and started sucking my cock. It was slightly better than the previous night. Once my cock was hard, she climbed on top of me, and simply heaved up and down until I came. She got off, sucked my cock dry, and went to sleep. I could see that a pattern was developing.

'The next night she stripped off, as usual, leant over and started sucking my cock. It was much better than the previous night. Once my cock was hard, she climbed on top of me and started gyrating, and then she simply heaved up and down. She got off, sucked my cock dry, and went to sleep. Some progress had been made.

'This went on for a few weeks. Talking to an experienced hand, he explained that family members train the girls that come over. They are taught to follow a set routine. He said, "You have to take control. Otherwise, they will follow that set routine forever". I asked him what they did on Sundays. He said, "They are out selling their bodies in the market so that they have some money for themselves. What you have to do is to pay them not to go out. I assume that you are doing that. Otherwise, you will pick up some nasty diseases".

'I was pleased that it was time to go home.'

Sheila said, 'How do you feel about using a woman's body now?'

Elvis, 'Tricky one — different times, different outlook, different culture, I'm more mature.'

Sheila, 'I meant about using my body?'

Elvis wasn't sure what to say, but he did say, 'I would love a second chance.'

Sheila said, 'This is the deal — you can enter my fanny, you can fuck me, but you can't come.' Elvis nodded. Sheila took off her dressing gown and bent over the chair. Elvis stood up, stripped, and placed his cock at the entrance to Sheila's cunt. Sheila moved backwards slightly so that she forced him to enter her. The entry was easy as his story had got her well lubricated. He started fucking. Sheila could sense that he was going to lose control. As things were getting more animated, Sheila said, 'Stop, stop now.' Elvis, with a huge look of disappointment, stopped and withdrew. She said, 'How did that compare to your little oriental tart?'

Before he could answer, Sheila got up and left the kitchen with a swagger.

The moral of the story is, "Careful — what you find in your bed, is not always golden".

The Neighbour: Part 3

Sheila had a much better sleep, but was obviously still very saddened by the loss of her friends. The good news was that Wormy had got through the worst. Sepsis had been caught in time.

She was also quite pleased with her encounter with Elvis. It appeared that his real name was Alvis, after the British car manufacturer, but his name didn't survive the torments of school. She wondered what hold Greta had over him. Anyway, she now had a hold over him as well. If you enter a woman's vagina, there are always consequences, and she giggled.

Sheila finished tidying up her flat as she was expecting a visit from Anna. It was going to be difficult with the loss of Jack and Jerry, but at least she had a bouncing baby boy. She wondered what Anna was going to call it. Sheila was still wondering what actually happened at the hospital while she was behind the curtains.

Sheila then entered that strange period where everything was tidy, all of the snacks had been organised, drinks were prepared, and mood music had been selected. In fact, it took longer to choose the music than anything else, but Burt Bacharach won. "I say a Little Prayer" was gently playing in the background. It was that strange period of anticipation. Everything was ready, waiting for the knock on the door, and when the knock came, it was a surprise.

There was a knock on the door. Sheila was surprised. It wasn't Anna, but Elvis from next door. He wanted to know if Sheila could come out to play. Sheila explained that she had guests coming, but she might be able to play later. She would ring him. Just as she shut the door, Anna knocked. Sheila thought, *'Strange, how often things like that happen.'*

They hugged and laughed, although there were some tears. Sheila cuddled the baby. They just smelt so good. What is it about them? Sheila always felt slightly broody after a baby hug. They talked about weights, and sleeping, and breast feeding, and baby clothes, and nappies, and parents, and the future. They discussed names, and Anna said, 'Go on, guess what I'm going to call him.'

Sheila pretended to think, and then said, 'Jack.'

Anna said, 'You are right, how did you know?'

Sheila said, 'Just a good guess,' 'and they laughed and laughed.

Both of them actually needed a good laugh. It had been a funny, few weeks, but life goes on. Sheila asked if Anna had any problems. Anna said that she needed to find somewhere to live, as she couldn't tolerate her mum and dad for long. She explained how her hatred for her parents had developed into an appreciation of their world. Their struggles. Their needs and hopes. The way they were brought up. They were controlling, but they weren't the evil demons that they once were, and they idolised "Little Jack".

Anyway, money was not a problem. Anna said, 'Guess what my biggest problem is?' Sheila couldn't. Anna, 'I desperately, desperately need a fuck. I need a huge cock up my fanny.' To say that Sheila was shocked was an understatement. Anna, 'I find it hard to believe that I want a fuck after just giving birth. I want it more than ever.'

Sheila said, 'Why do you think that is?'

Anna, 'I'm not sure. As you know, I've always had a lot of sex. It helped pay my way through university, but I rarely had orgasms, until Jerry showed me the way. Now I'm hooked on orgasms. They are a bit like a drug. I also think I need someone to make love to me, to prove that I'm still attractive.'

Sheila said, 'But you are gorgeous. No one would believe that you have just given birth.'

Anna, 'Thank you for that, but it's at a more fundamental level. I know that I'm talking nonsense, but I feel that this huge baby has just exited from my vagina. People talk about the pain, but it really is something else. It reminded me of the Alien film where all the bones extended. I felt my hips widen; I imagined hard, concrete bones separating. I needed my man holding my hand, or any man. Instead, I had that terrible hospital experience. Sheila desperately wanted to talk about that, but she decided just to let Anna flow.

'At quite a deep level, I keep imagining that my fanny is now massive. I had this dream where a man said, "Don't bother with her, she has a fanny large enough for a bus to enter". I woke up horrified that no man would ever want me again.'

Sheila cuddled her and said, 'Honestly, everything goes back to normal; I've had three children, I know.'

Anna said, 'It must be different down there now? Will I enjoy it so much?' And the tears continued to flow.

Sheila said, 'Do you want me to find you a man?' Anna looked surprised. Sheila said, 'I will find you a man now. I will walk your boy around the block for an hour and come back. How does that sound?'

Anna, 'I'm terrified, but I desperately need to have a

man.'

Sheila said, 'This is what we will do. You will have a bath and get yourself ready. I will sort my bedroom out.' Anna nodded and went to the bathroom. Sheila pulled the sheets back, closed the shutters and curtains, and took the bulbs out of the light fittings. She sprayed some perfume around the room. Anna luxuriated in the bath and prepared herself for an hour of love-making. She kept playing with her fanny, trying to decide if it was larger or not.

Sheila told Anna to get in the bed stark naked and wait for a man to appear. 'Don't say a word; just let him fuck you.' Anna eagerly agreed. Sheila made sure that "Little Jack" was wrapped up warm and prepared for their neighbourhood walk. Sheila then phoned Elvis.

Elvis answered. Sheila said, 'Now listen. Later, I will be waiting for you next door in my bedroom. I will have a bath. I will warm the bed. I will draw the curtains. Then I just want you to come in and fuck me. I don't want any chat. I just want a long, hard fuck. Do you understand?'

Elvis just responded, 'Yes, madam — should I bring the chocolates?'

Sheila said, 'I will slam my door when I'm ready, you have a key.'

Sheila prepared herself for a quick getaway. The pushchair was ready. She slammed the front door and ran for the lift. Elvis quickly showered and probably put too much Brut on. It might have been the quickest shower he ever had, as he was next door in minutes. He unlocked the door and quickly snuck into bed.

Elvis, in his mind, had planned the love-making campaign. He was going to massage Sheila's entire body gently. He would then lick and suck her breasts and vagina. He would gently finger her fanny until she was fully aroused. He would then gently enter her and gradually increase the rhythm. He would dedicate himself to her needs, although he had every intention of coming. He was going to fill her up with his love juices.

That didn't happen. Anna used her martial arts skills to pin him down. She sat on his loins and forced his cock up her fanny. It was aggressive. It was nasty. Anna rode him hard, very hard. He was her plaything. He had never experienced anything like it. Anna used her vaginal muscles to grab his cock. It was being squeezed and squashed. It was being pulled and pushed. Elvis had never experienced so many female orgasms before. She had one after another. The piercing screams were terrifying. They made his hairs stand on end.

Anna was ruthless, brutal and demanding. Elvis came, but she wasn't going to let that stop her from having fun. She sucked him back to hardness and rode him again. He wasn't as hard as before, but she didn't care. Again and again, she came — hard, unfettered fucking. On and on it went. Elvis was exhausted, tired beyond any previous experience. That didn't stop her. She started biting him all over. She was going to eat this man.

Elvis slipped out of bed and managed to crawl to the front door. He wasn't sure how he freed the lock, but he managed to drag himself along the corridor. He was fighting pain. His body wanted to sleep, no demanded it. It was a Scott of the Antarctic moment. He wondered why he couldn't meet a normal woman. Then he saw Sheila getting out of the lift with a pram.

Elvis' mind couldn't comprehend it. Sheila said, 'What are you doing lying naked in the corridor?' Elvis tried to talk, but his vocal cords had either dried up, or they had been fucked to death. Sheila helped him up. He was stuttering and muttering, 'Rape, she-devil, succubus, sex-fiend,' and other demonic names.

Sheila was surprised by how many scratches and bite marks there were on his body. His penis was black and blue, and it had shrunk. It looked like it was trying to retreat back into his body. Sheila helped him into bed. This was not the man she knew. He had clearly been through a major trauma. It could take years of psychological re-structuring just to get his confidence back. After a second look at his penis, she wondered if some corrective surgery might be needed.

Sheila got him a coffee and a hot water bottle. She rubbed some saltwater on his wounds, which he didn't seem to appreciate, as everyone knows that it is a magic cure-all. She had to leave him. She wondered what state Anna was in.

She returned home to find Anna fully dressed. Everything was back to normal. Sheila said, 'How did it go?'

Anna said, 'Not bad, but he lacked some stamina. I was just getting a second wind when he disappeared. It was, however, just what I needed. I think everything is OK down there. In fact, I think I now have better control of my vaginal muscles.'

Anna said she had to go, but they agreed that they would get together again to discuss their last hospital experience. Just as Anna was leaving, she said, 'Next time I'm here, could you organise another session?' Sheila said that she would see what she could do.

The moral of the story is, "A curry is often better than a succubus, but both have worrying side effects".

The Hospital Visit: Part 2

Sheila was listening to Desert Island Discs on a podcast. She had always been a great fan. Then, she heard a short review of Nicolas Parson's life. She was amazed to learn that his father was a doctor, whose claim to fame was that he delivered Margaret Thatcher. *'Funny old world,* 'Sheila thought.

As she was listening to the programme, the phone rang. It was Elvis. He said, 'What happened yesterday?'

Sheila said, 'What do you mean?'

Elvis, 'You know, that she-devil.'

Sheila, 'I'm not sure what you are talking about; you'd better come around.'

Shortly afterwards, there was a knock on the door. A person who vaguely looked like Elvis stood there. From what Sheila could ascertain, he had two black eyes, a badly cut face, and a very swollen lip. Sheila said, 'Who did this to you?'

Elvis, 'Come on, you know, the person in your bedroom. My face is nothing compared to the rest of me.'

Sheila said, 'What are you talking about?'

Elvis said, 'You invited me around.'

Sheila, 'That's true, but only after the door was slammed.'

Elvis, 'Well, a door was slammed.'

Sheila, 'That's strange, I was out walking a friend's baby, while she was at the dentist.'

Sheila felt an urge to protect Anna, although she was

surprised by the level of injuries he had sustained. Sheila, 'Well, what happened?'

Elvis, 'I used the key I had to your flat to let myself in, and I got into bed. A sex maniac then attacked me. It was horrible.' Elvis started crying. Sheila hugged him and asked him to continue.

Elvis, 'It's hard for me to recall, it was a sexual blitzkrieg. I was pinned down, abused, raped, scratched, bitten, licked, sucked, chewed, gnawed, crushed and debased.'

Sheila, 'I assume that it was a woman.'

Elvis, 'It was a woman all right — she had my cock in her fanny. It was squashed, munched, beaten, ridiculed and squeezed. She almost ground me to death. I've never been treated in such a rough, brutal, inhuman way before. It hasn't done my nerves any good. What sort of inhumane woman would treat a man like that?'

Sheila, 'She must have been strong?'

Elvis, 'Clearly, she was some sort of ninja. I had no chance. It was just the callous, unfeeling way I was treated. I was just a toy. She just took what she wanted.'

'I wondered if you had her number. I would love to see her again.' Sheila managed to shuffle him out of the door as Anna was coming back to discuss what happened at the hospital. She thought it best to keep them apart. Elvis will need some time to recover. She wondered what he was going to tell his wife.

Anna arrived. Sheila had a chilled glass of prosecco waiting for her. "Little Jack" was sleeping, so they could have a good old chat. Anna said, 'I don't suppose that you've had a chance to fix another session with your man-friend?'

Sheila, 'I need to have a chat with you about him. He has

sustained some serious injuries. He is not in a good state. What did you do to him?'

Anna, 'Well, I can explain. With the baby and everything, I felt exhausted, and in no time at all, I was fast asleep in your bed. Then suddenly, this man got into the bed. My martial arts self-defence training just kicked in. I kicked him in the groin a few times, gave him about a dozen slaps around the head, stuck two fingers in his eyes, and kick boxed him in the mouth. He was looking a bit shaky, so I jumped on top of him, and then I felt his cock stirring. So I just used him.

'I fucked him real hard. He got a severe grinding. He won't rape another woman. That certainly taught him a lesson. Then he had the audacity to come. I wasn't having that, so I head-butted him and had a biting spree. I was just about to bite his genitals when they started stirring again. So I gave his cock a quick suck to harden it up. I then pounded away at his cock, as I've never done before. I'm not sure what it was. It might have been the relief. It might have been the violence. It might just have been the pure power I had over this whimp, but I had one orgasm after another. It was heavenly.

'I went to the loo. When I came back, he was gone. I need more, that's why I asked you to fix another session. How much does he charge?'

Sheila had always seen Anna as a friendly, down-to-earth sort of girl, not this outrageous predator. She decided to move things on, and asked, 'So, what is your version of events at the hospital — it's all rather confusing?'

Anna, 'Well, I arrived slightly early. I had allowed extra time, as I was so heavily pregnant. I had reached the stage where even walking was an exhausting experience. When I say walking, it was very duck like. I was confronted with a

273

delighted, smiling Jerry. You can say what you like, but he smiled to the very end.

'I immediately gave him an enormous hug as we had been lovers, as you know. He really seemed to appreciate the hug. It brought back the good times we had together. I could tell that he wanted more, but I was concerned about his injuries. I asked him how he was, and he went through this ridiculously long list of issues.

'From memory, it included cracked ribs, memory loss because of strangulation, a burnt foot, skin grafts from his bum, black eyes, and extensive bruising. But the real problem was his genitalia, which as you know, I had intimate knowledge of. Jerry offered to show me the problem. I wasn't keen, but out they came — two of the largest multi-coloured testicles I have ever seen in my life. The sheer size was daunting, and the colour was mind boggling. They also seemed to be hanging rather low. I wouldn't like that. You could easily sit on them by mistake.'

Sheila said, 'I know what you mean. You would have to be careful. And I agree that the mix of blue, black and yellow colours was quite impressive.'

Anna, 'It reminded me of a recent trip to the Tate Modern. I've never seen goolies that big or colourful before. I wanted to take a photo, but my better judgement kicked in. Then, to top it all, one had a bungee cord sticking out of it. It's hard to believe, but it's true.

'I mean, what sort of evil bastard could do that? Who would be wicked enough to stick a bungee cord in a man's private parts? It really is foul play.' Sheila wondered how she could say all that after the way she had treated poor Elvis. Sheila asked Anna to continue.

Anna, 'Then, Inspector Knight and Jane arrived. She looked to be as pregnant as me, about to burst. As you know, I'm not the sort to gossip, but I would never put those two together in a thousand years. There must be a thirty-year age gap. And he is a right bore. I guess he must have a big cock.'

Sheila said, 'Why do you think that?'

Anna, 'I can't think of any other reason that Jane would marry him. Anyway, they had a good chat with Jerry, and they both viewed his genitalia. It became the theme of the day. I noticed that the Inspector had a very close look, and spoke of satanic forces at work.

'Then you and Linda arrived. I must admit that you looked your normal, immaculately dressed self. Then you both experienced the visual delights of seeing Jerry's bollocks. I was a bit surprised to see Linda staring at them.'

Sheila, 'Linda has lived a very sheltered life. I'm not sure if she has ever seen men's bits before, let alone testicles that size. It was enough to put you off your dinner.'

Anna, 'Why did Linda start poking Jerry's reproductive organs with a pen?'

Sheila, 'I don't have an answer to that, or why she bit his testicle.'

Anna, 'Have you found out since?'

Sheila, 'No, she was sectioned, and I've not made contact yet. However, I do know that they are keeping her away from men.'

Anna, 'I saw the Inspector pull her away, but it was a bit late. There was lots of blood everywhere. I saw you mopping the blood up and getting your lovely clothes all bloody.'

Sheila, 'I was a bit annoyed about that, no one else helped.'

Anna, 'Most of us were too pregnant to help, including Jane's dad's bit of stuff. I later learnt that they were called Horace and Blondie. As you know, I'm not a gossip, but who would put those two together, and she's not blonde. I know a bottle job when I see one.'

Sheila, 'This is where I lost contact. I was covered in blood, so I went to change. Eventually, when I came back, everyone had gone. What happened next?'

Anna, 'Well, it all turned into a farce. Horace and Blondie, who didn't know Jerry, asked him how he was. By then, things had got a lot worse. There was blood pouring out of Jerry's private parts. Then the blonde woman pulled at the bungee cord. I've no idea why she did it. She pulled the cord hard. Jerry's testicle followed, and then the rest of Jerry followed the testicle. He had no choice.

'That wouldn't have been too bad, except that he landed on top of me. I hadn't expected that. All of Jerry's twenty stones literally came crashing down on top of me. My waters broke. To be honest, I had been expecting it for a while. The baby dropped about three weeks ago. The good news was that I could breathe a lot better, but I've been peeing twice an hour ever since. It had started to be a real pain. And talking about pain, the cramps were getting really nasty.

'On the way to the hospital, I had to stop twice because of diarrhoea. You know on tele, the pregnant woman is always having a romantic dinner when her waters break, then the contractions start. Well, I had been having contractions for quite a while. Anyway, I don't think Jerry landing on top of me helped.

'A nurse was on hand almost immediately. One way or another, I was going to give birth there and then. The nurse shouted out for someone to get a doctor. The Inspector let go of Linda so he could go and get help. I couldn't work out why Linda was covered in white foam. I'm not sure what happened next, but Jerry started screaming really loud. He was making a terrible noise. It's not what I wanted, as my contractions got more intense.

'Then I heard Jerry say, "Get that mad woman off me now", and he pushed Linda out of the way. I had a restricted view, but I think Linda landed on top of Jane. Then I heard someone shout, "Her waters have broken, get some hot water". By now, my contractions were getting really bad. I was warned about the pain, but this was something else. My back really, really ached. I was just amazed that lots of women have more than one child.

'The doctor arrived, and checked me out; things were going OK, but now they needed another doctor for Jane. There were shouts and screams from all over the place. There was now a considerable abundance of water, which no one seemed to want.

'I was getting used to the pain, if you can, as it had a regular frequency. But Jane was making a lot of noise. Jerry was making even more noise, as it looked like Linda was chasing him around the room. I might have got the sequence of events wrong, as my contractions were getting worse, but I saw the Inspector drag a very reluctant doctor into the room. He had him by the cuff of the overall and was pushing him into Jane's groin.

'I noticed that Jerry had a testicle in each hand. Linda was dropping foam all over the place. The Inspector was shouting at the doctor, "Do your stuff, I don't care that you are a podiatrist. Feet can't be that different". I'm not sure if the man could breathe or not — the Inspector was losing it. Horace started using saucepans to deliver the hot water that no one seemed to want. I was sweating like an extremely hot pig in the Sahara. I didn't know that I could pant like a dog.

'The podiatrist was struggling now. I'm not sure if he was having breathing difficulties, or he just didn't like fannies. I won't say what he said, but I got the impression that it was the latter. The Inspector lost the fight with the foot doctor, and he went flying. He smashed into Horace, who was still holding two saucepans. All this was going on while I was in the final stages of childbirth. I felt like someone was punching me in the back and the stomach at the same time. Sometimes, it felt like the air had been forced out of my body. There were severe stabbing pains in my fanny. To be honest, I more or less lost control of my body.

'Another part of me was trying to keep track of what was going on. I couldn't see everything at once. Jane was still screaming. Jerry had tripped over one of his testicles and was exhausted. Linda was lying on the floor, possibly dead. Then I saw Blondie removing a wet coat. She shouted that her waters had broken. Well, I didn't get my jacket that wet.

'My mind couldn't work out that all three of us had gone into labour at the same time. That's just weird. Then, someone was telling me to push. Then another push. I might have nodded off. It looked like I could shove in my sleep. 'Then a wet, slippery thing was placed on my breast. I might have nodded off. The nurse grabbed the slippery thing, which might have been a boy, and put it in a cot. I was happy, but just so tired, so very tired. I think there was also lots of cheering. It might have been about my baby.'

'Then, the Inspector woke me up, shouting. He shouted,

"That's not a doctor, it's that hardened criminal, the one from the restaurant".

Sheila said, 'Stop, are you saying the guy who had been in prison was there?' Anna nodded. Sheila couldn't believe it, and said, 'What happened to him?'

Anna, 'It gets a bit confusing now.'

Sheila said, 'What do you mean confusing now, it is like a farce.'

Anna, 'I agree. The Inspector chased the criminal with a fire extinguisher.'

Sheila, 'Why a fire extinguisher?'

Anna, 'No idea, but there was more cheering as Jane had a baby girl. I don't want to go into the gory details, but childbirth is not a particularly tidy process. There were bodily fluids scattered all over the place. The whole process is damn right embarrassing. I leaked from every orifice.'

Sheila said, 'I know, been there, got the T-shirt.'

Anna, 'Well, I'm just trying to create the scene. Everywhere was pretty slippery. Then, this fearsome-looking woman came running into the room with a huge pair of scissors. I vaguely recognised her, but wasn't sure. It turned out to be Jane's mum. She was shouting, "Off with the balls, off with the balls". Well, I thought, Jerry's were almost off.

'She then collided with the Inspector. The extinguisher exploded, and the contents sprayed everywhere. Jane's mum collapsed on the floor, and I think the criminal landed on top of the scissors. I'm not exactly sure what was happening, but there was a lot of laughing. Someone was shouting, "Serves you right for impersonating a doctor".

'Doctors were everywhere, patching people up and delivering babies. The blonde woman gave birth. Someone was trying to explain that a niece and aunt had been born on the same day, but I just wanted to sleep. All the babies were collected up, as people tried to clean the room. Jerry was screaming an awful lot.

'It ended with three successful births. Two of the babies had two parents. I was on my own.'

Sheila said, 'What an amazing set of events. It's hard to believe.' They had a second glass of prosecco and called it a day.

The moral of the story is, "*Picture This*, a *Sunday Girl*, *Hanging on the Telephone*, has *A Heart of Glass*, when *The Tide is High*".

The Hospital Visit: Part 3

There had been a couple of calls from Elvis, which Sheila had ignored. He was still after the telephone number of the person who ravaged him. Sheila was hoping that this entire issue would disappear after his wife returned from her training course. Just to make it worse, Anna had phoned to see if "her man" was available. Sheila sometimes thought that the world would be a much nicer place without sex.

Elvis was feeling much better; most of the facial bruising had disappeared. He wasn't sure if he should tell his wife that he had been mugged, or just hope that all external evidence of the sexual blitzkrieg would have cleared up by her return. He decided on the latter, as he couldn't face calling her. He couldn't really face her coming back either. He had considered doing a runner, but she would track him down. She had the nose of a bloodhound.

He was also worried that she might want a bit of slap and tickle when she came home. It had happened before. He tried to think of suitable excuses, but none were forthcoming. He might have to give her one. That thought alone was ruining his day.

Anna had put a deposit down on a rental property while she continued to look for one to buy. She was surprised by the lack of suitable houses on the market. "Little Jack" was now officially called Jack. She was a bit surprised that there was no family resemblance at all. Not even an ear in common. But her biggest problem was still her libido; she urgently needed a man, or rather a fuck.

At Jerry's inquest, the cause of death was put down to natural causes. The hospital had been liable, Linda had been liable, and even Sheila thought that she was liable. But there was no one to argue his case. In fact, there was no one. He just about had enough money in his account to pay for his funeral. It reminded Sheila of Eleanor Rigby.

Sheila wondered if she was gradually turning into Eleanor.

Jane and her husband were superficially happy, but Jane was still craving for a real man, ideally someone her age. On the other hand, the Inspector was dedicated to his son. They named him Daniel but planned to call him Dan, although they started calling him Dannyboy. They were a bit surprised that there was no family resemblance at all. Not even an ear in common.

Jane's mum was in rehab again. She was lucky that Wormy wasn't pressing charges. On the other hand, he might have been done for impersonating a doctor.

Horace and Blondie were totally unsuited for each other, but totally in love. It was quite charming seeing them together. They idolised their daughter, whom they named Jackeline.

Sheila did go and see Linda. She was still restrained in a psychiatric ward. She couldn't be released, as she would immediately attack the nearest pair of testicles. All she would talk about was men's genitalia. Sheila had known her for years. They used to do the school run together. In all that time, Sheila could honestly say that there was not a single discussion on the penis, or even testicles. It was almost a taboo subject.

Sheila wondered if she had some deep-rooted genophobia or coitophobia. Here, the person has a physical or psychological fear of sexual relations or sexual intercourse. Some women are even afraid of their vagina. It wasn't a problem that Sheila had, although the odd cock had put the fear of God into her.

Sheila was a bit annoyed that Linda wasn't interested in the grapes. She had invested four pounds in that bunch.

While she was in hospital, she decided to go and see Wormy. He had several questions to answer. She walked into the ward angry, but soon softened when she saw the pathetic figure of a man in front of her. He was in a sorry state. She thought, *'Death warmed up,'* but this was far worse. It was more a case of grave robbing. Rather than drop the body off in the morgue for dissection, they had accidentally put it into a ward for the living.

Then, she wondered if it was someone else. There was no mistake. It was Wormy. Then she realised that Wormy was speaking. His voice was hushed and squeaky. *'There didn't appear to be any way you could turn the volume up,'* she laughed to herself.

It appeared that Wormy felt that the world had mistreated him, and all he had tried to do was good. He started talking about his issues: 'I had the entire contents of a table shoved up my arse, including a cruet set. I had the embarrassment of having it extracted in public. I have been accused of rape. I have been gang-banged in prison. I have lost my car. I could go on, but now I've got a pair of scissors up my arse. What is it about my bottom that seems to attract alien objects? This is not what I expected from retirement.'

Once again, Sheila was trying to stifle a laugh. Laugh

stifling was not her strong suit. Sheila said that she had to pop out for a minute. Outside, there was an outbreak of merriment. She came back sombre, but then had to dash off for another outbreak. She returned, telling Wormy that her tummy was a bit dicky.

Wormy said, 'A bit dicky. How would you feel if you had a huge pair of kitchen scissors up your rectum?' Sheila had to dash out again. These outbreaks of merriment can be quite serious. They are not usually fatal, but nevertheless, they should be treated with a fair amount of caution.

Sheila came back and said, 'It can't be pleasant.'

Wormy, 'Pleasant — that's a fucking understatement. What's happened to me is serious. I need to get this point across.' Shelia thought, *'Well, most of the point is up your arse.'*

Sheila said, 'Let's get to the cut and thrust of your argument — you feel you have been hard done by.'

Wormy, 'I certainly do!'

Sheila, 'I have to ask, why were you parading around the hospital in a doctor's outfit? In fact, why were you in the hospital?'

Wormy, 'I was trying to ascertain what horrible act you were planning for me next. I never expected another brutal attack on my arse.'

Sheila, 'You think that this was all planned as an attack on you. I didn't even know that you were in the hospital.'

Wormy, 'That just shows how devious your plan is. Well, I'm holding you directly responsible for my condition.'

Sheila, 'This is all nonsense, I'm going. Good luck to you.'

Sheila left. She was glad that she hadn't invested four

pounds in grapes for Wormy.

While she was in the hospital, she had got a call from Chas, who she worked with during the *Snow White* pantomime. They commiserated with each other on the loss of Ken. They both agreed that he was a fine man. Chas wanted to know if she wanted to come for an interview for a sex education film. She accepted, of course.

The moral of the story is, "Laugh, and the world laughs with you; weep, and you weep alone, is not strictly true".

Sex Education: Part 1

Sheila had been told that there would be an interview, but as her references were so good, it was very likely that she would start straight away. So, she was all ready to kick off her film career. At least it wasn't a porno, but a sex education film for adults might be pretty similar.

Sheila arrived on time. She was always on time. The studio was in a converted aircraft hangar. There were lots of pictures of the Second World War bombers. She was quite chuffed that she recognised a Lancaster. There was also a library of self-help video films of the more adult type.

Mr James Wright came down some spiral stairs to meet her. He was a large, balding man in his sixties with a slight limp. He shook her hand in a limp sort of way and had a rather limp smile. He asked her to follow him up the stairs into a conference room. In the room were six men and two women chatting away to each other. They stopped when James entered the room.

He introduced Sheila to everyone and stated that "subject to a satisfactory interview, she would be the new Miss Nipple 2020". Everyone clapped except Sheila. She wasn't sure if she wanted to be Miss Nipple. James asked Sheila to sit down and explained that he would be asking her a series of questions.

He started the questioning process; all he required was a nod of the head. Are you happy to appear fully nude? Are you happy to have sexual intercourse on film? Are you happy to have multiple sexual partners in a day? Are you happy to have sex with a woman? Are you happy to have sex with two partners at once? Sheila enthusiastically nodded to each question. She probably would have nodded to anything in the end.

James said, 'Now that is all cleared up, could we ask you to strip please?' You could see that most of the men in the room were suddenly more attentive. In the past, Sheila would have asked for a dressing room. Nowadays, she just stripped. Off came the dress, leaving bra and panties. She seductively removed her bra, allowing her cleavage to bounce freely. There were certainly no complaints in the room.

The men were licking their lips as the panties gradually came off. Sheila did the classic of showing her bum first, then her fanny. James said, 'Very nice, very nice indeed. Do you mind if I have a look at your fanny?' Sheila nodded. 'Come around boys,' 'he shouted. All six of the men were staring at Sheila's vagina as James prodded around. He had his fingers in and out of her pussy, he was fingering her clit, and he even entered her anus. He asked Steven what he thought of the colour.

Steve said, 'Nice mixture of brown, red and pink, it will do nicely.'

He asked Sheila to parade up and down the table. She then had to crawl, then put her bum up in the air, then open and close her legs, and so it went on. James said, 'Any objections to Sheila being Miss Nipple?' There were none, although Sheila thought about it.

James then asked the girls what they thought. The brunette said, 'Pretty face, nice smile, great hair, shapely legs, fabulous boobs, cute arse, curves in all the right places, but can she fuck?'

James said, 'See if Big Dick' is available.' It turned out that Big Dick was. James said to Big Dick, 'Would you mind fucking this young lady?' Without a word, Big Dick pulled his chopper out of his trousers, spat on his hand and rubbed the spittle all over his cock. He literally pulled Sheila off the table, bent her over the chair, and entered her from behind. Sheila now knew why he was called Big Dick.

Sheila was getting a serious fucking. She responded as well as she could, but he was just so big. She was a bit like a ventriloquist's doll. She was moved in whatever direction he moved. She was simply an extension of his cock. However, what he was doing was certainly working, as she could feel her orgasm build.

Big Dick turned to James and said, 'What do you want? Do you want me to come in her? Do you want her to have her orgasm? Do you want me to spray my spunk all over her?'

James said, 'Let's go for two and three.' The audience was now very keen to see how he performed. Big Dick upped his thrust rate. There was so much skin to skin friction that Sheila thought she might catch fire. She was hoping to make him come before she did.

Sheila upped her game, matching his thrusts with strong vaginal squeezes. She could sense that he was about to come. She focussed so much on him that she forgot about her brewing orgasm. He gave one powerful thrust, and Sheila came with a pulsating scream. Big Dick withdrew and sprayed Sheila with spunk. He sprayed the table and chair with his spunk. He sprayed the curtains with spunk. He would have sprayed the audience with spunk, except that they were ducking and diving all over the place. There was a serious outbreak of cheering, clapping, and laughing. James even got a dollop of spunk in his eye. Sheila had spunk globules all over her. It was a spunkfest.

Big Dick said, 'She can fuck OK.'

The brunette said, 'Fucking ain't a problem.'

And James said, 'I think we have found Miss Nipple.'

James asked Sheila if she could start work tomorrow. It was a Saturday, but she said, 'Yes.' She found the communal unisex toilets and cleaned herself up. She swaggered home, knowing that the pay was good, and she got a share of any film sales.'

The moral of the story is. "You need to get abreast of Miss Nipple".

Sex Education: Part 2

Sheila woke up the next day with a sore fanny. She blamed it on Big Dick's big dick. It wasn't good news, as she was likely to get another pounding today. It's not easy having a career.

Sheila arrived on time at the studio. She was always on time. She quickly stripped off and made herself available to the director. She was pleased that she was allowed to wear a dressing gown between shoots, just to keep warm.

A previous actress had covered the anatomy of the female body. Sheila's first shoot was the standard missionary position, which is never that easy to film. Sheila was introduced to Gerald, who was going to be her film partner. Sheila thought it was all a bit formal; basically, he was the bloke who was going to shag her.

Sheila was called, and she laid on the bed as instructed. The director issued the following instructions:
- Gerald to suck both of Sheila's breasts
- Gerald to lick and suck Sheila's vagina
- Close-ups needed of Sheila's clitoris being sucked
- Gerald to put his finger in Sheila's vagina
- Close-up needed of a finger in the vagina
- Close-up of Gerald's penis at the entrance to Sheila's vagina
- Gerald to put his penis in Sheila's vagina
- Gerald to start intercourse with Sheila, then stop.

The director called for action. Gerald had no problem getting an erection, as Sheila just looked so inviting. Gerald knelt, and caressed both of Sheila's breasts, and then sucked them. The director told the cameraman to get some close-ups of Miss Nipple's nipples being licked.

Gerald then went south and started licking Sheila's labia and fanny. He then moved onto the clit, which was getting Sheila hot. The cameraman came in for a close-up. He was almost in her fanny. At one stage he re-positioned the labia to get a better picture of the clit. Gerald continued to lick. His tongue was well-entrenched in Sheila's fanny. The actors didn't have to make any noises as these were dubbed in later, but Sheila couldn't help making small grunting noises which encouraged Gerald.

Gerald's finger entered Sheila's sweet little cunt. It made embarrassing squelchy noises as Sheila was very moist. Again, close-ups were taken of the finger in the fanny. Gerald was not asked, but he entered a second finger in her fanny, which caused Sheila's hips to gyrate. The director said, 'Go for it,' 'and Gerald continued to masturbate her. Sheila was squirming and writhing with pleasure. The director was shouting, 'I love it, I love it. Quick, get the penis in.'

Gerald was keen to obey, and his over-hard penis was ready to enter Sheila's well-lubricated fanny. The director stopped him for an entrance shot, and then he said, 'Go.' Gerald was in, and then the serious fucking began. Both of our players were near orgasm, when the director shouted, 'Stop, it's a rap.' Both Gerald and Sheila were devastated. The director was thrilled.

After a nice cup of coffee and a cherry Bakewell, the

Director issued the next set of instructions:
- Gerald to start with his penis in Sheila's vagina
- Gerald to withdraw at the point of ejaculation
- Gerald to spray Sheila's genitals with semen
- Sheila to lick Gerald's penis
- Sheila to let semen run out of her mouth

A fully dressed young lady sucked Gerald's cock back to full hardness. He had just received the services of a fluffer. Sheila thought that it was a bit unfair, as she was just expected to continue without any further stimulation. The director shouted, 'Action.' Gerald placed his cock back in Sheila's fanny and carried on with the fucking. Just before he came, he withdrew and sprayed Sheila with a mountain of spunk. Again, it seemed a bit unfair as he got his rocks off, leaving Sheila frustrated.

Anyway, Sheila had a job to do. She grabbed Gerald's cock and sucked it. She was never really sure if she liked the taste of semen. She had noticed over the years that there are many tastes. Apparently, it relates to the type of food the man eats. Gerald obviously liked eating salty bars of iron. Sheila could always detect a metallic taste. Anyway, she let some of the semen dribble out of her mouth. The director shouted, 'It's a rap.' Gerald thanked Sheila for a delightful experience.

The director instructed a young man to clean Sheila up. Apparently, this was the standard procedure on a shoot. He was soon on his hands and knees, giving Sheila's fanny a quick wash. She wasn't sure if his fingers were supposed to be in her fanny, but it was quite lovely. He dried her down, put some talcum powder around the edge, and used a professional lubricant on the entrance to the fanny itself.

The director called Sheila over and said, 'That was very

good; have lunch, but I need you back in an hour for the next position.' Sheila enjoyed her fish and chips. She was soon back on the bed to continue the filming.

Sheila was introduced to Jason, who was going to handle the doggy position. This is a much more comfortable position to film.

The director issued his instructions:

- Sheila to position herself on her hands and knees
- Sheila to wiggle her bum in an encouraging manner
- Jason to fondle Sheila's dangling breasts
- Close up needed of stiff nipples
- Jason to rim Sheila
- Jason to suck Sheila's vagina
- Jason to put his finger in Sheila's vagina
- Close up needed of a finger in the vagina
- Close up of Jason's penis at the entrance to Sheila's vagina
- Jason to put his penis in Sheila's vagina
- Jason to start intercourse with Sheila, then stop.

Sheila thought it was really "same old, same old". Sheila got on her hands and knees as instructed. It was a beautiful sight. Sheila's dangling breasts were just yummy. Jason wanted to eat them. One or two of the guys wandered around the back of Sheila to get a good view of her arse. It was definitely worth their effort. Jason was often stuck with some old tarts, but here he had a real beauty on his hands.

Sheila wiggled her bum in a very provocative manner. There were quite a few bystanders who had erect cocks. They usually were fairly hardened to this sort of thing, but Sheila was exceptional.

Jason stood behind Sheila and bent over to grab her boobs. They were delightful, full, firm, but dangly. The nipples quickly stiffened. The cameraman went in for a close-up. The director pushed her breasts together to get a particular shot he wanted. Jason's cock was already pushing against Sheila's fanny. He couldn't help it, considering his position, and Sheila offered no resistance.

The director shouted, 'Sucking, not fucking.'

Jason bent down and licked around Sheila's anus. Sheila wasn't used to this, but it was quite nice, in fact, very nice. Jason then started sucking Sheila's fanny. He was moving a bit too fast, and the director had to slow him down. If truth be known, Jason wanted to get onto the fucking stage. His cock was ready to burst. Jason then went wild. He totally ignored the director, and just started fucking Sheila.

The director tried to pull him off, but Jason was holding onto Sheila's hips. He was determined to get his way. They could do what they liked afterwards, but he was going for it. He fucked and fucked. The director got a bucket of cold water and threw it at them. They were both soaked, but Jason carried on fucking. His cock was on fire.

The director wrestled Jason to the ground. He was determined to save his film — this was outrageous. Jason was glued to Sheila. He wasn't going to let her go until he came. A band of spectators were cheering, and then Jason came. It was glorious, brilliant, fantastic. It was the best fuck of his life. Sheila was a goddess. He wanted to marry her. Sheila, however, was not happy — she had been soaked, and now she was covered in spunk again. Jason was removed off-site by Security before he could propose to Sheila.

Sheila wasn't sure what to do next, so she went to the loo.

She decided to do a runner and disappeared in the dressing gown they gave her. She had lost another dress. It was happening far too often. At least it wasn't covered in blood this time. Sheila reflected that it wasn't really a sex education film, it was just another porno, and that wasn't for her.

The moral of the story is, "Jason, without his Argonauts, still needs careful direction".

Common People

Sheila woke up again with a slightly sore fanny. She still blamed it on Big Dick's big dick, although since then, both Gerald and Jason had given it a bit of a battering. But fundamentally, it was Big Dick. No woman should have to put up with a dick that size, although given another chance, she would consider another bout. At least this time she would be prepared.

They always say that size doesn't matter. It's what you do with it. But Sheila knew, given a choice between two gifted lovers, she would go for the bigger one. Somehow, it's quite satisfying having your pussy stretched. There is a sense of satisfaction that you can handle it. There is a sense of achievement, as the giant cock enters inch by inch.

Sheila was starting to feel quite randy, which wasn't good news, as Elvis was coming round. She couldn't keep ignoring his calls. Part of her was also annoyed. There are so many circumstances where the needs of the woman are just ignored. Both Gerald and Jason had their orgasms, but what about her needs? Once they came, they were more or less useless for a while, but she could still go on and on. At least Big Dick was more considerate of a woman's need. She realised that she had been turned on, but was still on.

There was a knock on the door. Sheila thought that it was too early for Elvis. She wasn't even dressed yet. She checked through the peep-hole, and it was the man himself. She opened the door and said, 'You are early.'

Elvis said, 'It was deliberate — I was hoping to catch you in your nightie, and I have succeeded.'

Sheila said, 'I will go and get a dressing gown.'

Elvis said, 'Don't bother, I plan to get into that fanny of yours; I need some action before my wife comes home tomorrow.' He more or less pushed his way in.

Sheila made him a cup of coffee, while at the same time she was trying to protect her modesty. She was wearing a skimpy yellow nightie that barely covered her bottom. If she bent down, you could see everything. There were matching knickers, but she couldn't be bothered wearing them. Sheila said, 'So you plan to use my fanny — what do I get out of it?'

Elvis, 'I'm going to give you the full works — you will have an orgasm that blows your head off.'

Sheila, 'I would rather keep my head on.'

Elvis, 'In that case, you will get my eternal gratitude.'

Sheila, 'That doesn't pay the gas bill.'

Elvis, 'Did you want money?'

Sheila, laughing, said, 'How dare you?'

Elvis, 'Sorry, I didn't mean to offend.'

Sheila, 'How about another story — I quite enjoyed hearing about your Singapore adventures.'

Elvis said, 'How about you let me enter your fanny, and I will tell you a story while we are fucking?'

Sheila, 'I'm not sure if I trust you. You know what men are like, their needs seem to take over.'

Elvis, 'If you shout stop, then I will stop, scout's honour.'

Sheila said, 'OK, let's give it a try.' Sheila was still feeling quite randy.

Sheila slowly removed her nightie and walked towards the bedroom. Elvis was removing his clothes on the way. Sheila told him to slow down. She then said, 'How do you want me?'

Elvis said, 'What do you mean?'

Sheila thought, 'He's a bit dim sometimes.'

Sheila, 'Look, you are going to be telling me a story, you need to be comfortable.'

Elvis looked perplexed, but said, 'I would like you on your back with your legs in the air. Your legs can then rest against me, and we both get deep penetration.'

Sheila said, 'OK, but you have to lick me out first.' Elvis readily agreed. He lifted Sheila's legs and got his head between her thighs. He licked every part of Sheila's cunt. Sheila was surprised by how gentle he was. She was getting that very nice warm tingly sensation, but she wanted to slow things down. Sheila said, 'Elvis, you can enter me now.'

Elvis carried on licking away.

Sheila said, 'You can fuck me now.' Elvis had his tongue deep down in Sheila's pussy.

Sheila almost shouted. 'Time for the fucking now.' Then she realised that he couldn't hear as her thighs were tight against his ears. She decided just to let him continue. A gentle orgasm ripped through her. He continued. A larger orgasm then ripped through her. He continued, and a bigger orgasm ripped through her.

Elvis took a breather, and said, 'Shall I enter you now?' He had no idea that she had orgasmed, which she thought was a bit peculiar.

Sheila managed to say, 'Yes, please.' He stood up and gently pushed his cock into her fanny. There was no resistance at all. His full length slid straight in. Sheila said, 'Just leave it there a moment.' She really wanted a good hard fucking, but she had to train this man.'

Sheila said, 'Just leave it there and start the story.' She could feel his cock throb. It wanted action. Sheila said, 'Start the story now.'

Elvis said, 'OK,' and started.

Elvis, 'I used to work in the offices of an electrical wholesaler. Good job, but the money wasn't that impressive. Probably the equivalent of minimum wage nowadays. What was good was that they had flexitime, and you could choose your hours of work.' Elvis tried to get away with a few gentle strokes, but Sheila told him to stop.

'In the offices, I worked with an attractive woman called Corine. She was in her early thirties and had a great figure. Very pretty, fabulous bum, long legs and a great pair of tits. There were, however, two problems. Firstly, she was always showing her bits off. Her low tops meant that I had an intimate knowledge of her boobs. In the summer, she rarely wore a bra. When she bent over, you could see two bouncy beasts, with a cherry on top. You are probably surprised that I seem to be complaining. I'm not, but she was very distracting. It was very hard to concentrate on your work. I would probably have left that job earlier if she wasn't there.'

Sheila was now allowing some simple strokes. Elvis was enjoying the intimacy of the situation. In his mind's eye, he wasn't sure if he was fucking Sheila or Corine. He could picture Corine's tits. He wondered what happened to them. Sheila used her hips to urge him to continue with the story.

Elvis, 'It wasn't just her tits that were a problem. Her bum was never adequately covered. Her mini-skirts were so short that rarely an hour passed without me seeing her knickers.

Sometimes, she wore a thong, which meant that her fanny was on display. It never seemed to bother her. Her main objective was to get attention from the truck drivers. She would walk across the yard, making sure that she was always the centre of attraction. She would deliberately drop things so that, in picking it up, she would display herself. She probably had some sort of mental condition that made her act this way. Perhaps her father molested her. Who knows? I wasn't complaining.'

Sheila, without realising it, was letting Elvis up his thrusting rate. Both of them were getting hot, very hot. Sheila felt the signs of yet another orgasm, the big one she needed. Elvis' cock seemed to be getting longer and harder.

Elvis took a deep breath, and continued, 'She was a lovely girl, kind and considerate but very common. I hate using that term, but it might have been invented for her. Whenever I hear the Pulp song, *Common People*, I think of Corine. She had crisp sandwiches for lunch and a can of red bull. She frequently picked her nose. Her only handbag needed a good wash. B.O. was sometimes a close friend. Despite all of that, I was desperate to give her one. Do you know what I mean? Really desperate.'

Sheila could tell that Elvis was getting a bit carried away. She decided to slow him down. She said, 'Elvis, I fancy a position change.' She pushed Elvis' prick out of her fanny with a plop and turned over.

Elvis said, 'Did you want bum sex?'

Sheila said, 'No, just part my buttocks, and push your todger into my fanny. You will like it.' Elvis did as he was told. He did like it.

He said, 'That's great, you can feel your fanny, and it's

quite tight. This is good, I like it, and I'm enjoying the feel of your arse.' And the fucking continued at a slower pace.

Sheila said, 'What was the second problem?'

Elvis said, 'What do you mean?'

Sheila,' 'You said that Corine had two problems.'

Elvis, 'Oh, yes, she was a heavy smoker. In those days, you could smoke in the office. It wasn't so bad in the summer as you could undo the windows, but in the winter, it was shut. If I ever got lung cancer, it would be down to her. I was a serious, passive smoker. On the other hand, I thought to see her bum and tits made it all worthwhile.'

Elvis was gradually upping his work rate. Both of them weren't far away from their orgasms, but Sheila wanted her story first. She told Elvis to slow down. Reluctantly, he did as he was told. He wasn't keen because the train was ready to rock n' roll. It thought it was rushing towards the terminus, but the lights turned red.

Sheila said, 'So, did you get to screw her?'

Elvis, 'I did, and it was all down to a packet of cigarettes.'

Sheila, 'Go on.'

Elvis, 'Well, Corine came into the office in a particularly bad mood. I mean a foul mood. She wouldn't say why, but during the day the mood just got worse and worse. After lunch, she admitted that she had no fags, and that she had no money to buy some. I offered to get her some, but she said that it was against the rules.

'I asked what she meant. She said that both her salary and that of Fred, her husband, were needed to pay the bills. Anything Fred earned extra went on drink. Whatever she earned extra paid for the fags. Apparently, the extras had been sparse recently. They were both suffering.

'I asked what Fred did to earn a few extra bob. Corine said he made a profit on selling pallets and beer barrels if he could get them cheap. Occasionally, the odd item would fall off the back of the lorry. Then without prompting, she said, "I pay for my cigs from what my fanny earns".

'I nearly fell off the chair. She could see that I was surprised, but continued, "I charge twenty pounds for a fuck. I know that it is a lot, but it's an outstanding quality cunt. I think it's good value for money".

'I couldn't resist asking who her customers were. She said that they were usually friends of her husband. A couple of older men, who are friends of her mum, occasionally popped in. She had a couple of younger ones, but tried to avoid them, as she didn't want to get a reputation.'

Sheila was enjoying the story, and the long deep thrusts of Elvis' cock. She wasn't sure who he was fucking. Probably Corine, but she didn't care. Sheila said, 'So, did you fuck her?'

Elvis, 'I rustled up some courage and said, "For twenty pounds I wouldn't mind a go". Corine looked at me astonished, and said, "But I thought you were gay". I asked why she thought that. She said that in over a year, you had not made any sort of move. She then said, "It will cost you twenty pounds, and I want it upfront". I handed over the money. She said, "We need to go to my house now before the kids come home from school". There was a slight diversion to buy some fags.

'Sometimes, people are "common", but their houses are immaculate. That wasn't true of Corine's house. It was a dirty, untidy mess. She kept saying that we had to be quick. They had a kitchen/diner with a leather sofa in it. She asked if I just wanted her knickers off or everything. I decided to go for everything. As you know, I had seen large chunks of her body for over a year, but fully nude, she was a stunner. She could easily have been a page three girl.

'She bent over the arm of the worn sofa and opened her legs wide. I just wanted to admire her, but she urged me to hurry. I unzipped my trousers and let Johnny-be-good loose. He was hard, fit and raring to go. I was soon in her fanny. It looked good, it felt good, it was good. She urged me to get the job done, when the back door opened.

'In walked her mum, and her two young children. I immediately stopped the fucking and just stood still. I had no idea what to do or say. Corine said to the kids, "Did you have a good day at school?" They both nodded.

'Her mum said, "Because it's the parent-teacher meeting tonight they got out earlier".

'The little boy said, "Is that a new friend?"

'Corine said, "Yes, he is just giving mummy a massage, as my back hurts a bit". 'I started rubbing her back. Fortunately, the kids couldn't see anything inappropriate.

'Her mum took the kids next door to watch TV. Corine urged me to hurry. It was a bit tricky, as the old boy had deflated, but it wasn't long before he was up to his old tricks. I tried my best to get things going again, when her mum came back into the room. She said, "Don't worry about me; I'm just going to put the veg on". That was done, and she sat on a chair talking to her daughter. I tried to continue with the fucking, but it was hard to concentrate.'

Sheila was now concentrating on her orgasm. She didn't care about his. She just needed him to continue with the deep thrusts. She told him to keep going.

Elvis, 'I wasn't sure what to do. Then Corine said to her

mum, "I think you'd better leave, as I don't think Elvis can get the job done with you here". I was so grateful. I decided to really go for it, when the back door opened again. It was Fred. My erection collapsed in seconds. I was expecting a good beating. He said, "Looks like we are back in the fags". He nodded to me and went upstairs.

'I don't think Corine was impressed with my performance. She said, "Are you going to come, or shall we call it a day. Either way, you are not getting your money back". I continued, but mentally I wasn't sure if I could get the job done.'

Sheila was close to getting the job done. Really close. A few more strokes should do it.

Elvis, 'I was struggling a bit when her mum came back into the room. She said, "Looks like he is struggling a bit. Shall I give him the finger punch?" Corine nodded, and her mum calmly walked behind me, and without any warning, forcefully stuck her finger up my arse. It was a total shock. I shot my load immediately up her fanny, with tremendous force. Somehow it made Corine come.'

Elvis subconsciously re-enacted the movement with his todger. This sudden violent movement pushed Sheila over the edge. She had a smashing, lights-blazing orgasm. Her orgasm pushed Elvis over the edge, and he came, and as he came, he shouted, "Corine". His orgasm pushed Sheila into a second one. There was a serious outbreak of orgasms.

Sheila and Elvis cuddled for a while in a post-orgasmic bliss. They were exhausted and happy. Relaxed and sleepy. Sheila said, 'Well, what happened next?'

Elvis, 'I was invited to tea, as by then I knew the entire family. I accepted, but it wasn't the most hygienic of environments. What did make me laugh was the little boy. He was hammering a six-inch nail into the kitchen table. His dad told him, in a furious manner, to stop it. As little boys often do, he continued. His dad told him to stop it for a second time. He then grabbed the hammer and said, "I've told you before not to waste those nails".' They both laughed.

Sheila, 'And did you use the facilities again?

Elvis, 'I may have gone on a few cigarette runs. I became the target of final choice. When she was desperate, she would offer me two for one. She had a beautiful body, but there was little else.'

Sheila, 'Why did you stop?'

Elvis, 'I learnt from someone else that she was not on the pill. Her two children were from different men. Her husband couldn't have children. I didn't want to become a dad.'

Sleep demanded attention from both of them.

The moral of the story is, "A good drag sometimes leads to impregnation".

Tears for Fears

Things seemed to be going well, and then suddenly, they weren't. There was so much good news around, and suddenly things turned sour.

It all started with the death of Sheila's father. They had never been close, but it was still a shock to find that he had died. As a child, Sheila thought that she was "the one", as she was always helping him. She would be there at the weekends, helping him build his brick flower beds. She would bring him his hot mug of tea.

He was a strange man. Short, but very strong, with a very pronounced nose. He had a George Formby look about him. He was intelligent, but uneducated, leaving school at fourteen. He was an excellent advert for dyslexia, not that he could spell the word. He had probably never even heard of it. His father, a military policeman, died in the war. Her father and grandfather belonged to the "children should be seen, but not heard" brigade. To be honest, they would probably prefer to not even see the children, given the option.

Late into her teen years, it was expected that Sheila would be in her bedroom before he got home from work. He was an engineer, designing brick-making machines. Untrained, uneducated, but naturally gifted. But not gifted in the art of human relationships, and especially parenting.

Sheila thought she was "the blessed one", until one day he

sat her down and told her that he never really liked her. There was no point in telling her. There was no logic to it. It was an act of sheer nastiness. It was a callous thing to do. The bond between father and daughter, which had been tenuous, was broken. The fragile love that might have existed simply evaporated.

Sheila regretted his death, but felt no emotion. As far as she was concerned, he had died many years ago. She would have liked to know the cause of his death. She would have liked to know when he died, and where he was buried. But what's the point in visiting a corpse, when you never visited the living?

She thought that she might have shed a tear, but the well was dry.

Her thoughts then turned to Anna. What a thing to happen! It turned out that Little Jack's heart was not fully developed. As a consequence, not enough blood was flowing to the brain. This had already led to irreparable brain damage. That news was bad enough, but then to find that he was not her son was devastating.

Little Jack needed a blood transfusion. Obviously, Anna volunteered. After checking both the blood and the DNA, it became apparent that they were not related at all. Little Jack was not her son. Anna immediately took a dislike to him. The font of deeply embedded love for her son shrivelled up. Anna dropped the "body" off at the hospital of his birth, and said that this is your problem now, and walked away.

She thought that she might have shed a tear, but the well was dry.

Anna started the process of tracking down her baby. Her initial thoughts were that Jane and the Inspector might have it.

During the hospital debacle, the babies might have been incorrectly distributed. When she contacted Jane, there were shouts and screams and threats of legal action. This was because, deep down, Jane had always suspected that her son was not theirs. She felt it at a deep biological level.

When Jane told her husband, he went mad with anger. Jane had never seen him this agitated before. He started blaming it on "that hardened criminal", and started listing the things he was going to do to him. She didn't' think that one man could bear such depravities. Jane knew that her son would have to be returned to the "legal owner" one day. She felt it in her blood. She also knew that their marriage would not last, especially as she had an eye on someone.

She thought that she might have shed a tear over the marriage, but the well was dry.

The Inspector didn't want to swap a good model for a damaged one. He was going to resist the repatriation of his son, no matter what. Then the circumstances changed again. After DNA tests, it showed that he was not the father of either child. He didn't have a son. It dawned on him then that the rightful mother would win in a court of law. He wanted retribution, but technically neither of the children were his. He wanted the marriage to continue, but he couldn't cope with the thought of bringing up someone else's child.

He felt sad, very sad indeed, but he didn't shed a tear, the well was dry.

Anna did some research and was shocked to find out just how common the wrong baby is given to the wrong parent. In the UK alone, it has been estimated that there are twenty-eight thousand cases a year. Mind you, there are four million births a year. There was lots of advice on the internet on how you sue the hospital, but not much on how you retrieve your young one. However, she had an inner confidence that her son would be reunited with his mum. At the same time, she felt sorry for Jane. But it had been tough on her, and she felt that she needed a chat with a friend. She decided to go and visit Sheila. She might even bring her new boyfriend along.

The Inspector was not having a good day. His actions during the Garibaldi affair had been reviewed again. He was not the hero that had been originally portrayed. He had been accused of deliberately targeting Wormy in a malicious, spiteful, malevolent and uncompromising manner. His callous, hateful actions against this one individual were unacceptable in today's modern policing environment.

Inspector Knight was put on garden leave. He knew, however, that his days were numbered. He also knew who was going to suffer. He didn't see himself as a vindictive man, but the time had come for justice. He had heard from his police contacts that Wormy was going to be in Sheila's flat.

Retribution was on its way. Wormy would be shedding a few tears, assuming that his well wasn't dry.

Talking about Wormy it was the worst day of his life. He had experienced a few "worst days", but this was the "worstiest" ever. Even worse than the cruet set up his arse. Even worse than the prison gang-bang. Even worse than the scissor incident.

Wormy had always been a keen, but inept, motorcyclist. He had purchased a second-hand bike that was far too big for him. He could hardly lift it. A bigger problem was his pathetic sense of direction. There had been several occasions, on relatively local trips, that he had got so lost that he had to book into a hotel. Then he travelled the twenty miles back the next day.

He refused to buy the proper motorcycle leathers and ended up with frostbite. He had always prided himself on his electro-mechanical skills and decided to upgrade the bike's battery. This would generate more heat, that he could direct towards the steering mechanism. This would help to keep his hands warm. He got used to ignoring the mild electrical shocks that occurred regularly.

However, the fateful day happened. He left his still running motorcycle against the wall of his residence. He went upstairs to get a shopping bag, and without thinking, started tinkering with his latest concrete construction. This is what artists do. This sudden burst of creativity pushed him into an immediate slumber. He loved his dozy, snoozy catnaps. In fact, they were more common than his periods of lucidity.

Fortunately, the fire brigade was able to disturb his slumberous siesta and rescue him from both a kip and the fire. Nothing was saved except for one motorcycle battery. Wormy had lost all of his possessions.

Unfortunately, Wormy had cashed in his pension and all of his shares. Nearly thirty years' worth of poorly performing shares had been redeemed. Wormy had played the stock market for years. He had the unique skill of identifying disastrous stocks, sometimes years ahead of anyone else. Shares that were solid and safe became quagmires of financial ineptitude. Eventually, Wormy decided that he had had enough, and cashed them all in. After the crash, Wormy had no faith in banks whatsoever, so he reverted to the punters preferred safe-place: the mattress.

He had lost everything. He cried so much that there were no more tears. The well was dry.

To make things worse, Wormy had started an affair with Linda in the hospital. Initially, it was a love/hate relationship. Linda had just about recovered from her breakdown, although she still had a strong urge to attack testicles. Wormy had only been attacked once. Linda wanted a man, but he had to be relatively docile and innocuous. He had to do what he was told. Wormy was the perfect candidate.

Linda took him back to her home. It was a dull, dreary, innocuous place that had a continuous ringing sound. It sounded like someone banging a pipe. Linda claimed that it was the central heating.

Over tea, Linda had a relapse and went for Wormy's testicles. Wormy was not expecting that. He tried to resist, but she was so strong. His trousers and pants were ripped off, literally ripped. She began the hunt for his genitalia. He had a huge anus, but a tiny penis and a couple of walnuts. She shouted, 'This won't do, this won't do at all.' She went for the kitchen knife. Wormy ran, with the remains of his trousers dangling around his legs.

Wormy backed down some steps towards a cellar. He was trying to keep Linda at bay, but she was getting increasingly violent, always grunting, 'It won't do, it won't do at all.' He undid the cellar door, and for the first time, the central heating stopped ringing. Tied to the wall was a naked man. His genitals had been shaven and painted bright yellow. He seemed happy enough and asked if Wormy was the postman.

He was surrounded by half-eaten packets of food and empty bottles of water. Wormy had no idea who he was. He managed to hold Linda off and called the police. To Sheila's shock, they identified him as Ken. He was alive after all, but still not the Ken she knew.

This whole episode made Wormy wish that he had some sort of weapon to protect himself. Even some tear gas would have helped.

Wormy asked Sheila if he could stay with her. She only had one bedroom, and the last thing she wanted in her life was her ex-husband. As Wormy had nowhere else to go, he decided to go to Sheila's flat, regardless. Linda was still trying to track Wormy down. She was determined to find him.

Then things got worse. Elvis' wife returned. It wasn't a training course, after all. Greta had been in hospital having a sex-change operation. She was now George. And what was worse, he brought back his new girlfriend with him. It turned out to be Jane's mum. The one with the drink problem. She had been in rehab a couple of times, but, effectively, she had not been sober since Horace left her.

She had to drink to stop the tears. Her well was still very wet.

Elvis wasn't sure what to do, so George decided for him. His bags were packed, and he was evicted. Effectively, his whole life was in three cases. To make it worse, he had just been evicted from his property. He knocked on Sheila's door to see if she would take him in. He had the door key, but he didn't want to appear too presumptuous.

As she wasn't in, he decided to be presumptuous. He opened the door and was knocked unconscious. It brought tears to his eyes.

So who is left? Horace and Blondie. They seemed happy enough, but there were undercurrents. George, who used to be Greta, is going out with Jane's mum, who is still Horace's wife. Horace didn't mind his wife being an alcoholic, but he didn't like her being an adulterer, although he was committing adultery. It was his wife. She was his possession.

Horace was going to track his wife down, even if it brought tears to his eyes.

And just to drive the knife in further, Anna was going out with Blondie's ex-fiancée. She had no right to be jealous, but then jealousy is a very strange bed-fellow. She thought, *'I don't want him, but I don't want you to have him.'* Anna knew nothing of the connection, but the ex-fiancée did. Blondie's confidence was low due to stress-induced alopecia. Horace had a morbid fear of bald women, which didn't help.

Blondie was going to confront the two of them. She had a little cry, but she knew that nothing dries faster than tears.

The moral of the story is,' "A tear dries quickly when it is shed for the troubles of others".